RUBY
OF
LAW

Forbidden Conflicts
~~ Book Two ~~

ANN M PRATLEY

BY ANN M PRATLEY

Forbidden Conflicts Series
Amethyst of Youth
Ruby of Law
Diamond of War
Sapphire of Prejudice
Emerald of Wisdom

Power Moore Investigation Tales
Resolution of Happiness
Home by the Sea
Tiger in our House
Catch a Catfish Killer
DJ of Incapacity
Hoonigan

Freedom of Flight Series
Christian
Brandon
Trinity

Painful Deliverance Series
Painful Deliverance
Darkness of Heart
Friendship of Desire

Chisholm Manor Series
Alessandra
Elizabeth

CHAPTER 1

Phillip Leadbetter sat on the edge of the wharf and looked down at his reflection in the water below. At 29 years of age, he felt he should be living a life different from the one he was. He loved his family, and he'd never shirked his responsibilities as the oldest of five siblings. His father was alive and healthy. His mother was the strongest woman he'd ever known. There was much for him to be thankful for. But of all the things his family could have encouraged him to be successful in, why did that thing have to be crime?

His father had raised him in the art of stealing. That was how they survived as a family. Mark Leadbetter, at 49 years of age, was as strict and tough as Phillip could imagine any father to be. When he spoke, everyone listened. When he gave instructions or orders, everyone obeyed. Being a man of power, he'd made sure that each of his children, from a very young age, were put to good use. Learning to steal was one of the first things the Leadbetter children were taught. Not English. Not Mathematics. No, the most important thing in Mark Leadbetter's mind was teaching his kids how to be successful in theft. That was the way he'd been taught as a child. That was how he'd gone on to teach his own children, just as generations of Leadbetters had done previously.

Phillip had long ago accepted his role in the family. He looked out for everyone, especially his two younger brothers and his two younger sisters. He wasn't the only one looking out for them though. His family extended wide, partially in people who were actually related by blood, and further still by people who had been recruited in their youth. It was his family, yes, but

1

it was also just as much a gang. He didn't like the word, but when he looked at what they did and how they lived, he knew his family and the people extending out from it were just that. They were a gang. The Leadbetter gang.

He raised his head and looked around. In the distance, he saw his youngest brother, Rex. Phillip jumped up and immediately started to walk toward him. As he neared, he could see a look of excitement on his youngest brother's face. That could only mean trouble. Rex was only a kid in Phillip's eyes, but he had taken to the gang life like it was something to be truly celebrated.

Phillip caught up to him at the intersection of the wharf and the road that ran along the edge of the waterway.

"Hey," he called out and immediately saw Rex stop and turn.

"What are you doing?" Rex asked, surprised to see his oldest brother so close by. He had thought he was being discrete. He should have known better. Phillip was always in his face for one thing or another.

"I could ask you the same thing," Phillip replied.

He waited, knowing Rex would tell him what he'd been doing that had put a smile on his face. It was always the same with him. He would stand tall, staunch in his determination to keep something secret. Then he would cave in as he realized that he *wanted* people to know whatever it was that he was hiding.

Today was no exception.

"I have something amazing to show you. Do you want to see?" Rex asked, in his excitement forgetful that moments ago he'd wanted to keep things to himself.

"Of course I do," Phillip replied. He knew how to work his brother. It was always best to pretend to be excited by whatever it was that held his present attention. When Rex believed he had something that excited others, he became excited himself. In his excitement, he then became forgetful of discretion.

They walked four blocks in silence, not even bothering with small talk. Rex had kept something to himself for months, and he was bursting to tell someone. He needed someone to know how cool it was, what he'd done, and what he had.

Finally, they stood in front of a large row of storage units. Phillip remained silent, not wanting to startle his younger brother before the door was rolled up.

Rex proudly unlocked and pushed the roller door high. As he did, Phillip saw the source of his younger brother's pride and excitement. It was a car - a bright yellow car with two black stripes down the center length of it.

Inside the privacy of his mind, Phillip moaned. He knew the car, and he knew the cops had been looking for it. As always with Rex, Phillip had to think before he reacted or spoke. It was vital. If he just barged at Rex, he would find nothing out because the kid would startle and then bolt. He took a moment to think, under the guise of walking into the storage unit, and walking around the car as if impressed. He knew the car had disappeared the same day there had been a shooting in the large supermarket in town. The thought of Rex having possibly had access to a firearm and then going crazy shooting like that scared Phillip.

"Isn't she a beauty!" Rex exclaimed.

Phillip looked at him with as much of a slight smile as he could manage. He had to find out information. He couldn't screw things up by reacting in a way that would make Rex feel like he'd done something stupid. Not yet anyway.

"She is," Phillip agreed.

In that, he didn't have to lie. The car had been restored beautifully. Its owner - its *true* owner - must have been devastated when it had been stolen. That was one of the worst aspects about what their family did. It was one thing to think about the items they gained through stealing, but Phillip's mind sometimes wandered to the people who'd had something stolen from them. He hated knowing he might have caused someone misery by something they loved suddenly not being there anymore. The gang justified it by claiming that those people hardly looked at all the things they owned, so would never miss anything. In Phillip's heart, he'd never quite believed that to be true. Yes, some people had far too much to sometimes even remember what exactly they'd purchased and owned, but not everyone. Some people had little - and that little had been taken from them ... by his family.

Rex looked at his brother with eager anticipation. He'd thought Phillip would be impressed, but he gave no such reaction. It annoyed Rex. No matter how hard he worked to put what he'd been taught into reality, it was never good enough. Sure, his father had stressed that they should only steal small items - preferably jewelry because it was tiny, easy to conceal, and easy to sell. What fun was in that? This was something else. Stealing a *car*. He should get a pat on the back for this theft.

"How long have you had this, Rex?" Phillip asked, choosing his words and tone carefully.

"Ages. I'm waiting to paint her before I take her out," Rex replied.

Phillip nodded as if he thought it was a good plan. Then he couldn't hold back his concerns and anger any longer. His face changed, revealing his feelings. Rex saw it and took a step backward.

"The cops have been looking for this for months, and you've been hiding it here all this time?" Phillip asked and immediately saw Rex nod meekly. "They came to our house. They questioned all of us about the car and about that shooting. Was that you?!"

Rex looked at his brother in horror but shook his head. "No."

"I'm going to ask you one more time, Rex. Was it

4

you who pulled a gun out and SHOT AT PEOPLE IN THAT SUPERMARKET??"

Rex took another step backward. Sometimes he hated his older brothers, but other times, like at that moment, he feared his oldest one. What was he so angry about anyway? They were supposed to steal. That was what he'd done.

"No!" he responded but could see that his brother didn't believe him.

"You have to get rid of this, Rex. When the cops find this, you are going to be a suspect in that shooting. You could be put away for attempted murder…"

"NO!" Rex yelled out.

Before Phillip could reach him and do to him whatever it was that his anger was going to drive him to do, Rex turned and ran.

Phillip watched his little brother take off. He was angry, but not just at Rex. He was also angry at his father for forcing them into the life of crime they'd become part of. Even more so, he was angry at himself for having handled the previous few minutes so badly. Now Rex had run, there was no way of knowing when or if he'd come back. He was 21 years old, so should have been savvy enough to look after himself, no matter what. But something in Rex had always worried Phillip. With Rex, his maturity hadn't quite caught up with his age.

Phillip turned and looked toward the car one more time. He didn't touch it. There was no way he wanted his fingerprints on it. He hoped that the shininess of it meant that Rex had done a good job of making sure *his* fingerprints weren't on it. Phillip looked inside, dreading he might see proof of something to do with the shooting - maybe even the gun. As far as he could see, there was nothing. Even the interior was pristine.

Slowly, with his mind working about what to do, he walked outside and carefully closed and locked the storage unit. Rex had left the key in the lock when he'd unlocked it. Good. That meant he wouldn't be able to do something stupid like come back, take the car, and drive it out for all to see.

As he walked away, Phillip wondered what to tell his father and mother. He then wondered *if* he should tell his father and mother. Once again, there was a mess made by one of his siblings, and he was the one who had to decide what he should do with the knowledge of it.

~~~~~

Daisy Leefton rushed around in her usual early morning routine. To her, it was organized. To anyone else who could have watched her, they'd have said she was crazy in the mornings. At 29, she lived alone in a one-bedroom apartment. Six months earlier, she'd lived happily with the man she'd intended to marry. She'd thought they'd been happy - both of them. That belief had been shattered when Pete had sat her down and told her he wasn't happy at all. Her work kept her busy far too much. He wanted to spend more time with her, but she just couldn't do it, so it was over.

Even with six months having passed since then, Daisy occasionally thought back to that conversation. Pete had said so much to her that she had just been completely oblivious to. She worked too much. She always had to have things her way. They never did things together. He'd gone on and on that night, as if he'd been saving it all up to let it all out in one long rant. As the words had flowed out of his mouth, there hadn't been one thing that she could argue with.

She'd worked and studied hard to get to where she was. She was a respected lawyer. Did she still have a lot to learn and a long way to go? Absolutely. But she was determined to work as hard as she could to earn even more respect in the legal profession. She was a woman in power, and she loved it.

Glimpsing at herself one more time in the mirror, she tucked a loose strand of her blonde hair back behind her ear and then stood still. She took a deep breath and closed her eyes. When she opened them, she just looked at herself. She was almost 30. She wondered if the stress she sometimes felt in her job was aging her. Would she ever be attractive to any man again?

She shook her head and let a slight chuckle leave her lips. She'd only just gotten out of a relationship. There was no way she was going to race into another one.

~~~~~

Mark Leadbetter sat in his office. Head of the family, he'd been thinking about his kids all morning. Phillip and David, in their late-20s, were good kids. Sasha and Rex - well, they were still young and finding themselves in trouble more often than he'd like, but they'd grow out of that. Then there was little Anya. At 15, she seemed like a normal teenager, but already she was a master pickpocket. He knew that from the ever-growing mountain of acquisitions in her room. She'd not once been caught, though. That told him she had skills that none of her older siblings had. If any of them could be considered for a large job, ironically it would be her - the youngest - that Mark would think most suited and trustworthy in it. Not that they often did big jobs, of course.

Sometimes he heard about large-scale jewelry coming into the city that he dreamed of attempting to steal, but he never ventured there. It seemed like almost every time something like that was around, someone *else* jumped in and stole it. He didn't know who the guys were who worked such high-caliber thefts but he was envious of them. He'd never admit that to anyone but there was a part of him that wished he had the skills and the courage to do something larger than the small burglaries that his family primarily did. He didn't even really know why his family lived like they did. His parents had raised him to be like that, so he had naturally raised his own kids to be the same.

He was a Leadbetter. That's who he was. But sometimes he just wished he'd become a guy who went to work from nine till five, Monday to Friday, and went golfing on Sundays.

"Where's your head at?" he heard Rhett ask from the other side of his desk. Although not related by blood, Rhett was as close to Mark as any family member. They'd met when they were in high school. Rhett had lived on the streets after his parents had thrown him out and told him never to come back. He'd had no-one, so Mark had brought him home to stay for a couple of nights. That was long enough for the senior Leadbetters to see potential in Rhett and invite him to live with them permanently.

Mark smiled at him and opted not to talk about the concerns he had about his kids.

"I was thinking back to when we were first initiated," he said.

Rhett instantly groaned in response.

"Oh, fuck that. Don't remind me!"

The third person in the room chuckled. Greg was Mark's cousin and had also been a part of the family gang since he was a teenager. "At least there's no such thing now. You were good to get rid of that carry-on," he said to Mark and received a nod in return.

Outside the doorway, Rex approached but halted in his quest to speak to his father. He could hear the three-way conversation. It would be good fun to hear what the oldies were talking about.

"I agree," Rhett said, his voice more serious. "I know we did everything we were told to, but fuck, forcing a woman to have sex as a way to get into a gang - that was just sick."

Rex's ears picked up even more. The conversation was getting even better. He next heard his father's voice add to the conversation.

"I know," Mark said, nodding. "I've never forgotten it either, but that was the initiation for generations. To them, it was just a normal thing to do. Rape a woman to prove your worthiness to the family and the other members. I won't ever let that be something that's allowed. Never again."

Rex had heard enough. The last sentences he'd heard come out of his father's mouth, he instantly disregarded. He had a way to get people to do what he wanted. An initiation! Yes! He would be the coolest guy around if he could get people interested in becoming a gang member. And all they'd have to do was mess a woman or two up and take from her what they probably wanted anyway. Win, win.

He walked away with a smile on his face. The fact that everyone else considered the concept an ancient act of sickness meant absolutely nothing to him. He was young, and he was free. He was going to do whatever the hell he wanted.

~~~~~

"Hey, I heard that there's a gang initiation tonight," Rex started to tell guys he ran into over the afternoon. "Are you in?"

Within a couple of hours, he had five guys interested, although he suspected some of them were all talk and no action. Still, he moved forward with his plan. He told them where to be and when. That was when they would start looking for the right target to fulfill their purpose.

~~~~~

"Come on, girl! It's been long enough. Get off your ass and find yourself a man!"

Daisy laughed at her closest friend, Emma. Since the engagement had ended and Daisy had set herself up in her own apartment, Emma had been singing the same tune, over and over.

"I am perfectly fine on my own, thank you very

much," Daisy threw back at her friend as they enjoyed a meal at La Revolution Restaurant.

"Hmm, no, actually I agree with Emma," added in the third of the party, Nicola. "It's been far too long. If you aren't ready for a relationship, you do at least need to get laid."

Daisy spluttered in the combination of drinking and laughing at the same time.

"Cheers to that!" Vinnie called out as he raised his glass and encouraged everyone at the table to do the same.

"Cheers!" Daisy heard her three friends call out loudly, making her giggle and simultaneously try to hide as people turned to look at them.

She was professional in her job. She was good at what she did. But when she could find the time to get together with her friends and let her hair down, she loved it. Having all gone to college together, the conversations they had were never boring. Her job suited her serious side of her nature. Her friends suited the rest.

"But enough about me," she said, turning to Vinnie. "This one has a new lover, I hear. What's his name? Brad? Chad?"

Vinnie laughed out loud. "Nice try, but you aren't getting any information out of me about my *lad*."

"Nice try, *you*, but come on. Let's have the gossip."

The three women indulged in hearing the latest adventures of Vinnie before the waiter came and removed their main meal plates and took their orders for dessert. Indulgence. It was sometimes needed. When their sweets had been delivered, the talking stopped, just as it did every week at the same time.

"Oh … my … god!" Nicola said.

Daisy looked at her and saw rich red berry sauce running down her friend's chin. She wondered whether to tell Nicola how messy her face looked at that moment.

She decided to not say anything. The look was too priceless.

"This meringue and berry mix is incredible. Here, try this…"

After a long while of indulgence, the four stood up to leave.

"Same time next week?" Daisy asked and saw her friends nod in reply. "Who's deciding next time?"

"I am!" Vinnie called out. "I'll text you all Thursday and tell you where we'll be dining next Friday."

Daisy waved her three friends off and made her way toward where she'd parked.

~~~~~

"Come on, man," one of the guys said to Rex as they stood in the three-story car parking structure. "No woman's coming here. This is a waste of time."

Rex spoke again to the three guys who stood near him. Each of them had felt excitement at the plan, but as time passed, they started to feel like it was just some kind of joke. Rex hoped something would go right because he himself didn't want to be on the wrong side of the guys he'd invited along.

~~~~~

Walking through the streets in the dark was something Daisy was used to. Did she question her mind, walking around so confidently when the sun was down? Absolutely, but she'd grown up in the city, and she often had to work late. It was just the way life was.

She entered the structure she parked her car in each day. When she was close enough to her car to see it where she'd parked it, she felt apprehension flow over her. As the hairs on the back of her neck stood up, she felt her heart start beating heavier. She stopped walking and looked around in fear.

As she turned, she saw four young men walking toward her. They hardly looked older than teenagers, but there were four of them. She glanced at her car, wondering if she could sprint there before the guys reached her. She was too late. Within an extremely short period of time, they'd surrounded her.

"Hey, baby," Rex called out as they started to circle her like a pack of wild dogs. "I'm sure you're looking for some action, huh?"

As Daisy looked at him, she wondered if she might faint.

~~~~~

From behind one of the large concrete columns that seemed to hold the structure up, Phillip watched. He'd tailed Rex when he'd seen him leave their home. The two of them hadn't spoken again, but something about Rex had him on edge. Phillip had needed to see what it was that his little brother was up to.

What he saw alarmed him. Rex and three friends had a woman surrounded. The words they were all throwing out at her left Phillip in no doubt about what they planned to do. He felt sick at the thought of his brother even considering such a thing. He had to act.

When the pack moved in closer and were within touching distance of the woman, Phillip stepped forward.

"Stop!" he called out, alarming everyone. He moved his body between the woman and Rex. "Stop this, and go home," he said, looking right at his brother.

"Get out of our way," Rex replied with a menacing tone in his voice. He hated his oldest brother at that moment. He was going to ruin *everything*.

"No," Phillip said as he moved back so that his back was almost touching the woman. "I said, get out of here!"

All four young men moved toward Phillip. One of them attempted to throw a punch. He was immediately knocked to the ground. A second one moved in to hit Phillip. He also went down. At that point, Rex and the fourth guy turned away, but not before Phillip saw the look on Rex's face. He was angry. He looked wild. He appeared so irate that Phillip wondered if he might have it in him to kill someone, right there and then.

After a long standoff, the four boys ran off, leaving Phillip and the woman alone. He watched them run till he could see them no more and then turned around. The woman was shaking, and she was white. Phillip started to approach her but immediately saw her raise her arms as if to shield herself from an expected attack.

"I'm not going to hurt you," Phillip said quietly. He stood back from her to make sure she didn't become any more distressed. "Are you alright?"

Daisy was in shock. The four young men were gone, but now before her was an older man. He was muscular and solid. He could probably break her in two.

Phillip saw her start to wilt, almost as if she were about to faint. Without thinking, he rushed forward and placed his arms around her to steady her.

"Oh, shit. You aren't okay at all," he mumbled but stood still, terrified that any sudden movement could cause her to shut down completely.

They stood as they were for a long time. Daisy felt his arms on her. She waited for the pain to come. Whatever he was going to do to her, she hoped he would do it swiftly so that she wouldn't have to endure the agony for too long. She closed her eyes and stood perfectly still, waiting…

"Are you alright? Can you stand by yourself?" she heard him ask quietly. It didn't *seem* to be the voice of a guy who intended to hurt or kill her. When she opened her eyes and looked right at him, she heard him speak again. "I think you're in shock. Is your car here somewhere? Can I walk you to it? I'd like to make sure you're safe before I leave you."

Daisy looked at him in disbelief. Now he *really* didn't sound like he wanted to hurt or kill her. She forced herself to focus fully and pull herself upright so that she wasn't leaning on him. She stepped away tentatively, wondering if there was still something awful to come. Slowly she walked toward her car. She could sense him walking behind her. Not too close. Not too far back.

When she approached her car, she reached into her handbag to try and find her keys. She was flustered and couldn't focus. The keys should have been easy to find, but she was muddled and started to get even more flustered in frustration.

"Let me," Phillip said, reaching out for her handbag. He saw her reluctantly hand it to him and was sure she expected him to run off with it. While he unzipped it, he maintained eye contact with her as much as he could. Inside the bag, his hand rummaged around until he found the familiar feeling of keys and then pulled them out. "Are these your car keys?" he asked and saw Daisy nod.

Phillip handed the keys to her and watched her unlock the driver's side door.

As Daisy reached in and sat on the seat, she wondered if that was going to be the moment. Was he going to hurt her in the car?

"Don't forget this," she heard his deep voice say softly. When she turned to look at him, she saw he was handing her handbag to her. "Are you okay? Will you be able to drive? Do you want to call a friend to come and help you?"

As he voiced his questions, Daisy found herself calming and returning to normal. Feeling her heart slowly ease in its pounding, she looked closer at the guy. He hadn't hurt her. He hadn't even stolen her bag. He looked tough. The tattoos up his arms made him look like many of the criminals she'd helped to put in prison, but his eyes were *kind*. The contrast surprised and stunned her.

Finally, she found her voice. "Yes, thank you. I'm

fine. I might just need a drink when I get home," she said, trying to fake a slight laugh.

Phillip backed away. "Alright. Well, I hope you *are* okay. Lock your door," he said before he closed the driver side door for her. Instantly he saw her nod and activate the door lock from inside.

Daisy took a deep breath and started the car. She turned to look at him once more before slowly driving forward to exit the building. As she did, she looked in her rearview mirror. He was still standing as he had been, watching her leave. With her head finally clearing, she could look at him more clearly.

And he looked good.

~~~~~

Late into the night, Phillip tossed and turned in wakefulness in his bed. He was angry at his brother. How much more stupid could he get?! Now Phillip had to decide whether to mention to their parents about anything of his brother's recent antics. The car? The attempted assault on a woman? Despite what they did as a family, they generally never went to prison. He wondered if Rex was going to change that at the rate he was going.

Before he went to sleep, Phillip let his mind wander back to the woman. She'd been Rex's target. Thinking back now, Phillip tried to remember what she'd looked like, but he couldn't picture her at all. All he could remember was her expression of fear. His memory couldn't get past that and formulate any kind of actual image of her. Although saddened by the thought, he had to admit that if he ever saw her again, he probably wouldn't even know it.

He turned over in his bed again. Eventually, his mind found peace and he drifted off into slumber.

CHAPTER 2

"*What* happened??!!" Daisy heard Emma shriek down the phone the next day. After getting home safely the night before, it had been a long while before Daisy had fallen asleep. She was glad it was Saturday. That meant no work today - well, not yet anyway. Anything could happen at any time when it came to people breaking the law. In truth, she loved the thrill of her job. She thrived on it and was more than happy to step up to anything anytime. Even so, after what she'd been through, she did hope for a quiet, uneventful weekend. Her mind needed a little peace, and perhaps complete escapism in the form of non-stop movies and tubs of ice cream.

"I told you already. Now quit asking. I'm fine," she said, actually feeling blessed that she was indeed okay.

"Well, okay, but who was the masked man who saved you?" Emma asked.

Daisy laughed softly at her friend's attempt at humor.

"He wasn't masked!" she exclaimed.

"But he saved you, right? Like Batman or Zorro?"

"Okay, you are out of control," Daisy replied, chuckling. "I was freaked out last night, but now I'm fine. I'm going to take it easy today and just chill. I'll be here all day, so if you feel like popping over, you know you can."

"But the masked man…? Who was he? Was he hot…?"

Daisy heard the questions and hung up. Generally, she regarded it highly rude to hang up on people, but it was part of the friendship she shared with Emma. It was their own private way of ending conversations. When she considered the questions Emma had posed to her, she conceded they were reasonable ones. Who was he? Probably someone she wouldn't want to meet again, given the roughness of what he looked like. Was he hot? Hmm. *That* question definitely deserved some serious pondering further.

~~~~~

In the large Leadbetter family home, the head of the family, Mark, was enjoying brunch with his wife, Stacey. Their peacefulness was loudly interrupted, startling them both.

"Open up! Police!" Mark heard, along with pounding on the front door to their large home. He looked at Stacey. Her face clearly mirrored the fear he felt.

"I'll answer it," she said in response. They'd been through the routine enough times to know that she was more patient than he was when it came to their kids being accused of something.

Mark watched her leave the kitchen. He sat still, silent, waiting to hear who was in trouble now. Generally, it was Sasha who was noticed by the law most often. Her quick temper seemed to fairly constantly land her in trouble. He hoped that was what the cops were at the house about. Her semi-violent outbursts at least usually resulted in a mild charge, if any at all.

"Can I help you, Officer?" he heard his wife ask after she'd opened the front door.

"Ma'am, we need to talk to Mark Leadbetter. Is he here?"

Mark heard Stacey begin to make an excuse. He ran out before she would downright lie to the officer. He loved her. He didn't want her to get in trouble for trying to protect him.

"I'm Mark. What's this about?"

"We understand you are the lessee of a storage unit at Downtown Storage…" the officer started to say.

"No, I don't believe I am."

The officer produced a document and handed it to Mark.

"This says otherwise."

Mark unfolded the page and looked over it. It certainly was his name on it. That confused him since he definitely hadn't rented any storage space. His eyes moved to the bottom of the page. The signature told all. It was a mild attempt of his scribble, to say the least, but it was the handwriting beside it that told him clearly who had used his name and forged his signature. That kid was *really* going to get it this time.

For now, though, what was he to do? He turned and handed the page to Stacey, hoping she would also know from the scribble who the culprit was. If she did that, she might be far more quick thinking in how to get out of whatever it was that Mark was about to be accused of.

He turned back to the officer. "Is there some problem with the storage unit you are asking about?"

"Oh, I think you know, Mr Leadbetter. I need you to come with me to the station."

Mark looked at his wife again. On her face, he could see frustration. The long years they'd been together had made them both aware of what their facial expressions meant. He could see she'd interpreted the page in her hand exactly as he had. She knew what had happened - and who had done it.

"Of course," Mark said, his heart pounding in his chest. Inside his head, he was shouting, "FUCK!!" but no such anger or words came out of his mouth. He obliged and made no attempt to resist. The look that Stacey gave him said that she would investigate. That gave him time to find out what was going on. She was an incredible woman. When they'd met, she had been a sweet young thing. Over their years together, she'd hardened. She would give their kids as much of a working over as was needed to get the information she wanted.

As soon as she'd watched the patrol car back down the driveway and drive off, Stacey started to call each and every one of her children. She knew from the handwriting on the form that it was Rex who was the culprit this time, but she wanted to give him time to admit it. She told each one of them to come home immediately. They would follow her command. They always did.

When they were all finally assembled, she shuffled them into the kitchen and demanded they sit around the large table. Each of them looked nervous. That told her a great deal. That told her they'd *all* been up to no good. It was a long term conflict with her. She knew it was the way of the Leadbetter family, to steal as criminals. While she'd accepted that before she'd married Mark, she also wished they wouldn't do it. She didn't want to lose any of her kids. They were troublesome, but only because the family they were part of made them that way.

"Your father has been hauled off by cops and one of you is to blame," she said as she looked at each of their faces. She wouldn't let on yet that she knew which one had forged Mark's signature on the form.

"What?" Phillip and David both asked at the same time.

It wasn't lost on Stacey that only her two oldest children seemed instantly concerned about what she'd just said.

"Dad's in jail?" Anya finally asked. She was a tough little thing, but she did love her dad.

Stacey looked at her youngest and nodded. "He could be, for all I know. I haven't heard anything since they took him away."

"But why?" Sasha finally asked and immediately saw her mother look pointedly at her. It panicked Sasha, wondering which thing she'd done lately that could have possibly resulted in her father being blamed for it.

Stacey held up the piece of paper that the officer had left with her. It was only a copy, she noted, but that wouldn't matter. Hopefully, the culprit would see it and step up to admit what he'd done. She hoped he would. Surely he wouldn't let his own father take the blame…

"This."

"What is that?" Phillip asked, not understanding anything that was going on.

Stacey passed it to him and watched his face. When she saw him glance over it, he went white. For a moment, she wondered if she'd assessed incorrectly. Was Phillip the one to blame? No, when she saw him immediately glance at Rex, she knew she was right. What she hadn't counted on was her oldest son knowing about it.

"You know something," she said directly to him.

Phillip gulped. He was torn between wanting to be honest with his mother but knowing it wasn't good to have to report the stupid thing his kid brother had done.

"I do," he said quietly, silently urging Rex to speak. Phillip sat in silence for a long while. His brother wasn't going to speak up. He really was willing to let their father take the blame for the theft of that stupid car. "What did the police say?" Phillip asked, trying to ensure everyone realized what had happened.

"They came here and took him off, like I said. Apparently, he rented this storage space. The only problem is that he *didn't* rent it," Stacey said and paused to see if her youngest son would yet speak up. Silence. "*Did* he, Rex?" she continued.

Rex saw his mother looking directly at him. His nerves had him on edge. The longer he sat silent, the more he realized that everyone had turned and was looking at him.

"What did you do, Rex?" Anya asked.

Rex turned on her and gave her a deathly glare that clearly interpreted to, 'Stupid baby sister'.

"Your father is at the cop station!" Stacey yelled at him as she slammed her hand down on the table in front of him.

Rex jumped. She'd never been the most loving mother, but he feared her when she got angry - and she was definitely angry.

"Why did you do it?" Stacey went on to ask. "Why did you forge his signature on this? Did you really intend for him to be arrested?"

"No!" Rex cried out.

"Then why is his name on this? Why not yours?"

"Because…"

Stacey looked at him in disbelief. They were a family of criminals. She'd never tried to tell herself otherwise, but they'd never turned on each other. This was a first.

"That isn't good enough. How far is this going to go? Will you let your father go to jail for you?" she asked further but could see that her youngest son was shutting down.

"What's there, Rex?" David asked quietly but forcefully. He saw Rex turn and look at him with a look of discomfort on his face. "What's in that storage unit that has caught the attention of the cops?"

Rex looked at all the faces around him. Fuck he hated his family. Always picking on him and blaming him for everything.

"A car," he finally said, after having a good long rant silently inside his mind.

"Tell them," Phillip said. When he'd let some time pass where his brother said nothing, he repeated his words. "*Tell* them!"

"A car that I stole, okay?! I stole a car, and it's stored there," Rex finally admitted.

"Keep going," his oldest brother said.

Rex looked at him in distaste. Fucking older brother. Always in his face.

"Tell them why the cops are so interested in *that* car, Rex," Phillip urged.

"It's nothing…"

Stacey watched the interaction between her oldest and youngest sons. Rex wasn't going to give away as much as it seemed he needed to.

"You tell me," she said, turning to Phillip. "He isn't going to."

Phillip took a deep breath. He was angry at Rex for putting him in the position he was in.

"It's the car that the cops came and asked about months ago," he said.

"The car that went missing when the grocery store was shot up?" Stacey asked and saw Phillip nod. She turned to Rex. "You? You had a gun? You shot at those people who were just buying food for their families?"

"No!" Rex shouted as he stood up abruptly.

"SIT DOWN!!" his mother commanded.

Rex briefly considered just bolting. Another moment to think told him to not do that. Instead, he sat down as his mother moved closer to him.

"Were you the shooter?" Stacey asked.

"No."

"Tell me the truth!"

"*No*! It wasn't me!" Rex exclaimed. "I took the car that night. It was in the carpark out the front of the supermarket. No-one was around. It was there, so I took it, and I hid it. That's all."

Everyone looked at Rex. No-one was sure if he was telling the truth about being part of the shooting or not. All each of them knew was that they themselves hadn't been a part of it. But Rex? At 21, he was young, but he was capable of anything.

"But, Rex, why did you forge Dad's signature on that form? Why would you do that to him? You must have known he would be the one they thought…"

"No! I didn't know the cops would find anything," Rex replied. "I didn't think they'd come here and take him away. What do you think I am?"

"Well, you didn't sign *your* name on that piece of paper, so I'm thinking you actually *did* consider the cops might see it," Sasha added in.

Everyone glared at Rex. He felt like he was a kid again, being scolded for eating all the cookies. He had nothing to say. What *could* he say? His mother wasn't going to let him get away with it though.

"How are you going to put this right, Rex?" she asked.

"You need to go to the cop station…" Anya added in before Rex cut her off.

"No way! I'm not going down there!"

"And what of your father? Should he take the blame for what you did?" his mother asked him.

Everyone could hear in her voice that she was trying to maintain calm, but she was almost at boiling point inside. When Rex didn't reply, her voice went up an octave.

"SHOULD HE??"

Rex remained quiet. Inside he was panicked. Only one word kept flying across his thoughts. Fuck! Fuck! FUCK!!

~~~~~

At the police station, Mark found himself led into an investigation room. It wasn't the first time he'd been in one, but he'd always walked out free. He wondered if, on that day, he would. The most frustration came from not even knowing what the deal was with the storage unit. Drugs? Weapons? What the hell had his youngest son done? What had he gotten himself into that had the cops so on edge?

He looked up as the officer who had come to the house sat down in front of him. The second person to enter the room looked more like a detective. That realization put fear into Mark. There was definitely a difference between a normal cop asking questions and a detective being involved.

The latter looked at him as he opened a file on the table in front of them all. Finally, he spoke.

"Your name is on a lease form for a storage unit, Mr Leadbetter."

"So I hear," Mark replied.

"Why don't you tell me a little about that."

Mark looked at the detective. He hated the law with a passion on any day of any year, but he hated it even more at that moment - especially since he hadn't done anything wrong.

"I can't. I didn't rent it," he said. "Someone has signed my name, but that isn't even my handwriting."

"Whose handwriting is it?" the officer asked.

Something about the tone of the question made Mark sharpen his thoughts. They didn't think he was the one responsible for whatever was inside at all. No. They had pulled him in to find out who *was*.

He sat silent, his mind active to a point where it was almost scrambled. He'd have to take the wrap. The only other choice was to throw his youngest son to the law. He couldn't do that. Even if Rex deserved some attention from the law to stop him from doing such stupid things, Mark just couldn't do it.

"What's in that storage unit?" he dared to ask but got no response. "It must be something big. Maybe if you tell me that, I might be able to think about who would benefit from forging my signature on a document like that one."

The detective looked as if he was considering his options. Mark expected to hear nothing in response to his question. He was wrong in that assumption.

"In that storage unit is a car," the detective replied. "It's the same car we came and asked your family about months ago. Do you remember?"

Mark nodded slowly, suddenly panicked. What the *fuck* had Rex done??!!

"That car was sitting outside the Main Street Supermarket when the building got all shot up. And you know what? That car was gone the next day. We think the shooter came back to get it that night. Was that you, Mr Leadbetter? Was it you who pulled the trigger on innocent people who just happened to be doing their grocery shopping at the wrong time on the wrong day?"

"No!" Mark exclaimed. He was horrified at the idea. His family were criminals, yes, but they weren't murderers. They weren't even *attempted* murderers.

"Really? Because at the time, a witness thought it was your family who were responsible. As yet, we haven't been able to prove that. We haven't found one shred of proof you were involved." He paused for effect. "Until *now*, that is."

Mark sat quietly. He wouldn't admit to anything. He wouldn't say anything. Like the detective had said, they had to prove he did something wrong. In that, he knew they couldn't because he hadn't done anything that they were accusing him of.

The three men sat in silence. Mark wasn't surprised when they let him go. Taking him to the station had nothing to do with them thinking it was him who'd done it at all. It was a warning to whoever *had* done it, that their time of hiding was running out. The cops were closing in.

~~~~~

Mark walked home. He could have called Stacey or one of the kids and told them to come and get him, but he needed the time to calm down. He forced himself to breathe deeply. He had to think, but his mind was a mess of emotions. Anger. Disappointment. Anger. Frustration. *Anger*. What had he been thinking to raise his kids the way *he'd* been raised? He should have done things better. Rex had stupidly taken the car, but Mark knew that ultimately *he* was to blame for his kids getting into trouble when they did.

By the time he reached their family home, he felt more deflated than angry. He didn't often experience the sense of loss he felt. It shocked him to the core. He felt like he was done with all of the life that they lived. The idea of being that nine to five guy sounded appealing. Hell, it sounded like a *holiday* compared to the stress he went through doing what he did.

As he opened the front door of their home, Stacey immediately came up to him and threw her arms around him. He welcomed the move. They'd been married for 30 years and never had she turned away from him in intimacy. Even at the age they were, they still made time to be alone together, to join together and love one another. And he did love her. Deeply. There was a part of him that wished she was still that innocent thing she'd been when they'd met. He wished his family's way of life had never changed hers - but it had.

Stacey pulled a little away from him and then kissed him. She didn't care who saw. She'd been scared to hell and back, worrying he might go to jail. She was going to give him the biggest damn tongue-in-mouth kiss she felt like giving him.

Mark was surprised by the oral attack on him but welcomed it. There was nothing like kissing his wife, especially when she used her tongue on his like she was. Well, *almost* nothing like it, but that wasn't the right time to be thinking about that. He let her indulge and then decide when she would pull away.

Once apart again, he could see on her face just how worried she'd been.

"What happened?" she asked, desperation evident in her voice.

"Are they here?" Mark asked her quietly, disregarding her question for the moment.

Stacey nodded and said nothing more. She knew her husband. He had things he needed to say. She wouldn't try and stop him from saying them. She felt his hand lightly caress her arm, and his lips touch her forehead as he walked past her, heading toward the kitchen at the far end of the hallway.

Rex heard the arrival of his father and found himself panicked. When he'd signed that piece of paper, he hadn't even considered the *remote* possibility that his father would find out what he'd done. It was too late to run. He had no choice but to stand his ground and take whatever was coming to him. Once again, that all too familiar word repeated in his head, getting louder by the second. Fuck, fuck, *FUCK*!

Mark walked in and saw all of his children seated at the kitchen table. Every one of them looked at him as he entered. None of them smiled. None of them said anything. All they did was wait. They looked at him, and then they all turned and looked at Rex.

"You!" Mark said with a tone that was almost deathly. There was no doubt in anyone's mind who it was directed at. "Come with me," he continued and then walked out the back door.

Rex saw all eyes on him. He was scared to go outside with his father. He didn't want to. He could run. The way was clear between the kitchen and the front door...

"Don't even think it, Rex," his mother said to him, quietly but forcefully. "Get your ass out there and talk to your father. You got him and you both into this mess. Now it's time to own up to what you've done."

Rex looked up at his mother's face and saw the disappointment. Slowly he stood, hung his head, and walked out the back door to go and find his father in their large yard.

Stacey looked around all of her other children. They were no longer children at all, but still her babies at heart.

"Do you want us to stay?" Phillip asked, voicing the thoughts of everyone in the room.

He saw his mother turn her attention to him. All of a sudden, she looked much older than she was, and much older than she usually did. He stood up, walked to her, and put his arms around her.

"Are you okay, Ma?" he asked softly and felt her arms enclose him. He'd been taller than her for a decade but still felt like a little boy on the rare occasion that they hugged.

Stacey pulled away from him and smiled sadly.

"I'm fine. None of you have to stay. Your father will deal with this, but please, none of you give Rex a hard time about this. It isn't your place, and you could make things worse. Let this go. Forget it for now. It's all in fate's hands if anything will happen."

One by one, each of them stood and followed Phillip's example by giving their mother a hug before they said their farewell and left. In general, they never hugged. They weren't that type of family, but all of them could see that whatever was going on, it had hit their mother hard. Only Anya remained behind, looking uncertain.

"What are you going to do, little one?" her mother asked her, trying to smile at her.

"Leigh asked me to meet her at the mall, but I can stay…"

"No. Thank you, Anya, but go. Have fun with your friends," Stacey replied and saw her youngest stand and begin to walk out. "And don't get caught!"

Anya turned and laughed softly at her mother, breaking some of the tension. After she waved, Stacey heard the front door close.

From the kitchen window, she could see Mark and Rex talking. They were down the far end of the yard, next to the woodpile. She hoped and even prayed that things would work out. Usually, they did, but she knew their family had missed a few bullets in their time. They had all gotten away with things they'd actually done. It was only a matter of time before that luck changed.

~~~~~

"What were you thinking, Rex?" Mark started to ask, determined to maintain calm in his voice.

"I didn't want my name on the form in case something happened…"

"You could have used *any* name. Why mine? What made you think it would be okay for *me* to get arrested for what *you* did?"

Rex was speechless. That wasn't what he'd been thinking at all, but he could see that it certainly looked that way. It looked like he'd set his own father up to take the fall for something he'd done.

"Look, I don't know what's going to happen with this," Mark said. "It's all in the police's hands now. We can't go near the storage place, and we can't go near that car. *Understood*?" he asked. He saw Rex nod but Mark knew that didn't necessarily mean anything. "You have choices. You can right now turn and run away from this situation and wait for the cops to catch up with you, or you can take some time to consider other, more mature options."

Rex watched as his father opened the shed. When he came out with an axe in his hand, Rex was briefly startled. Images of his father doing something drastic came to mind. Just how much had Rex upset him?

Mark saw the expression on his son's face when he turned to face him, axe in hand. He was angry and disappointed in Rex but still had to work hard to not smile at the look on Rex's face at that moment. It was tempting to let Rex worry longer. Mark decided instead to put him out of his misery.

"Take this and start working on that pile of firewood - or you can run away and hide. If you choose the first option I said, you can stay here and not stop until all of that wood is chopped and neatly stacked against the shed wall. While you're doing that, take some serious time to figure out what is going to be a solution because I'm not going to jail for you, Rex."

Rex looked horrified at the insinuation that he'd actually wanted that to happen. Looking into his father's eyes, he was intensely regretful of everything.

"Take the axe, or don't take it. You decide," his father continued.

After contemplation, Rex stepped right up to him and accepted it. He did actually want to run, but he wouldn't.

"Don't step foot in that house again until this is all done," Mark said, his word final.

Rex nodded meekly, and his father walked away from him. It wasn't usual for Rex, but he felt tears come to his eyes. He didn't often admit it, but this time he had to. He'd screwed up. Badly.

~~~~~

Stacey had watched the conversation through the window. Even though she'd not been able to hear it, she could tell by Rex's body stance that he was finally starting to feel bad about what he'd done. That was a good thing. It was one thing to live as a criminal. It was another to try and get one of your other family members in trouble for what you did.

She turned as Mark came in the back door and closed it behind him.

"Has everyone else gone?" he asked and saw her nod. The look on her face told him the extreme level of emotion that was happening inside of her. He walked up to her, took her hand, and led her into his office at the side of the house. There he put his arms around her. "We'll get through this. We'll be alright."

As she kissed him again with passion, Mark indulged in it. Thirty years of marriage hadn't altered his desire for her. His body instantly reacted to her lips and tongue. He'd always let her set the time and the pace of their lovemaking, but he already knew where she was at in her mind and her body. He knew, even before she whispered in his ear, "Fuck me."

Those two simple words enflamed him every time he heard them. Sometimes she was soft and demure, and he loved that. Other times she was forceful and forward, like she was when she let those two words flow from her mouth. He loved that equally.

Stacey saw his eyes change and already could feel him hard against her. As always when something happened that pushed her emotions to the brink, she needed him. She slowly walked backward with him following her. As they made their way toward the large wooden desk in the room, she alternated between kissing him and removing clothing. When she was naked, Mark watched her as she lifted herself onto the edge of the desk, lay back, supported herself on her elbows, and widened her knees.

Mark was entranced. Fuck he loved her when she was like that. He heard her say the two words again, pleading him to strip and plunge into her, but he wouldn't rush like that. He stood before her and touched her clitoris lightly with his finger. No other parts of their bodies were touching.

"Oh, no, my beautiful woman. I'm not giving it to you yet. Look at these juices that are already running. I'm going to drink my fill first," he said as he pulled a chair to directly in front of her. There he sat and leaned forward to taste the nectar he'd loved for three decades.

Stacey closed her eyes and let her head hang backward as she moved her fingers to her nipples. The combination of that, along with his tongue working its magic, resulted in her reaching orgasm quickly. Thirty years of frequent lovemaking had ensured he was perfect in pleasing her. Always he could make her come quickly if he wanted her to. He kept licking as if cleaning her with his tongue before he stood up.

Opening her eyes, she looked at him as he removed his shirt, jeans, and underwear. Before her stood a beautiful, muscular man who she'd adored for most of her life. He had tattoos up both arms. Another tattoo of a large serpent wrapped around his shoulder and back toward his chest. To her, he was utterly beautiful. No amount of aging had made her love his body any less.

Mark leaned over her and kissed her as he pushed into her and instantly heard her groan as she accepted him.

"Hmm, you are so deliciously wet and warm," he said quietly against her lips before plunging his tongue into her mouth.

Stacey wrapped her legs and arms around him and found herself lifted. He'd done that right from when they had started sharing their bodies with each other all those years earlier. No matter how much her body had changed over their lifetime together so far, he'd always been able to lift her up and walk with her bouncing on his erection. She loved it, and he knew it.

"How 'bout today *you* take control?" he said huskily as he walked them to the sofa. There he carefully sat down, not losing the connection with her for a second.

Mark leaned back and watched as she adjusted herself to get comfortable and then started to move on him. He loved her body so much. Over time she'd changed from the skinny girl she'd been when he'd first laid eyes on her. The years had provided her with a more curvy body, and he adored it. Putting his hands out to caress her breasts, he loved how fully they fitted into his hands. He loved how hard her nipples were. She looked glorious as she moved up and down on him. They were both not far off 50. He knew - or at least *hoped* - they'd still be doing the same thing when they were 90. No other woman had ever caught his eye. No other woman ever would.

Stacey leaned close to him, kissing him long and hard while she continued to ride him. She had no desire to take it slow at that time. No, that was for other times. That day, she wanted the excitement, not the loving caresses. They had a blend of it in their lovemaking, and it kept things alive. There had to be slow, loving days. There equally had to be what she termed in her mind 'simple hard-fuck days'. Both were needed at differing times, so both they indulged in.

"Again," Mark said quietly as he moved his head to her breast and started to suck on one nipple. As he simultaneously moved one hand to the other nipple and lightly squeezed it, and his other hand to her clit again, he heard and felt her begin to shimmer around him.

"Come with me," she said as the wave started. The second orgasm in such a short time meant it was a strong one. The ripples came on slowly and then engulfed her. Just as they did, she felt him climax deep inside her, moaning heavily as he did.

Mark clung to her, holding her tightly against him as he focused on the feelings flowing right through his whole body. He could feel her holding him equally tightly. It felt good to just be with her and not have his mind thinking.

Stacey leaned down and kissed his lips softly. She loved him so much. The thought of him going to prison had always been in the back of her mind, given the way their family lived. That thought had seemed infinitely closer and more real on that day.

"I'm here, and I'm okay," he whispered as if he'd heard her exact thoughts. "I love you too much to leave you, Stace. This will get sorted. Promise."

She looked at him. She knew he couldn't make any such promise, just as he knew it, but she loved him for at least trying to pretend everything was alright. She closed her eyes and enjoyed the feeling as his finger lightly caressed her cheek and then her lips. When she opened her eyes, she found herself pulled even tighter against him. Neither moved or said anything more for a very long time.

CHAPTER 3

Phillip left the house with his emotions in turmoil. He was over living the life that he was, but did he have any real choice about how to live his life? Did *any* of them? He was almost thirty years old. Guys he'd gone to high school with were settled in decent jobs with a wife and kids beside them in a nice home. He had nothing to show for his life so far - absolutely nothing.

He wandered around aimlessly, his mind working far too hard before he decided to go and see his boss. For almost ten years, he'd been a mechanic at the local workshop, going in to service and repair cars when his boss needed him to. It had taken him a long time to find something he could be passionate about that earned him an honest wage. Cars were it. Not only did he love it, but he was good at it.

"Hey, Phillip!" Enrique exclaimed when he walked into the large garage. "How's my best mechanic doing?" he asked with a cheeky grin on his face. He only ever said that when another mechanic, Steve, was around and within listening distance.

"*I'm* your best mechanic!" Steve's voice threw out from underneath a '56 Chevrolet he was working on. All three men laughed. It was a silly ongoing joke, but it always relaxed them.

"I'm doing okay, Enrique," Phillip said. "You got any work for me?"

"Tired of being a lazy bum, huh?" his boss teased him further but toned his voice down a little when he studied Phillip's face. "Yeah, I got some work for you. Come in tomorrow, and you can start working on that little convertible over there," he said, his head nodding toward a topless car that could only be described as fluorescent pink.

Phillip laughed. "Seriously? Who has a car like *that*?"

Enrique laughed softly and shrugged his shoulders. "Hey, they're paying to have it serviced and a new radiator installed. I don't ask questions. Do you want it or not?"

Phillip smiled and held out his hand. "Of course I do. I'll be in nice and early tomorrow," he said as his boss shook his hand firmly.

He walked out and stood still as he raised his face toward the sun. It was a warm day, and the heat felt good. Looking around, he decided to head to the café down the street to pick up a salad roll. Knowing he had some work coming up had instantly changed his demeanor. Even if it was work for only a day or two, it was something - and it was honest.

As he strode down the busy footpath, he slowed when he neared the café. It looked busy, but he had all the time in the world. Entering and joining the queue, he didn't take any notice of other customers. Most of them looked like they worked in offices in the area, given their attire. He didn't care about that either. He was hungry.

"What can I get for you, Sir?" he heard one of the counter assistants call out to him over the heads of several other customers who were waiting for their orders.

"Oh, hi. Can I get a ham salad on rye … oh, with mustard, not mayo…" Phillip called out and saw the counter assistant nod at him.

Once the words were out of his mouth, he became aware of the woman in front of him turning around. When she looked right at him, he gaped in what felt like shock. He had thought he'd never recognize her if he saw her again. He was wrong. *Oh,* how he was wrong! He looked at her, and she was looking straight back at him.

He felt his heart pound, wondering what he

should do. If there was any chance at all that she would freak out if he said something to her, he most certainly didn't want to do that. He looked directly at her, uncertain. Finally, he saw her smile. Was she smiling at him though? He turned around to look behind him, just in case. She was probably there with someone and didn't realize who she was so close to.

"I'm looking at *you*, not anyone else," he heard her say. When he turned back and looked at her, he couldn't deny the fact anymore. "I was hoping I'd one day have the chance to thank you. I guess one day just arrived."

Phillip was momentarily speechless. He looked at her face and could see just how beautiful she was. She was wearing corporate gear again. The knee-length skirt caught his eye, as did the shapely legs revealed from under it.

The full-length glance he gave from her eyes down to her feet and back up again wasn't missed by her.

"Umm, hi," she heard him mumble, his nervousness extremely evident to Daisy.

She smiled at his shyness. When she'd mustered up visions of him since that night, he'd appeared strong and fearless. It was almost comical to see him so timid.

"Hi right back at you," she said. "Would you like to join me? I'm on my lunch break, but I have another 20 minutes till I have to leave."

"Oh, um, yeah, sure…" Phillip said as her order appeared to be called out and she left him to move to the counter. His order was called shortly afterward.

"There are some seats in the park over there. What do you think?" she asked, pointing at the seating that nestled around a large fountain nearby.

"Yeah, that sounds good," he said, still feeling unsure about what was happening. "Lead the way."

Without speaking, the two of them walked out of the noisy café. Once on the other side of the street, life seemed to become more peaceful again as they walked toward the fountain.

"I really do want to thank you…" Daisy started to say as they sat down together on a wooden park bench. Her words were cut off both by her observation of how long his eyelashes were, and him chuckling softly.

"I think you already *have* thanked me," he said. "But you really don't need to. Could we start somewhere else? Like … what's your *name*?"

Daisy felt drawn to him. He was as rugged as she'd remembered him to be, but his face in the more relaxed state was like a magnet to her. And those darned long eyelashes…

She heard him chuckle. "Name?" he prompted her again.

Phillip saw her blush before she stammered out her reply.

"Oh, yes. Sorry! I'm Daisy."

He liked it. She suited the name perfectly. He smiled and held out his hand.

"It's a pleasure to meet you, Daisy. I'm Phillip."

They shook hands and gave themselves permission to relax as if starting over and meeting for the very first time.

"And what do you do, Phillip?" she asked. It was a normal question that she always asked new people she met, and new people she met always asked her. She didn't think anything of it.

But he did.

Instantly, Daisy saw his face start to shut down, but then he seemed to recover somewhat as he looked into her eyes and replied.

"I'm a mechanic," he said. "I fix cars over at Enrique's."

She smiled broadly at him. Muscular, long-eyelashed, *and* good with his hands … hmm!

"And you?" he asked.

Daisy found herself also not quite willing to say what kind of work she was in. Being a lawyer was something she was proud of, but she knew not everyone had reason to like lawyers.

"I work in that office over there," she said, pointing to the tallest building in the nearby block. She purposely said nothing more. She was happy to lead him to believe she was an office worker - perhaps a receptionist or a secretary. She hadn't lied. She just didn't want to tell him the truth.

Phillip noticed the absence of details but didn't press. What did it matter anyway? He might not see her again. They forgot the aspect of work and moved to safer topics. The weather. The food. The coffee. The café. Specific details of jobs and families were off the discussion agenda.

"Oh, I have to get back to the office!" Daisy said when she heard the large town bell ring at the three-quarter hour mark. She was reluctant to leave, but it was time for her to move. Before she walked away, she looked straight at him. "Would you like to meet up like this again? Maybe tomorrow?"

Phillip was surprised but nodded.

"I have to work tomorrow, but I can get away for lunch. What time?"

"Just after twelve? Here?"

"Okay."

"Okay, then. Well, bye," Daisy said and finally began walking away.

Her heart was fluttering, but she had to get to work. A large case was being handled by her senior manager and she'd been asked to help out with it. As she moved closer to her workplace, the hot guy she'd just spent twenty minutes with faded from her mind. Woman mode turned off. Lawyer mode reactivated.

Phillip remained on the seat. Watching her as she walked, he finally started to notice details about her. She filled out that knee-length skirt well, and her calves were almost chiseled in the high heels she was wearing. Her blonde hair was up with tufts well placed at the crown of her head. She wore a simple but classy blouse. Around her neck was a black scarf, knotted in a way that made him think of a flight attendant.

She was more than well-groomed. She was downright polished to perfection. Watching her ass as she walked further and further away from him was no difficult thing for him to do. No indeed. For the first time in a long while, he felt his body twitch. It wanted to leap to attention. He willed it not to. It had been so long since he'd last been with a woman that he really didn't know *when* exactly it had been. They crossed his path now and then but other than a few girlfriends who had stayed around for a few months here and there, he'd never really had anyone serious in his life. When an opportunity arose, and it suited both, he happily took advantage of sex if it was on offer, but he didn't particularly like intimacy that way. It might have been by mutual consent to mean nothing, but the 'mean nothing' aspect of it always left him feeling more than a little unfulfilled.

Realizing she'd fallen out of view completely, he stood and decided to head home. He hoped that whatever had gone down there, it was over with. He knew he shouldn't even still be living at home at his age, but with the life that he lived he felt stuck. It always seemed like options just didn't exist.

Almost all the way home, he thought about Rex and that stupid situation. Annoyed about the anger associated with that, he forced himself to instead think about Daisy - particularly how she looked from behind when she walked in that skirt.

CHAPTER 4

Max Stonewarden was resting in his large family home when he heard a solid knock on the door. Looking outside the window of the living room, he saw a police car. The sight caused a brief panic in him. He was the only one home. Not too long before, his kid sister, Charlie, would have also been at home at that time. Now she was gone. She'd gone and fallen in love and was now married with a kid on the way. Whenever Max thought about that, he shook his head. Unbelievable! But he was happy for her. If anyone deserved happiness and freedom from the Stonewarden family business, she did.

He opted whether to open the door or not, but it was best to just get it over with - whatever *it* was.

"Max Stonewarden?" the officer asked.

Max nodded. His heart was pounding. He hoped he wasn't going to have to go to the station and answer questions about his father or brothers. It seemed not that long ago that they'd had a close call on one of their jobs. That still made all of them a little jumpy when they saw cops. "I've come to tell you we've found your car."

Max gulped. *That* wasn't what he'd expected to hear.

"And? Is she alright? Where is she?"

The officer looked at him as if he were crazy, talking about a car as if it were a woman.

"Your car is fine. We've just impounded it as evidence. It's going to be held for the moment as the investigation into the shooting continues. It could still be a while till you get it back, but I just wanted to let you know it's safe, and it'll be coming home."

Max smiled. He suspected by the tone of the officer's voice that he might also be a 'car man'.

"Thank you."

"No problem. Someone will call you when you can come and get it but, like I say, it could be weeks, maybe even months."

"Got it," Max said, nodding. "Thanks anyway."

Max closed the door and smiled. His girl was alright!

CHAPTER 5

Phillip worked hard on the pink convertible the next morning.

"Someone looks like they're in a hurry," his boss teased him. "Got a date, Leadbetter?"

Phillip only smiled but made sure he left work with plenty of time to get to the fountain before twelve. When he arrived, he saw Daisy already there.

"Hey," he said tentatively. She was wearing a dress. Black with three-quarter sleeves and an incredibly low v-neck, it definitely showed ample cleavage. Her blonde hair was pulled back into a formal and immaculate bun. "You look … beautiful," he whispered. He hadn't intended to say the words out loud, but when he heard them come out of his mouth, they didn't sound wrong. Her face reaffirmed it.

"Thank you," she said with a slight blush. "How are you? Had a dirty morning?" she asked, finding the confidence to slip in a little cheekiness to relax the moment.

Phillip laughed softly at her as he looked down his front. He'd left his overalls behind at work, but he was still a mess. If she could look past what *he* looked like at that moment, he'd be a lucky man indeed. "I *have* been a dirty boy, I'm sorry to say."

They sat and chatted lightly. As Phillip told her as much about his family as he dared to, he could see Daisy's eyes flicking all over him. She kept returning her gaze to his eyes but around that, she was glancing at each of his upper arms, and then his lips, down to his chest. She was looking *everywhere*. All the while, he was watching her face. Her eyes were a brilliant green. He'd never seen eyes that color before.

"Do you wear contacts?" he blurted out, unthinking before he spoke. He saw her look startled and confused at the question. "Your eyes are amazing. I thought you might be wearing some kind of colored contacts."

Daisy laughed at him. "No. These are definitely *my* eyes. There's nothing special about them…"

"There is. They're beautiful. *You're* beautiful…"

Daisy was silenced in her surprise. She'd only just been thinking the same thing about him. He was rough. He looked like he'd kill someone if the situation demanded it, but he was beautiful too.

"So are you," she said and saw him look completely surprised by her comment.

Both of them burst out laughing. It was just too soppy a thing for either of them to have admitted.

"I have to get back to work," Phillip said before he stood up. "Thanks. I enjoyed this."

"Tomorrow?" Daisy asked and, in return, received the broadest grin.

"Sure," Phillip replied. "I look forward to it. Have a good afternoon, Miss Daisy."

Daisy remained where she was and watched him walk away. Hmm. *That* butt definitely looked good in jeans.

~~~~~

"Daisy!" she heard her supervisor call out to her when she returned from lunch. "The police have a suspect in the supermarket shooting. I want you to find out all you can about him. Find out who he is, who his family is, and what motives he might have had in shooting the place up that day."

"Isn't that the job for the police?" Daisy asked timidly. Most of the time, she felt powerful. When she stood in front of her supervisor, who seemed infinitely *more* powerful, she sometimes felt like the meekest person on the planet.

Her supervisor relaxed a little and smiled at her.

"It is, but we've been called to prepare the case for prosecution. The more we can find out, the better. If you can find out what you can without having to go near the police, that would be a huge help to me."

"Right," Daisy responded, nodding. "I'm on it."

As she walked away, she felt her heart pounding. She was a qualified and experienced lawyer, but in the profession as a whole, she was still a newbie. Little jobs she handled herself. On the bigger cases that her firm secured, she was the little guy running around for the big kids. She didn't mind. She loved watching the lawyers who had been doing the job for years longer. Sometimes she felt it was like watching an artist create. Every brush stroke she saw them deliver intrigued and excited her.

She spent the afternoon making phone call after phone call. The person the police had in custody was only 21. He was just a kid. What could have made him go and let bullets fly on a supermarket in the middle of the day?

~~~~~

After work, Phillip arrived home to see his parents holding each other tightly. It wasn't a scene he'd witnessed often in his lifetime, and it surprised him. His mother was visibly upset. The tears on her cheeks and the redness of her eyes told him that.

"What's happened?" he asked when they both turned and looked at him.

"Rex is with the cops," Mark said. He looked grave. "They came a couple of hours ago and took him away."

Phillip gulped, wondering if there had been anything he could have done since learning about that car that could have prevented such a thing from happening.

"They arrested him?"

"They've taken him in for questioning."

"But we have to *do* something! Why aren't you down there…"

"Phillip, there's nothing we can do," Mark said. "Now it's up to Rex. He has to handle things by himself."

Mark saw Phillip look at him in disbelief. He read the look and felt guilty. He'd already been feeling like a failure as a father. That feeling was quickly compounding. He was glad Stacey was happily nestled in his arms. She made him feel safe. She made him feel like he wasn't a bad father - like he was okay.

Stacey looked at her oldest son for a long while, saying nothing. Day to day, she didn't take time to study her children. They were a wayward lot - as they'd been brought up to be. They'd each stopped needing her long ago.

As she looked at Phillip, she realized that he was a good-looking guy. He almost looked like his father had at that age. A part of her wished they'd never raised their kids like they had. Phillip and David, at least, should have already been married and happy raising their own families. David had a girlfriend and stayed with her a lot. Phillip seemed settled at home. To Stacey, looking at him as she was, it seemed a waste. She knew that in his heart, he was a good kid. He was a good *man*. Someone should have already been benefiting from that heart.

"How are you?" she asked him and saw him startled by the question. She moved out of Mark's arms and moved closer to her son. "Is everything okay with you?"

Phillip let out a deep breath. For his mother, he mustered up a small smile and nodded.

"I'm fine," he replied. "I've got some work on at Enrique's this week."

"Good. It'll help keep your mind busy. Don't worry about your brother. He'll get out of this. He always does," she said and pointed at the stove. "There's some casserole in the pot. Help yourself. We've already eaten."

"Thanks. I'll have a shower, and then I'll grab some," Phillip replied.

He moved forward and hugged her briefly before pulling away and moving toward the bathroom. He could feel the grime of the day all over him. It was the downside of working on cars.

As the water warmed up, he stripped down and looked in the mirror. His mind wandered to Daisy. She was gorgeous. Why she wanted to see him again and again, he had no idea. She could have anyone she wanted - someone who wore a suit, or at least someone clean. He wondered what her body was like under that corporate clothing. It was easy to imagine her standing in front of him and slowly hitching up that skirt.

His hand moved down. He was already getting hard at the thought of her. In actual fact, he was horny as. It had been quite a while since he'd felt that way. Stroking himself quickly, it took almost no time at all before he let loose his ejaculation into the toilet. The climax left him weak, it had been so long since he'd last had one, but it felt good.

He climbed in the shower, shampooed his hair, and soaped his body. Already he felt better. That release had been long overdue.

~~~~~

As Daisy readied herself for work the following morning, she found herself humming. She felt happy. She felt excited. After six months of feeling like she wasn't sure what she was doing, she found her focus sharpening again.

She thought about Phillip. She was meeting him again at lunchtime. The tingle that thought caused was pleasurable to her. When she'd gone to bed the night before, she'd laid back and touched herself while thinking of him. She'd never gone for a rough guy before, but he had her attention. She wanted to know more about him, and maybe Emma had been right - it *was* about time she got laid. It had been quite long enough.

~~~~~

Again they met up on a seat near the large water fountain. Phillip had made a quick dash into the supermarket before he met her. When he produced fresh strawberries and a tiny box containing just four chocolates, he'd made her smile. It was such a small gesture, but she liked it. How many guys had she dated over the years who always did big gestures - huge bunches of flowers, oversized boxes of chocolates, or drives in a stretched limo. A stretched limo?? She *hated* that one. It was like they were all following the same recipe that had been drummed into them. They all had the same formula for success - bigger was better. Bigger would get the girl. She was tired of grandiose. She'd much rather have a good man who was subtle than a jerk who could give her the big things in life.

"So, Miss Daisy, tell me about the men of your life. Am I safe in assuming since we are spending this time together, that you aren't involved with anyone? Or am I stepping on someone's toes?" he asked her as they ate together.

She looked at him, thinking it was a funny thing to ask. She supposed she could have been offended at him implying she might be cheating on someone, but she didn't think he *was* asking that - not like that anyway. He just wanted things out on the table.

"I was engaged until six months ago," she said. "Now, I'm single."

"Do you want to talk about what happened?" he asked.

His voice was so quiet and steady. It seemed in one way to not match the roughness of his appearance. It made Daisy think of a kids' movie she'd seen years earlier - Aladdin - and an expression that had been used

48

in it. Diamond in the rough. That was what the man beside her was appearing to be with the more time she spent with him.

"Oh, well, I like my job, and I work a lot," she said. "He didn't like that so much. He wanted me to give all my attention and time to him, I think. When we met, I think I didn't have much confidence. Working in my current job, I've gained more. I don't think he liked that much either. He wanted someone meek and yielding. I don't want to be like that."

Phillip listened and was surprised. It was difficult to imagine her without confidence. She was stunning. How could someone like that not be confident? He sat silent, saying nothing.

"Does that bother you?" she asked, wondering if she'd just turned him off to getting to know her more. When he asked what she meant, she continued. "Do you also prefer women who are weak?"

Phillip laughed softly.

"I think … hmm … I think that you have to be who you are," he said. "People pretending to be weak and subservient when it actually isn't their nature could only result in a recipe for disaster if you ask me. Be honest with yourself. That's all any of us can do."

"But what about *you*?" she asked again. She could see he still wasn't quite getting her question. She decided to be more pointed. "If you know that I'm not a woman who will bow down and do whatever is asked of me … would you still want to see me again?"

Daisy saw the surprise clearly plastered over his face. Finally, he understood she was asking specifically about the two of them, not men and women in general. His face expressed several emotions before she saw him move closer, ever so slowly, as if gauging her response to make sure he hadn't misunderstood. Finally, his lips met hers. She naturally tried to move along the seat toward him, but he pulled away, chuckling.

"Don't come any closer. You're clean. I'm not," he said and saw her smile.

"Okay. Lips only then," she replied, looking into his eyes.

"Lips only," he said with humor evident in his voice.

When Daisy kissed him, the feel of his lips moving against hers drove a jolt right down her body. She was instantly aroused. She'd only had an orgasm the night before, thinking about him. She started to feel like she needed to release again, but she couldn't stop it. Her tongue moved into his mouth slowly, and he accepted it. She could hear his breathing deepen. It turned her on even more.

Phillip fought to not pull her against him. He maintained control. She was immaculately dressed. Imagining her returning to work with oil and grease down the front of her crisp white blouse made him laugh against her lips. He pulled away, apologetic.

"Sorry. I can't stop worrying about you getting dirty," he said.

Daisy laughed. Getting dirty with him was *exactly* what she'd just been thinking about.

"Maybe sometime we could get together when I'm not dressed like this," she said quietly.

She'd, of course, meant that she'd like to meet when she was dressed in more casual attire. Knowing that didn't stop Phillip's mind from immediately producing a self-built image of her without *any* clothes on. He shoved the thought aside in his head.

"Maybe," he said. "I'm not working tomorrow. Are you?"

"Weekends are always a bit of unknown for me," Daisy replied. "Generally I'm not needed, but sometimes I get called in at short notice. What about after work today? I could meet you here just after five."

"I'll be finished work then, but I'll still be dirty,"

he said, grinning widely. Her enthusiasm was surprising but very, very welcome.

"You can come back to my place and shower," she said. "I live just a couple of blocks away."

Phillip looked closely into her eyes. She was asking him to go to her apartment with her? Should he read that as some kind of sexual invitation? Would he be a complete and utter jerk for assuming she meant it as a sexual invitation? He moved closer so that their faces were less distant from one another.

"I … I won't have any clean clothes to change into after that shower."

Daisy blushed slightly and smiled shyly at him. It was bold for her, but she couldn't stop herself.

"Maybe you won't *need* clothes after that shower," she said, almost in a whisper.

Phillip blinked. Okay, he wasn't just being a complete and utter jerk for thinking she wanted him. Or was he? Best to clarify a little more.

"Will … *you* … have clothes on after I shower?"

Daisy laughed out loud. The fear of misinterpretation was clear as day on his face. They were both lightly dancing around something that they both wanted.

"Phillip," she said.

"Yes?"

"I want you to come to my apartment today after we both finish work. I want you to take off your clothes and shower at my place, and I want to take my clothes off too."

He smiled at her. *That* was bold. He was enjoying the conversation too much. She looked open enough to be teased a little.

"So we'll *both* be naked?" he asked and saw her nod as her face grew redder. "Well, which room will we be in when neither of us has any clothes on?"

She giggled, and he loved the sound of it.

"I will possibly show you into my bedroom."

"Oh! Then what?" he asked as he leaned closer, his lips almost touching hers.

"Then I will want you to kiss me, again and again, all over my body."

That was Phillip's breaking point. He pushed his lips against hers and plunged his tongue into the depth of her mouth to find hers. It took all his strength to keep from moving his body closer.

In the distance, Daisy heard the town clock chime at the three-quarter-hour mark. She pulled away with reluctance.

"I have to go."

"Me, too," Phillip replied. "Really, I need a cold shower."

She giggled again as they stood up.

"Will you meet me here just after five?" she asked him. Her body wanted to move into his arms and hold him. It was torture that she couldn't.

Phillip nodded at her. She was surprising, but he had no intention of letting her down.

"I will."

Daisy smiled, nodded, then walked off in one direction. Phillip walked off in the other. Any onlooker would have found it difficult to determine which one of them had the biggest grin on their face.

~~~~~

"I'm going to be late to dinner," Emma said to her over the phone a short time later.

Daisy closed her eyes and sat in disbelief. For the first time in years, she had completely forgotten her dinner date with friends.

"Oh, Emma! I can't go tonight," she replied. "I'm sorry!"

"What? How? Why?" she started to ask, making Daisy chuckle while feeling regret.

"I … oh! I … I have a date."

There was silence on the phone. She thought Emma would chastise her for making a man a priority over friends. After a while, she heard a loud shriek come down the phone.

"Oh … my … fucking … god!" Emma exclaimed. "You are going to let laid. *Finally!*"

Daisy laughed out loud. She didn't even try to deny it.

~~~~~

Doing the final checks on his installation of the new radiator into the car he was working on, Phillip found his mind returning to his brother. Rex was still with the cops. Part of Phillip thought he should be doing something, but what could he do? He wondered if he should make that situation a priority after work, rather than going off for pleasure.

The night before, he, David, and Sasha had talked for a long time with their parents. It seemed the agreed consensus was that they had to just wait and see what happened. It would do Rex no good for anyone to go down and harass the police. That didn't stop him worrying.

He finished up and took a moment to consider his options again. He wanted to see Daisy. Even without the planned intention she'd expressed to him, he knew he'd have wanted to see her. Getting to know her was invigorating, and he sure did want to get to know her more. But what about his brother?

He made a quick phone call to his mother and was promptly told there was no news, nothing could be done, and he should try to relax and not worry about it. The concern was still evident in his mother's voice, but even in that, he knew he wasn't needed. His father had been oddly affectionate toward her recently. Perhaps he'd always been affectionate toward her. If so, it had always been behind closed doors - till now.

Forcing himself to switch off his mind to the

situation, he strolled toward the fountain. When he reached it, the large clock on the town hall showed 5.10pm. There was no sign of Daisy.

~~~~~

Daisy looked at her watch as she sat in her office. She wanted to leave. Hell, she wanted to *run*. She wanted nothing more than to get to their arranged meeting point, take Phillip home, and get his clothes off. Throughout the afternoon, her supervisor had asked her to investigate even deeper into the case everyone seemed excited about. As she had, a photo of the accused had made its appearance. The photo had made Daisy feel like she might faint. She was instantly pulled back in her memory to that night in the car park. The kid in the photo was the same one who'd approached her and tried to coax the other three guys to mess with her. It had only been luck that had saved her with Phillip being in the right place at the right time.

For a fleeting moment, she felt herself go cold. She felt shock, and she felt fear all over again. She forced herself to think about the good thing that had come from that night - Phillip. She had to focus on him. That would help. It was possible she could talk to him about the discovery. He would probably be the *best* person to talk to about the coincidence of it being the same kid, but she didn't want that night to always be the focus of whatever it was that was happening with Phillip. She wanted to forget that night. She was safe. She'd walked away unharmed. It would do no good to bring to anyone's attention what that kid had tried.

Glancing at her watch one more time, she grabbed her bag and started to run. She didn't want to miss him. It took less than ten minutes to get from the office to the fountain. That gave her ten minutes to turn her mind off to her work, stop being a lawyer, and start preparing to feel like a woman.

~~~~~

Phillip looked at the clock again. It was 5.20. He'd wait till 5.30, and then he'd leave. She'd told him her work was sometimes demanding. He allowed himself to believe that it was her job that was keeping her away. The possibility of her having changed her mind wasn't something he wanted to consider. It had been her idea. He hadn't pushed for anything. Why would she have suggested the invitation if she didn't want to see him?

Just as he prepared to stand up and leave, he heard her call out to him. When he turned, he saw her running toward him - well, *trying* to run. She was in high heels, so it made for a slightly comical scene, but he opted to not tease her. He walked in her direction until the two of them met.

"Sorry! I got held up at work," she said, almost breathless.

He smiled at her as he felt his heart racing.

"It's okay. You're here. I'm here. It's all good."

Daisy nodded and grinned while she let her eyes roam down and up his body. Yes. She needed that. She turned.

"Shall we go?"

Phillip nodded and started to follow her. He could sense some tension in her, so chose not to ask about her work. All he could do there was hope she knew she could talk to him if she needed to. When she asked him about *his* work, he indulged her to keep the conversation going, and the mood relaxed.

"This is it," she said as she opened a street-level door wedged between two clothing stores. "We have to go up two flights of stairs."

They made their way up in silence. When she unlocked another door, Phillip found himself in what felt like an alternative universe. Everywhere he looked were plants. Large. Small. Ground level. Climbing over frames near the walls. Hanging from the ceiling.

"Wow," Phillip exclaimed. He felt like he'd

walked into a glasshouse. The fact that she had such a paradise inside an apartment in the middle of a city overwhelmed him. "This is *incredible*."

Daisy turned to face him, ready for a smart comment to come. No-one ever appreciated her apartment with the level of greenery in it. When she looked at him, she had to revise that thought. He did look honestly impressed.

"Thank you," she said quietly.

"How… ?" he started to ask but found himself speechless as he refocused on her. "You're amazing," he breathed out as he moved closer. He almost put his arms around her but then remembered again his state. "And I'm still dirty," he said as he laughed.

"Right. Come with me," Daisy said as she led him through the room toward a doorway on the other side.

As she walked, Phillip saw her lift her blouse over her head and throw it aside, then step out of her high heels. He remained behind her. He was already hard. If it were possible, he might even say that he was *beyond* hard. Her back was toned, and when she turned the corner to go to the room off to the side, he saw her side on. She wasn't flat-chested, that was for sure. He gulped.

After they entered the bathroom, Daisy leaned over the bathtub to turn on the shower taps. As she did so, Phillip looked at her ass in the skirt. He looked forward to seeing that skirt come off.

When Daisy turned around, she saw his eyes immediately fall to her chest. She had her bra still on, and it felt too much. She reached behind her, unzipped her skirt, and let it drop to the floor before then raising her hands up her back and unclasping her bra. The look on his face as she dropped that and stood before him only in her briefs was incredible. He didn't move toward her. He seemed frozen until he finally seemed to rouse himself. She saw him pull his t-shirt over his head and reveal his chest to her. Then he moved to her.

"Oh no," she said, teasing him. "Those jeans are greasy. They need to go, too."

Phillip felt sheepish as he undid his belt and jeans, pulled off his shoes and socks, and then slid his jeans down. He saw her step toward him and raise her hands. She moved them over his chest, enjoying the firmness of that and his upper arms. He had tattoos right up his arms. Over his chest was a large tattoo of an eagle. It was phenomenal.

"It's beautiful," she said as she touched the image.

"*You're* beautiful," she heard him reply.

Phillip couldn't hold back any longer. He put his arms around her and pulled her to him firmly. Parting her lips, his tongue dived into the depth of her mouth. After a long while, aware that the room was becoming steamy, Phillip pulled away and looked at her.

"Pull these down," she said, her voice full of authority. Phillip liked the tone of it and instantly obeyed. As he pushed her panties down to the ground, he heard her voice again. "Lick. Just one stroke."

His senses felt muddled as he knelt down on the ground. When she moved her legs apart, he once again obeyed. One lick, she'd said. He spread her folds and did just that, beginning with pushing his tongue into her and then letting it travel upward and over her clit. There he rested for a moment to caress her until she told him to stop.

As he stood up and pushed off his underwear, Daisy looked at his erection and liked what she saw. His naked body, in its entirety, was stunning. The way he'd run his tongue over her also gave her an idea that he was going to be good in bed - *very* good.

Phillip took her hand and led her into the bathtub. They moved until they found the spot that worked for them. She didn't stop him from grabbing her body wash, soaping up his hands, and beginning to run them over her. He began innocently by caressing her arms and her back. She enjoyed feeling his hands move inwards and eventually caress her breasts. Her nipples were aching as he took his time caressing them. When he started using his fingers to flick over her nipples quickly but softly, he instantly heard her moan. He moved one hand lower and found her clit, where he kept his finger caressing until he saw and felt her climax against his hand. The sight alone almost made him reach orgasm.

Daisy grabbed her soap and returned the caresses. While her hands worked over him, he grabbed the shampoo he could see and quickly washed the dirt out of his hair. He could feel her hands working all over him. When he was clean, she knelt in front of him and took him in her mouth. He gasped at the sensation, then moaned loudly.

"Wait. Daisy, please," he said with the incredible sound of arousal deep in his voice. Daisy stopped her attention and stood. "I wouldn't last long if you do that, and the first time I come, I want to be buried deep inside you."

Daisy thought they were the most beautiful words she'd ever heard. She moved against him and put her arms around him. The feeling of his arms wrapping around him in return was welcome. She'd been alone for too long. For a long while, they stood still, holding one another and kissing deeply.

"I need you," she said as she leaned around him and turned the water off.

Phillip didn't argue, letting her lead the way. She'd told him she was a woman who knew what she wanted, and he respected that. Whatever she was going to ask of him, he knew he would oblige.

Daisy grabbed a towel and moved it over his body and hair. As she bent over to dry his legs, she took him in her mouth again. It was a taster. She ran her tongue and lips over him briefly before pulling away and handing him the towel.

Ordered to dry her body in return, Phillip did as he was told. Watching her walk from the bathroom to the bedroom with a small towel wrapped around her, he felt like he was in heaven. Once in the bedroom, she turned to him and let the towel drop before moving to him and pulling off the towel he'd wrapped around his hips. Straight away, he felt her hand wrap around him and start stroking him.

They kissed as they moved onto the bed. Daisy was full of longing. She'd had orgasms recently, but she hadn't had someone inside her for months.

"Lie on your back," she said as she pushed him back.

When Phillip was flat on his back, he watched as she swiftly wrapped him in a condom and then straddled him. She was fast, leaving him enthralled. It wasn't the usual order of things for him when he was with a woman, but if he had to lie back and watch her bouncing up and down on him, who was he to argue with her wishes. She looked incredible. Her breasts were beautiful, bouncing with each of her movements. Her head was back, and her lips were parted as she moaned heavily. It felt a little like she was detached from him, doing what she wanted to do, until he saw her open her eyes and lean forward so that she was lying down on him. Her kisses spoke of her hunger.

"I like the way you fit me," she said and heard him agree.

"And I like the way it feels to be inside of you," he said quietly to her.

He wasn't usually so inactive during sex, but he'd go with it for her, and it did feel incredible to have her moving on him like she was.

"Will you taste me again? Will you make me come with your tongue?" she asked and saw him nod.

"Yes, please."

Daisy moved off him and lay back on the bed.

After moving his body and kissing her briefly, he settled down the bed between her thighs. She was au natural there, and he liked it. Already he could see her clit enlarged, helping his tongue easily find its target. She was vocal as he licked and caressed her. He enjoyed feeling her use a hand on his head to push him closer or guide him to pull away slightly.

Daisy felt like she was floating in the feelings invoked. She'd suspected he'd be a man who knew how to please a woman, and she'd been right. With his tongue hitting exactly the right spot, she knew she would come quickly. Finally, she felt it flow over her. The third orgasm in 24 hours. It was powerful.

She reached down and guided him back up so that she could kiss him again. As she did, she felt him slide into her once more.

"Yes! Hard and fast," she said as he started to let himself go.

It had been so long since Phillip had been with a woman that he'd thought it would be over in two seconds, but it felt different with her. They fitted well together, but his body didn't seem to be in any hurry at all to finish. He kept thrusting into her while enjoying her vocalization that told him the harder he did, the more she liked it.

The feeling started to come on. He felt a tiny wave begin, and then it was crashing over him. Every muscle tightened in explosion. The sensations seemed to go on for an extended period of time before he slumped on her, feeling exhausted. His body needed to recover, and his mind needed to relax with the overwhelming emotions flowing through him.

Daisy caressed his back and ran her fingers through his hair. It felt good to have a man on top of her again, but it felt even better that *he* was on top of her. She knew so little about him, but she'd known before they went anywhere near her apartment that she wanted him and they'd be good together.

They lay together for a long time, unmoving. Phillip felt close to her, not just in body but in some other way. Like fate had always meant for them to join and be close. Her hands on him made him feel accepted and loved. It wasn't a real emotion, he expected. He wanted to grasp it and hold it for just a moment before distancing himself enough to make her feel comfortable.

Phillip raised his head from her shoulder. He looked into her eyes and kissed her softly. He was pleased she responded equally softly.

Daisy felt him move out of her and then lie beside her. Emma had been right. She definitely had needed to get laid but more than that, she'd needed to get laid by *him*. When she turned to look at him, he was lying fully on his back and had one arm folded up behind his head. She let her eyes drift down and over his body. It was like a piece of art with its broad array of images secure in his skin. When her eyes came back up and met his, she felt a little timid. He was strong and firm. She liked being a strong woman, but at that moment, she was happy to be feminine and let him be the one of strength. As if sensing her exact thoughts, he moved his arm and held it out, silently signaling her to move into his hold against his chest.

"You are a beautiful, sexy woman, Daisy," he said softly as his hands started to caress her idly. When she said nothing in return, he smiled and leaned down to kiss her gently. Her smile told him she was okay. More than that, she was happy.

"Could you stay with me?" she asked.

Phillip was slightly surprised but pleased.

"Stay the night? All night?"

"Yes."

He tightened his hold on her. It was long enough since he'd had sex with a woman. The last time he'd actually slept with one was way too far in the past for him to remember.

"I'd like that very much."

CHAPTER 6

After spending Friday and Saturday nights together, Phillip left her apartment on Sunday to return home. He'd shared incredible moments with her all weekend. They'd shared meals, shared showers, and gotten to know each other rather well in the bedroom. Amongst all of that, they'd talked, but still, she kept quiet about her job, and he kept quiet about his family. They each had aspects they didn't want to share. Each suspected the other had secrets. Neither cared.

~~~~~

"Daisy, we have a court date. Wednesday, we'll be going in. I want you there beside me. I'll lead, but you know the details, and I want you there as my wingman."

Daisy looked at her supervisor and tried not to laugh. It wasn't usual terminology that the law firm partners used, but it was always refreshing and made her feel relaxed. She hadn't told anyone that she'd previously been face to face with the kid who was accused of using a firearm, stealing a car, and attempted murder. She had to do her job. She had to distance herself from that night and focus only on the shooting and car theft that was their focus.

At lunchtime, she met Phillip at their usual lunch spot and told him she wouldn't see him again before Thursday because her work was going to be demanding for the following two days. He accepted it and didn't push for more details.

That night he sat with his parents. They were stressed. It was evident on their faces, and it worried Phillip. They were both incredibly strong people. He'd never seen them so worried about anyone as they were about Rex. After talking about everything, he went to his room and left them to their peace.

Mark encouraged Stacey to go to bed early with him. As soon as their bedroom door was closed, she made it obvious to him that she needed him to make love to her. Happily, he took his time undressing her and kissing her from head to toe and back again as she lay back on their bed. She wasn't in any hurry. What she needed was love and lots of it. He caressed her and gifted her with two orgasms before finally he slowly and gently slid into her. She welcomed him in with her warmth and wetness and he found a slow, steady tempo that coordinated well with them continuing to kiss and fondle without stopping. It was beautiful - just like her.

~~~~~

On Wednesday morning, Daisy felt nervous. She loved her work, but she was still intimidated at times when it came to being in a courtroom. She wanted to always be strong, but occasionally her shyness crept up on her. Regardless, she would do what her supervisor wanted her to do. They had spent two full days going over and over what would happen and what could happen. She was ready. Her part was uneventful and nothing to worry about at all. She just couldn't shake the feeling of unease that was also flowing through her veins.

Once in the courtroom, she sat where she was instructed to sit and made sure she knew where each piece of paper was that she would need. Her supervisor continued to give her instructions, and she focused on hearing and understanding what was expected of her. She didn't look around at all. She wanted no distractions. She just had to focus.

In the back row of the room, the Leadbetter family and supporters sat quietly and waited to watch and see whatever was going to happen to their little Rex. When the trial got underway, Phillip saw who was sitting at the front, preparing to help put his little brother in jail. He almost fainted as he looked in disbelief. His heart began pumping heavily in his chest. He wanted to run and hide. His head was screaming out, over and over again, 'FUCK!!!!' She was a lawyer? And not only that, she was there in the courtroom, helping in the attempt to prosecute Rex? Fuck, fuck, fuck, *FUCK!*

He ducked his head down, willing her to not look around and see him. What would she think if she realized he was Rex's brother? He'd only just met her, and they'd been getting on great. How could this fucked up event merge on that? He tried to focus on the words being said by all parties, but his mind tuned out to much of it. His mind wanted to focus on the beautiful blonde woman who'd turned him on and blown his mind for the entire past weekend. Even his body was threatening to react to seeing her.

With his head lowered, he was in disbelief. That stupid car. That was what all of this was about. A stupid fucking car. One that was painted to look like a Transformer, no less. It had driven Rex to steal it and hide it. The flow-on was now them being in court. Phillip thought over the stupid things he'd done in his late teen years and his early twenties, but he'd never gotten in trouble like Rex could be.

The hearing ran all afternoon. Phillip missed most of the details but determined to focus when the jury was done deliberating, and the verdict was called. Guilty. Rex was guilty of stealing the car. That was it. Nothing had been found to point to him being the shooter at the supermarket that day. Nothing had been found to show that he was anywhere near the supermarket at the time of the shooting, but he *had* gone back that night and stolen the car. For that, he'd get a small sentence. Phillip felt his mother slump beside him in relief. His father instantly pulled her to him, and Phillip saw tears begin in the eyes of both of his parents. Rex had missed a bullet. Surely now, their parents would see that they had to change their lives. They *had* to.

It was over. Everyone stood, and the legal professionals left the courtroom. As they did, Phillip kept his head down. He couldn't face Daisy. Not today. Perhaps not ever again. He finally stood and slowly walked out behind his parents. Rex wasn't coming home with them yet, but he would be coming home. That was a relief.

As they walked out into the large hallway of the courthouse, Phillip told his parents and siblings that he wanted to be alone. To let them get a head start, he ducked into the restroom to sit in a stall and catch his breath. When he'd closed his eyes for a long while, he walked out of the restroom with the intent of walking the long way home.

As he rounded the corner to make his way to the large wooden doors that led outside, he collided with someone. It took him a moment to realize who it was. By her face, he could tell that she was as startled to see him there as he was to run into her.

"Phillip! What are you doing here?" Daisy asked, obviously flustered.

"I … I…" he started to say, but he was silenced by his mind not being able to think at all.

"You're what?"

"I'm sorry. I had to be here for someone," he said, hoping she would leave it at that.

Daisy looked at him and thought about the case she'd just been involved with. That kid was the kid from the night she'd met Phillip. He'd fought the young men off, but he'd been there. Surely he wasn't … a *friend* of that guy…

Phillip saw her face change.

"Is there something that you and I should talk about?" she asked.

Phillip was uncertain what to do, but when he looked closer at her, he knew he had to take a chance.

He couldn't just walk away because it was easy to do. She might walk away anyway when she learned about Rex being his brother. At least then he would know for sure that it was what she truly wanted.

"Maybe," he said. "I don't know. Do you *want* to talk?"

Daisy nodded at him. He was in the courthouse. He probably now knew she was a lawyer. How would he feel about that?

"I do," she said. "I'm finished for the day now. There's a small restaurant next door. It's usually quiet at this time of day."

Phillip nodded and let her lead the way. When they'd sat down and ordered something small to share, he could see stress and concern on her face. He hated seeing her like that. He wanted to protect her, but he also thought it best to get it over with, whatever was going to happen. Like pulling off a Band-Aid - best to just get on and do it quickly.

"You're a lawyer," he said and saw her nod with a slight blush on her face.

"I am," Daisy confirmed. "I'm sorry I didn't tell you. I didn't want that to poison you and I getting to know each other."

Phillip nodded. He fully understood that logic.

"It's okay. I have nothing against lawyers."

"Why were you there, Phillip? Why were you in the courthouse just before?"

He took a deep breath and assembled the words in his head. He needed to think before he spoke.

"I was in the court*room*, Daisy - the same one you were in," he said and immediately saw her look confused - then downhearted.

"You know that guy, don't you. He's one of the guys who surrounded me the night that you saved me," she said and saw him nod in confirmation. "Is that some kind of game that you all play? Four of you pretend to attack a woman, and then the fifth one steps in and pretends to save the day, like some knight in shining armor? Is it some kind of joke?"

Phillip was astounded by what she was suggesting - and disgusted. It showed on his face.

"No! What? How could you think *that*?"

"I don't know what to think," Daisy said. "Why else would you be there today unless you were friends with him?"

"Because he's my *brother*!" he said forcefully, desperately wanting the conversation to be over with. He forced himself to soften his voice when he spoke again. "Daisy, Rex is my kid brother."

Daisy's eyes grew wide as she comprehended what he'd just said. She wanted to believe it was all a coincidence, them meeting and him wanting to spend time with her. It all seemed *too* coincidental. What were the odds that all of that would happen, and she would end up being in court in the attempt to get his brother imprisoned for the shooting? It couldn't be just some sick twist of fate, surely. Her mind was still in turmoil when the waiter put their ordered garlic bread on the table between them. She looked at it. Any other time it would have looked delicious, but she no longer felt hungry.

She didn't make eye contact with Phillip again. Instead, she stood, grabbed her coat and bag off the back of the chair, and mumbled an apology before walking out. Phillip remained where he was. He wouldn't go after her. She had every right to be upset. He grabbed a piece of garlic bread and just sat there. Slowly he ate his way through the whole lot of it. He didn't know where he wanted to go or what he wanted to do. Eating was as sufficient activity as any to simply fill in time while he pondered just that.

~~~~~

Daisy entered her apartment and sat on the sofa.

She could hardly remember her journey from the restaurant to her home, her head was so full of conflicting thoughts. As well as the distress that she felt from having just worked on a case that was centered around Phillip's brother, she also felt regret that she'd walked out and left Phillip in the restaurant. So many arguments flowed through her mind. He should have told her his brother was in trouble with the law. He should have told her his last name. He should have told her he was going to be going to court that week to watch a trial involving his brother.

On the flip side, she argued that she should have told him she was a lawyer. She should have told him about the case she was working on. She should have told him how much she loved her work because it often resulted in criminals being removed from the streets.

She cast her mind back to her research. The Leadbetters. She knew about them. The whole lot of them had been accused of something criminal at one time or another, but they never got convicted. Somehow they had either a huge amount of luck, someone on their side working for the police, or they just knew how to get away with things. The notes had given her the impression that at different times, the whole family had passed through police notice. When she tried to remember exact details, she couldn't focus on anything major to do with Phillip. Maybe he was the good one of the family. Maybe he wasn't a criminal at all.

As she pulled her high heels off and lay along the length of the sofa, she closed her eyes. She'd just spent an amazing weekend with an incredible guy who turned her on and had worked her body like he was a master of her instrument. Yes, he looked rough, but a criminal? What could possibly happen between them now?

He was on one side of the law.

She was on the other.

CHAPTER 7

"Max! Phone!" Mitchell Stonewarden called out to his son. It wasn't normal for people to call the landline in their family home anymore, so his curiosity was piqued. He decided to hang around and investigate when the call was finished.

"Yep?" Max asked as he picked up the call. Straight away, he heard a quiet voice that had a sweetness about it.

"Mr Max Stonewarden?"

"That's me. Who are you?"

"Oh, Mr Stonewarden, this is Christy from the Central Police Station. I'm calling to let you know your car has been released. You can pick it up from the station any time. It's being parked out front as we speak."

Max smiled, partly because his girl was okay and she was available for him to enjoy again, but also because he liked the voice on the phone - very much.

"Why, thank you, Christy. You have a really nice voice."

There was silence before she mumbled an obviously flustered reply. "Oh … oh, thanks … I guess."

"Are you at the station? Will *you* be there too when I pick up my car?" he asked suggestively.

Behind him, Mitchell couldn't help but smile to himself. His sons never failed to amaze him when it came to women.

"Umm … I guess that would depend on when you are going to pick it up."

"I can be there in twenty minutes," Max said. "Will you still be there then?"

"Yes."

"Great. And it must almost be time for your lunch break, right?" he asked.

Christy chuckled softly. She got a lot of different responses when she called people and said she was from the police station. She'd never had one like that before. "Tell you what, Mr Stonewarden. I'm the front desk receptionist. If you come in and see me, and you still want to take me to lunch, I'll go with you."

It was the most she'd said, and Max felt his blood heat up a little. It made no sense since he had no idea what she looked like, but he sure liked her voice.

"Deal," he said, grinning. "I'll be there soon."

He hung up the phone. With the shooting and the coma, it had been a long while since he'd enjoyed feminine company. The thought made him smile. The smile was cut short as he turned and saw his father standing there.

"Dad! It's rude to listen to other people's phone conversations," he said, half serious and half in jest.

"What was the call about?" Mitchell asked.

Max could tell by his father's voice that it wasn't a time to act playful.

"My car. It's ready for me to pick up. Can you give me a lift to the police station?"

"Did they say who is responsible?"

"No, and Dad, please don't go asking," Max begged. "I want to forget all of this. Please. I don't want any blood feud. I'm okay, Charlie is doing great, and now I can get my car back. Please let it go. If you or any of the guys react, things will escalate, and next time, the bullets might not miss."

Mitchell heard what his son was saying and nodded his head. Inside, he wanted to get revenge for whoever it was that had pulled that trigger. At the same time, he bowed down to Max's wisdom. He was right. If an all-out war started, more bullets could fly, and next time they might hit their target. It had been tough enough seeing Max in hospital. Mitchell didn't think he could survive seeing something like that again. They still didn't know if the bullets had been intended for Max and Charlie. It was an assumption that would remain so until the police discovered whoever had fired that gun. Mitchell had to concede that it still might turn out to have been a completely random thing that had happened and, it had nothing to do with his family at all.

"Alright, Max. I won't say anything to the others," he reassured his son. "Come on. From what I just heard, a young lass is waiting to meet you, so let's go."

~~~~~

Christy Jones laughed as she hung up the phone. She wasn't naïve. She knew that guy wasn't really coming to see her. Even if he did, as soon as he saw her, he'd turn and walk out. Hearing her voice, he'd probably imagined her to be slim, tall, and blonde. What a shock he'd get when he saw she was fat, short, and ugly. She laughed it all off but felt that familiar loneliness inside that she always felt when she was honest with herself. At 23, she'd never been in love. No guy wanted her. She'd accepted that long ago.

At the station, Max jumped out of his father's car and ran to his Bumblebee. She was in perfect condition, he was relieved to see. Whoever had taken her hadn't done so with the intention of cutting her up or running her to ruin. He smiled broadly and waved at his father when he drove away.

After a brief inspection, he turned and looked up at the police station. He didn't particularly like going in there, but he'd flirted with the girl on the phone. He should at least be a gentleman and follow through. He wasn't naïve. He knew that sometimes the girls with the most beautiful voices didn't have the looks to match. She was probably 50 and married. Regardless, he'd made a suggestion, and he'd go ahead with it. She might take one look at him and not want to chat to him anyway. He still had to be a gentleman. He began to walk inside.

From the front door, he looked around and saw the front desk. Behind it, he saw two women. One was older - much older. Her hair was grey. God, he hoped that wasn't her (but if it was, he'd be a gentleman!). His eyes drifted to the younger woman. She had her head down, but he could see the shape of her shoulders. She was overweight, no doubt about that. Not his usual pick of flavor, but at the most, it was only lunch. At least she'd have a good appetite. He heard those words in his head and silently cursed himself for being such a jerk before he finally moved forward.

As he approached the counter, the young woman looked up. Max was startled. She was overweight, yes - largely so - but she was stunning. She had brilliant blue eyes, and long, dark eyelashes. The mild-toned lip gloss drew his attention to her mouth, which definitely looked kissable. He felt a slight stirring in his jeans. Even he was surprised by that.

"Are you … Christy?" he asked and immediately saw the look of shock on her face.

Christy nodded, flustered.

"Yes," she said timidly, confirming by her voice that she was. "How can I help?"

"I'm…" Max started to say and found himself momentarily without the ability to speak. That *never* happened to him. "I'm Max Stonewarden. We spoke on the phone…"

"Max…" she said with a dreamy tone to her voice. The sound made him relax and laugh a little. His laugh in turn made her snap out of whatever trance she was in. She smiled at him. "Max Stonewarden. You were quite forward on the phone. I didn't expect you to come in here, you know."

"Sorry, I'm a bit of a flirt," Max replied. "But I meant it about lunch. Do you want to?"

She looked utterly surprised. He read from her

look that she had indeed expected him to either not show up or not want to really see her.

"Oh, it isn't quite my lunch…"

"Go!" the older woman threw at them from behind. "Christy, this handsome young man wants to take you to lunch. Turn him down, and I'll tell the chief to fire you."

Both young people laughed before Christy nodded, stood, and grabbed her handbag. She prepared herself inwardly for something horrible to happen. How many times in high school had some good looking guy pretended to like her just so that he could get her out in front of others and then humiliate her. She knew the drill. She was used to it, but she still hated it. Even though she was much older now and she knew people did respect her more, that teenage girl still resided in her. It drove her on in her lack of self-confidence and lack of self-esteem. It made her still expect that any guy who looked at her was going to go out of his way to ultimately make her feel like she was the most worthless and ugliest person on the planet. It wasn't an ideal existence, but it was hers.

Max watched as she came around to his side of the counter. She was short, and she was round. Her shape reminded him of an apple. She was exactly the kind of woman who had never caught his eye. He was ashamed to admit it, but he always went for the slender girls who emanated beauty, even if it *was* out of a can, or a bottle, or whatever it was that they all seemed to paint themselves with. They were the ones he always noticed. They were the ones he always dated. They were also the ones who often turned out to be the most boring women to spend time with.

"What do you feel like eating?" he asked her as they walked out of the large station doors.

"Oh, I don't mind," Christy replied. "There's a Mexican taco stand just across the street. They have some tables and chairs outside, but really, anything is fine."

"Mexican sounds perfect," Max said, smiling at her. He really liked looking at her. She had an innocence about her, but also a sense of sadness.

They crossed the road and ordered. Christy was in disbelief when Max paid for both of their orders. No guy had ever done that for her. It probably meant nothing to him, but for a moment, she felt a tear threaten. She shook it off. It wasn't the time to read too much into a one-off lunch … date? Nope, that word couldn't be used. She sat down and silently told her head to shut up.

"This is a great idea," Max said as he started to eat a taco overflowing with meat and salad vegetables. "I've never been here before, but this is amazing. How's yours?"

Christy nodded. Oh, geez, he was asking her a question just as she'd taken a bite. She felt horrified until he smiled and handed her a napkin to hide behind. Finally, she relaxed and laughed softly as she reached a point of being able to swallow.

"It's good," she said and they laughed together.

Slowly she felt herself relax a little and become a more easygoing version of her usual self. The negativity had to be kept at bay. Once it was, she felt okay as a person.

"How's your car? I can't talk about anything to do with the police or the station, but is it okay?"

"Yes! That's her there," Max said, pointing out the yellow Mustang with the black stripes running down it.

Christy looked and then turned back to him, grinning widely.

"It kind of looks like Bumblebee," she said and saw him nod and give her a brilliant smile. "Are you a Transformers fan?"

"In a past life. Since I lost that baby, I've been working on a ute. It's blue and red. I've named her

Optimus," he said and immediately saw her break out in a giggle.

"Okay, but you know that Optimus isn't a ute and Bumblebee isn't a Mustang, right?"

Max looked at her in surprise.

"What do you think Bumblebee is?"

"He's a Camaro," she said, smiling broadly at him.

"How…?" Max started to ask. He'd never met a girl who could identify that. "How do you know that?"

Christy shrugged her shoulders.

"I like cars," she said. The surprise that showed on his face made her giggle harder.

Max was enraptured by the sound of it. She intrigued him. She had some unique blend of happiness but extreme sadness going on about her, all at the same time. The fact that she liked cars pushed up his intrigue about her even more.

"I'd like to hear about you," he said. "I respect you can't talk about your job but do you enjoy it?"

She looked at him. No-one ever asked her that. She had to think before she answered, the question was so new to her.

"I do," she said. "I've been a receptionist since leaving high school, but I do like it. I like … I dunno … I want to help people. Not everyone wants help from me. Sometimes I deal with people who aren't so nice, but overall I like it. What about you?"

Max hated that question. He tried to never ask people about their jobs so that they wouldn't ask him about his. He always forgot, and he always asked. The words 'I'm a high caliber jewel thief' flashed across his mind before he smiled at her.

"I'm still finding my way," he said. "I've had a few part-time jobs in different things, but I do need to get off my ass and get a real job."

"It's tough when you leave high school, and there

are so many options out there. How are any of us to know exactly what we're supposed to do? I know I've been really lucky," she replied and looked at her watch as she wiped the last of her lunch from her lips, not knowing how much Max liked looking at those lips. "Oh, hey, I'd better get back. Sandra gets cranky if I take too long for lunch."

Max saw her stand up. She didn't look like she wanted anything more from him. He felt quite the opposite. He stood up and spoke before she turned to walk away from him.

"Hey, can I see you again?"

Christy looked at him with dread in her soul. He was going to do that thing the guys in high school did - lead her on and then make a fool out of her. "Thank you, Max, but you don't need to pretend…"

"Pretend what?"

"That someone like you could ever enjoy spending time with someone like me."

Max felt like he was bowled over. He realized how little kindness she must have received. It made him want to pull her into his arms and cuddle her. Then he told himself that he didn't want to find himself in *that* stupid situation of being involved with someone because he felt sorry for them, as if they were a stray kitten with big sad eyes. He had to think quickly. He had to assess which was driving his desire to see her again. The sad kitten thing? Or the attractive woman thing? He stepped up to her and looked into her eyes. No, not the sad kitten thing. *Definitely* the attractive woman thing.

"Why would you think I wouldn't want to spend any more time with you? I've enjoyed sitting with you and talking to you. Don't you believe that?"

Christy heard sincerity in his voice. She didn't believe it, but she wouldn't tell him that. She could at least be gracious.

"I do. Thank you. I hope you have a good day,

Max. I'm glad your car is okay," she said and started to walk away.

"Wait!" he said forcefully, making her turn back to him again. "Tomorrow. Can I come and see you tomorrow and have lunch with you again?"

Christy nodded. She knew she wouldn't see him again, but it didn't matter. She nodded and smiled, and then mumbled a farewell greeting before she turned and walked across the street.

Max watched her until she disappeared behind the large doors to the station. He was 22 years old, but already he'd been with a lot of women. Despite that, he'd never had the experience he'd just had. He felt different - and he liked it.

~~~~~

After Mitchell had dropped his son off at the police station, he drove to see Big John. In the flow of processes that happened with jewels after Mitchell and his sons had acquired them, Big John was always the second person to see the acquisitions. He was the master behind converting jewels that came in into different jewelry that went out. He was also one of the few people that Mitchell fully trusted.

"Mitchell, you need to let this go. Your son and your daughter both have their views on that. And you don't know for sure who it was who shot at them. The case is closed. The kid who had the car hasn't been found guilty of even being at the supermarket when it was shot up."

"But someone *did* shoot at them…"

"Did they? You don't know that either. It could have been some random kid who just took out his dad's gun and thought it would be fun to hit some windows. If the cops can't figure out who it was or why, you can't go thinking that you know better."

Mitchell rubbed his eyes. He was tired. It had been a tough year with Max being shot, and then Charlie challenging her place in the business. As if reading his thoughts, Big John spoke again.

"How's the little lass going?"

"Charlie … she's doing great, Big John," Mitchell replied. "I never would have expected my baby to be the first to fall in love and marry, but I do believe she's happy. She and Ash are doing good, learning to run the ranch. Tom only speaks highly of both of them in their work."

"And the baby?"

"The pregnancy seems to be going okay. I don't know how I feel about my baby having a baby…"

Big John laughed. "Mitchell, she's a married woman…"

"She's not even 20!"

"And? How old were you when Vic was born?"

Mitchell smiled at the memory. "That's different. Charlie's my little girl."

"She will always be your little girl, but soon you'll have a new little one - a grandchild. You'll be a granddad."

"Oh, don't call me that! I'm too young to be a grandfather."

Big John chuckled happily. "You should have been a grandfather long before now. What is going on with those sons of yours? Surely at least one of them must be getting close to meeting a woman they want to settle down with."

Mitchell laughed out loud. "They *love* women, Big John. That's the *problem*!"

"Well, they are all healthy, and they are alive," Big John said. "If you really do want my advice about the shooting, I'll tell you to forget about it. Max is okay. Charlie is okay. Everyone is fine. Don't make waves. You could be completely wrong in your assumptions, and you could start a war over them. You have a good family. Don't risk putting them in danger."

"I know. I *am* going to let it go," Mitchell said. "Don't worry. I'm actually thinking about heading away for a holiday. This past year has been crazy. I want some peace…"

"What you need is to find love again…"

"No! I love Caroline. That's all I need."

"Mitchell, it's been ten years."

"I don't care. I can't give my heart to anyone else," he said, standing up. "And right now, I need to go. I told Charlie I'd go and visit her today to see how she's doing."

"Well, please say hi from me, to her and Tom."

"I will. Thanks for listening. I do appreciate you being here for me."

"Always, Mitchell. Always."

~~~~~

The next day, Max woke with an urgency to do something. He'd followed the doctors' orders for ages, resting and not doing anything much except relax at home. He had his baby back, and she was still purring like a kitten. He was eager to take her out for a good long drive.

He thought about locations he could go to. Well, that was what he *wanted* to think about anyway. His mind had another idea. It kept bringing him back to the girl he'd met the day before at the cop shop - Christy.

When he'd gone home after their lunch, he'd still had the same enthusiasm to see her again. As the afternoon and evening had worn on, she'd drifted from his mind. He didn't want to be so fickle when it came to women, but he had to admit that he was. Generally, he just didn't look at women of Christy's body shape. He didn't like that about himself, but he was honest with himself about it.

As he lay on his bed and pondered options for the day ahead, he couldn't help it. His mind started to think about her more and more. Despite his logic telling him that he shouldn't like her because of her body shape, his *body* was telling him something else entirely. He could clearly remember her face - her eyes and her lips in particular. To him, she was stunning, and she'd affected him physically.

He considered reneging on his words to go and see her again. He quickly dispelled that idea. No matter what, he never treated women like that. He'd said he would go and see her again, and he would. He didn't have to ask her to see him again after they'd met the second time, but he'd follow through on what he'd already suggested. He was a gentleman. It was the right thing to do.

~~~~

At the police station, Christy hadn't given Max Stonewarden another thought. She'd filed away their lunch as a nice memory, but she knew he'd taken her to lunch more out of honor than enthusiasm. He'd made the suggestion before he'd seen what she looked like, and he'd followed through. That said a lot about the type of guy he was, but now that he *did* know what she looked like, she wouldn't see him again. That was okay. She should be grateful that some nice guy showed friendliness toward her.

She was surprised then when he walked into the station and stood before her, again just before lunchtime.

"Do you need to fill out some more paperwork or something?" she asked timidly.

Max instantly grinned widely. He'd remembered what she looked like. He hadn't quite remembered the effect she had on him.

"No, Christy! I've come to take you to lunch again. Are you free now or should I come back?"

Christy stared at him, blinking as if she wasn't sure what she was seeing. She'd almost fallen into a trance, looking right at him when she heard him laugh softly.

"Earth to Christy. Quit looking at me like that," Max lightly teased her. "When's your break?"

Christy blushed, feeling stupid for having stared at him like a complete idiot.

"Uh … um … so…" she said in her flustered state, unable to think.

Once again Sandra jumped to the rescue.

"Gosh, look at the time, Christy," she said. "It's your lunch break now. Off you go. I'll handle things here."

Christy relaxed and finally let herself chuckle. She could feel her face was red, but what could she do about it? Nothing. Knowing Max was waiting, she concentrated on grabbing her bag and not knocking anything over as she walked around to the other side of the counter.

"Oh, and Christy," the two of them heard Sandra call out. "I'm not taking my lunch break for another two hours, so for today, why don't you take a little longer for yours," the older woman said, winking at Max.

Max looked at Christy and smiled. She still had a pink tone to her cheeks. It didn't worry him. It only endeared him. If someone else were so embarrassed he might take the time to tease them, but he had no desire to tease her. He suspected she was out of her comfort zone quite enough.

"Do you have any preference for lunch since you have longer today?" he asked her and saw her smile at him.

"No. I really don't mind."

"Good, because since you *do* have longer today, I want to whisk you away. Ten minutes from here, there's a small food place right on the waterside. Are you keen?"

Christy nodded. She didn't know how she'd walk in her work shoes for ten minutes, and she dreaded that ten minutes to him was probably half an hour to her. She was literally looking at her feet when he seemed to accurately guess her concerns.

"My car's just over there."

Christy instantly felt relieved. She started to breathe again as he escorted her to the passenger side and opened the door for her. Shortly afterward, as he was jumping in his side and preparing to leave, she had to take a moment to consider what was happening. There was some gorgeous guy sitting beside her, in a beautifully restored Mustang that was painted like a Transformer. Apparently said gorgeous guy had the intention of whisking her away in said Mustang for lunch with a view.

She pinched herself. Was this really happening?

Max looked at her just as she literally pinched her arm. He laughed out loud.

"Relax, Christy. I'm hungry. Are you hungry?" he asked, trying to soothe her. When she nodded and attempted to smile at him, he grinned back. "Good. Let's go."

Effortlessly, he pulled out, and they were on their way. A fleeting thought in Christy's head was that the police station itself had footage of the guy who was taking her somewhere. If she never returned, at least they'd catch the guy pretty easily. She laughed inside her head and tossed that thought away. Sure, she had reservations about what Max Stonewarden was actually doing, seeing her again. but she didn't sense he was trouble - not of the physical harm kind anyway.

Fairly quickly, the buildings were left behind, and the scenery ahead was coastal.

"How's your work been today?" Max asked. "Sorry, I don't know what I can ask you about that…"

"It's okay," she replied. "I mean, it's okay for you to ask how my work is. You just can't ask me about what work I've been doing. If that makes sense."

Max glanced at her briefly and saw her get

flustered again. He felt kind of sorry for her, but at the same time, he found it refreshing. He always met girls who were overconfident, and it was sometimes a complete turnoff. It was kind of nice to meet someone who didn't already love themselves to the point where they had to look in the mirror every ten minutes.

He took a few minutes to try and frame a question about her work that wouldn't break any rules. He ended up laughing.

"It's really hard to ask you about your work without asking you about your work!" he said, almost giggling. "Maybe I can step back a bit. How was your evening last night, after work?"

Christy smiled at him. She liked the sound of him giggling. It seemed unexpected, given how he looked. The sound of it relaxed her.

"It was good. Two nights a week, I go to the homeless shelter and help serve their evening meal. Last night was one of those nights."

"You … serve meals to homeless people?" Max asked, his appreciation for her moving up a notch as she nodded. "You don't feel uncomfortable doing that?"

He caught Christy looking at him with curiosity plastered over her face. He glimpsed it briefly before they pulled into the carpark of a tiny building that resembled a shack. When the car stopped, he turned to her as he unclicked his seatbelt.

"Seriously?" he asked. "You feel comfortable around people who are homeless?"

"Yes, of course," Christy said, intrigued. "Do they make you feel *uncomfortable*?"

He looked at her, surprised and speechless for a moment.

"Wait," he said. "Let's go inside and order, and then I want to hear more."

Christy nodded and started to unclick her seatbelt. Just as she did, her door opened. For a moment, she felt like she was a princess, arriving at a ball in a limousine.

As they walked into the small shack, Max watched her face. As he'd hoped, as soon as they stepped completely inside, her face became alight in wonder. It was his favorite hangout for food. It had been his whole life, but more so since his mother had died. He'd taken a couple of girls there in the past. None of them appreciated it. In their individual ways, they'd all implied they thought it was a dive.

"Wow … it's … *magical!*" Christy exclaimed.

Before her, from wall to ceiling, was a coastal fantasy room. Briefly, she was transported back to a favorite movie from her past, The Little Mermaid. She was so in awe that she didn't even notice that she'd lifted one hand and placed it on Max's arm. It was something she'd never consciously have done, but it was easy. It was natural. It was *right*.

Max saw her eyes darting everywhere. She stood still and moved her face upwards, left, right, forwards, then behind. The whole time, she smiled, and he saw briefly that she had a small tear forming. He thought at that moment that she looked stunning. He wasn't sure which part of him was feeling what, but his body and his heart were both feeling *something*.

Christy grew aware of him standing beside her and quickly removed her hand from his arm. She didn't recognize that he hadn't moved away from her touch.

"Max, this place is wonderful," she said as they made their way to the counter to order.

He smiled brilliantly at her.

"Do you like seafood? If you don't, they do have other foods here…"

"I *love* seafood," she replied. "All kinds."

"Well, they do have an amazing seafood platter. We could share one of those if you're okay with that?"

Christy nodded. All of a sudden, she felt overwhelmed and utterly speechless. To have an excuse to hide her blush, she reached into her bag and pulled out her wallet.

"What are you doing?" he asked her, still grinning.

"I'm paying…"

"No, you're not."

"But you paid yesterday."

Max laughed at her.

"I'll tell you what. *You* find us the perfect seat, and I'll take care of this."

Christy started to object but decided not to. Why prolong the discomfort. Looking around, she saw a table beside a window. She walked toward it and automatically sat down. The view was breathtaking. She willed her mind to stop thinking as she let her eyes fall to the shimmer of the sun shining on the water.

"You picked the best seat," Max said as he sat opposite her.

"I didn't even know this place was here, and it's so close to work and home. How did you find it?"

"My mum used to bring us kids here a lot. It was like a once a month treat thing she had going on."

"Does she still come here with you?" she asked and saw Max's face change - sadden.

"She died ten years ago."

Christy softened.

"Oh, I'm so sorry, Max. Does it hurt to think about her?" she asked and saw him smile sadly at her.

"No. It always feels nice to think about her. Most days, I don't think about her, and then for whatever reason, she pops into my mind."

"But you must have been young…"

"I was 12 when she died," he said. "She'd been sick for a long time, so it wasn't unexpected, but yeah, it sucked big time losing her."

Christy watched his face. She knew she shouldn't have been, but she was surprised to see his eyes glisten with moisture a little.

Before the conversation continued, a large ceramic platter was placed between them. On it, Christy could see oysters, mussels, prawns, fish, crab stick, squid rings … the pile was high and broad. She couldn't help but smile.

"I trust you don't eat one of these alone when you come here," she said, teasing him.

"I probably could, but I haven't," Max said, chuckling. "Dig in. We have to keep an eye on the time, right?"

She nodded and smiled at him. For a guy who was going to somehow make a fool out of her, he was pretty easy going and likable. She didn't know if she particularly wanted to like him, not like that anyway. That never ended well.

She focused on the food and saw Max dive in, his fingers going straight for a squid ring that she could see the steam rising from. Before she could ask him if he was sure it was cool enough, he'd thrown it in his mouth. Right before her eyes, his eyes watered, and he started fanning his mouth with his hand. She didn't want to seem rude, but she couldn't help it. She burst out giggling and couldn't stop. His facial expressions looked comical, and it felt *really* good to laugh.

Max felt equal amounts of uneasiness in his mouth, with his natural tendency to laugh as well. Seeing her giggling at him drove him on to laugh more. That giggle was infectious, but even more than that - he thought it was sexy as *hell*.

A few minutes later, they calmed. Christy felt right at ease - finally. He was alright. If he was going to make a fool of her, at least she was having fun in the meantime. That was the best she could hope for. She'd make the most of the moment and have fun doing it.

Lifting a mussel to her mouth, she let it slide off the shell as she savored the flavor. She'd always loved seafood but hardly ever ate it. The flavor hitting her tongue made her close her eyes briefly and moan lightly in appreciation.

Max watched the whole movement, from her hand lifting the shell to her mouth, to the closing of her eyes and the small sound that came from her lips. He wanted to eat, but she was too easy to watch.

When she opened her eyes, Christy saw him looking at her. Immediately she blushed and then laughed softly.

"Sorry," she said. "I haven't had seafood for so long."

Max smiled brilliantly at her before moving his eyes to the platter and taking another item. He had to tone his body down. Inside his jeans, he was very aware of the effect she was having on him. When he looked at her objectively, he couldn't figure out what it was about her that was doing it. She didn't have the figure that other girls he'd chased did. She didn't have perfect hair, manicured nails, or even perfect makeup. Regardless of all those arguments, his body was screaming at him - loudly.

"Tell me about this meal for the homeless thing," he said, still intrigued by having learned that about her. "How long have you been doing that for?"

"About four years now," Christy replied. "I only do a couple of nights a week, and it's only for a couple of hours each night."

"But how did you get into that?"

"My aunt works with homeless people full time. She is one of the most amazing people I know. She's strong and funny and … *everything*. I've always been in awe of her. She was talking about it one day and asked if I'd like to come along one night. So I did, and I still do."

Max listened to her and encouraged her to keep talking. Her voice was melodic and hypnotizing. He could listen to her all day and all night…

"I'm stuffed. I can't eat any more, Max, but that was incredible. This place is incredible…" she said after a long while. She caught herself before the words 'you're incredible' left her mouth.

Max looked at his watch.

"You are very welcome. I'm glad you agreed to come. Let's go, though. I don't want you to get in trouble at work."

They stood and walked to the car. Still, he opened the door for her, and still, when they arrived back at the police station, he opened the door again. Christy was relieved.

As Max watched her climb out of his car, he thought back to his feeling earlier that morning that he'd see her that day but wouldn't ask her for a third meeting. He'd accepted that as his own decision on the matter. Except, as he saw her start to say goodbye, he wasn't so sure he liked his earlier thinking and decision.

"Thank you, Max," she said quietly as she forced herself to look directly at him. "I really did enjoy this. Have a good afternoon."

She turned to walk away. Even as he looked at her figure from behind, he was still reminded of an apple. He was also still unable to just let her walk away.

"Christy, wait!" He watched as she turned and faced him. "I … can I … would you consider giving me your mobile number? Can I call you sometime?"

Christy fought off the negativity. She had to. He was asking for her number. He wouldn't call, but what could she do? Refuse to give it? She nodded and watched as he opened his phone, typed her name into his contacts list, and handed it to her to enter her number. As soon as she had, he dialed it. Her phone could be heard vibrating in her bag.

She looked at him and saw him grin.

"Just checking," Max said, smiling at her. "Now you have my number too."

Christy smiled at him. She'd never call him. It just wasn't something that would be welcome, and she knew it.

"Bye, Max," she said quietly and turned to walk away.

Max watched her go inside. Hours earlier, he hadn't thought he'd want to see her a third time. He'd been wrong in that thought. Utterly wrong.

CHAPTER 8

Rex Leadbetter was finally home. Everyone settled around the large wooden table in the kitchen to enjoy dinner together. Phillip looked at each of their faces. David was his normal quiet self. Sasha was boisterous and foul-mouthed, as always. Anya was a 15-year-old - enough said. Then there was Rex. He was silent. To Phillip, it seemed like Rex might this time have had a genuine scare. Phillip hoped so.

He looked at his parents. They were sitting close to one another. Since Rex's arrest, they had been closer than Phillip ever remembered them having been before. His mother had always had a hardness about her.

During his school years, he'd wondered why she was so different from the mothers of his friends. Sometimes he would see his friends cuddled by their mothers, even kissed and soothed. His mother had never seemed to have that soft side to her. He still loved her. Just like she'd never been overly affectionate, she similarly had never been mean to any of them. She told them to harden up when they hurt themselves, but she never made them feel unloved. Sometimes he wondered if she'd always been like that or if she'd changed after she met his father. It didn't matter now, but he did like seeing her receiving the attention she was getting from his father. It was nice.

Seeing their loving mannerisms made him think of Daisy. That was still a mess. He hadn't seen her since that night in the restaurant. He remembered telling her where he worked, and she was definitely a woman who would seek him out if she wanted to see him. So far, she hadn't tried to see him. She might have already even forgotten him for all he knew.

He shouldn't have been saddened by her leaving his life so quickly, but he was. She'd made an impact on him, even in the short time they'd spent together. The sadness was exacerbated by the knowledge that they could now start over with everything open and honest between them. He suspected it was too late for that. They were from opposite sides of the social spectrum, and sometimes yin didn't complement yang after all.

After dinner, everyone scattered. Only Anya appeared uninterested in going out. When Mark looked at his oldest son, he could sense something was off.

"Phillip, can I talk to you in my office before you head out?" he asked. Phillip immediately nodded and followed his father. When the door was closed, Mark faced his son. "Are you alright?"

Phillip nodded automatically. That was what they did when they were asked that question. They had to be tough. Leadbetters were just that. Tough.

"Yeah, I'm good," he said. "Do you need a hand with something?"

"No," said Mark. "You just haven't seemed yourself lately. I really do just want to know if you're okay. Don't tell me you are if you aren't."

Phillip looked at his father in surprise. He'd never heard such a flow of words from either of his parents. It took him a moment to break free from the shock he'd immediately felt.

"Dad, I'm fine. Really."

"Alright. Well, I'm here if you want to talk about anything. And if you can't talk to me, you can talk to your mother. She'd welcome it. She's worried."

"Why?" asked Phillip.

"Because she knows all of you, and she can see something is different about you right now. If there is something wrong, talk to one of us so her mind can be put at rest."

Phillip nodded. "Okay. Do you need me for

anything then?"

"No. Go," said Mark.

When he left his father's office, Phillip went to the living room. Anya sat in there watching TV. He next went to the kitchen. There he found his mother, standing at the kitchen window, looking outside as if in a trance.

"Ma?" he said softly in an effort not to surprise and alarm her. When he saw her turn toward him, he walked up to her and hugged her. "Please don't worry so much. All of us are fine."

Stacey wrapped her arms around her oldest son.

"I know," she said. "I'm your mother. It's a mother's job to worry about her kids. I can tell something is off with you. Won't you tell me what it is?"

"It's nothing," Phillip said. "Just girl trouble. You know, the usual. Put your mind at rest."

Stacey didn't believe him, but she said nothing. It had to be enough that all of her kids had been home and all were healthy.

~~~~~

Phillip ventured to his room and lay on his bed. He wanted to see Daisy. He couldn't give up on her yet. He considered going to her apartment and forcing her to listen to him. The number of ways that could go wrong prevented him from doing it, but he had to do something.

The next day he went to the café and the fountain at lunchtime. He did the same the day after that, and the day after that. He just wanted to see her and talk to her. He wouldn't push her, but he had to hope that if she saw him, there might be a slight chance that she'd want to talk too.

On the fourth day, he saw her. She was sitting on the park bench, looking into the water flowing out of a stone gargoyle's mouth on the large fountain. When Phillip's eyes rested on her, he felt panicked. Should he approach her? He stood still, wondering what was the right thing to do. After a while, he became aware that she'd turned her head and was looking at him. When he focused on her, she stood. He thought she would walk away. Instead, she came toward him until she stood right in front of him. When her chest was close to his, Phillip looked down into her eyes.

Daisy looked at him. She'd taken time to think, and she didn't want to turn away from him yet. Despite the actions of his family, her gut still told her that he was a good person and a good man. Seeing he wasn't in his mechanic's state, she tentatively wrapped her arms around his waist. She pressed closer to him until she felt his arms wrap around her in return and pull her close and tight against him.

"Can we talk?" she asked quietly.

Phillip nodded but made no move to kiss her. "Yes."

Daisy pulled away and took one of his hands in hers. They walked together back to the seat she'd just vacated.

"How have you been?" he asked as he drank in what she looked like.

"I'm okay, but … I've been thinking about you … a lot," she replied in full honesty.

Phillip was pleased with the statement. He slowly raised his hand and lightly stroked her cheek.

"Me, too."

"Phillip, I can't protect your family," she said and saw the disbelief on his face.

"What?" he asked, wondering if he'd heard correctly. "Why would you say *that*? I can't believe … I don't … *Daisy*! What have you been thinking?!"

"I'm a lawyer. Your family…" she started to say. Her words drifted off to nothing.

"Stop," Phillip said. "Before we go into the world of your job, let's talk about me and my family if that's what's freaking you out."

"They … are … they've been…"

It was clear to Phillip that finding the right words was proving difficult for her - until she finally found the ones that suited what she wanted to say. "They're well known to police."

Daisy watched his face as he dealt with what she'd said. He looked thoughtful.

"Yeah," he responded. "My family aren't angels. I'm hardly going to deny that, but they have nothing to do with me getting to know you. I didn't know you were a lawyer until that day in court!" Pausing, he moved closer to her and took her hand in his. "I love spending time with you. I want to spend *more* time with you."

"I feel the same way…" Daisy said quietly.

"Then let's get on with it."

The large clock chimed in the background.

"I…"

"Yeah, I know," Phillip said. "You need to get back to work, but, Daisy, please. I don't want to just give up on you and me. I want us to work together to find a way that we can *work*. Can we at least talk properly?"

Daisy leaned toward him and kissed him deeply. She'd hoped that he wouldn't affect her so much, given what she'd learned about him and his family. As his lips caressed hers, she knew she'd been wrong. Even knowing what his family was like, she still felt the same. Pulling back, she nodded.

"I want that too," she said.

"Tell me. When? Where? Anywhere. I'll come."

"I don't want us to be too alone. I want us to really talk. If I'm alone with you, I'll be distracted…" she said and instantly saw him smile in agreement. The smile relaxed her a little.

"Okay," Phillip said. "There's a little Italian restaurant over there, just back from the road. Tell me a time and I'll meet you there."

"Five thirty?"

"Please," he said. "You mean today, right?"

Daisy nodded, her face still revealing uncertainty. "Yes."

Phillip said nothing more but ventured to kiss her softly before she stood up and walked away. She still looked amazing in that skirt, but it was far more important to him that she wanted to see him and talk to him.

~~~~~

"Hi," Daisy said as she approached him in the restaurant.

She noted that Phillip obviously gone home and showered, shaved, and changed. He looked and smelled good. With his tattoos hidden by the long-sleeved shirt he had on, there was little that made him look rough at all. He fitted right in with everyone else there, including the corporate crowd.

They were in a restaurant, but Phillip didn't care about food at all. He just wanted them to get past whatever was in their way. As he returned her greeting, he saw her sit at the other side of the table he'd been waiting at for half an hour. His mind had been active all afternoon, and he'd ended up being far too early, but when he'd gotten there, he didn't mind. It was a good place to sit and think.

Daisy let her eyes glide over him. Even just looking at him, she could feel her body wanting to respond. He looked beautiful. All afternoon she'd been nervous. She'd been glad that it was an afternoon where no-one particularly needed anything from her.

"You look yummy," she said without giving much thought to the fact that the words escaped through her mouth and weren't confined to just her head. She saw Phillip grin broadly.

"Thanks," he said. "So do you."

They ordered a light meal, and he waited for her to speak. She looked nervous. He found the unknowing unbearable. He decided he couldn't wait for her to speak after all.

"Daisy, please don't think that I've spent time with you because I somehow knew you were a lawyer, and I want something lawyer-ish from you," he said. He paused and reached out to take her hand in his. "I think you're amazing and beautiful and sweet, and I have enjoyed every minute we've spent together. That has nothing to do with what you do for a job."

"I know," she replied, nodding. "I do believe that. But you and I are on the opposite sides of the law. I became a lawyer because I want to make this world a safer place by putting criminals *away*."

After she said the words, she felt partially regretful. She didn't want to hurt him, but she knew she also needed to be honest.

"I…" He started to tell her he wasn't a criminal, but there were things she probably didn't even know about, given that his family hadn't been caught in some of their activities. He didn't want to lie to her, but he certainly didn't want to give that information up. "I don't believe that you and I can't get past this. We enjoyed that incredible weekend without your job or my family background invading our time together."

To Daisy, he made it sound so easy, and maybe it was. The question for her was, could she look past everything to find out.

When the waiter brought their small bowls of pasta, they quietly began eating.

"What if something happens like the last day we saw each other?" Daisy asked after a long period of silence. "You're in court to support someone you know, and I'm in court, trying to put them away?"

"I get why you're worried about this, but I don't want to do the what-if thing," Phillip replied. "It might never happen, and if it does, we'll work around it."

"I couldn't turn away from a case just because…"

"And I wouldn't expect you to. Your job is your

job. I didn't know about it before, and I didn't care," he said. "We can keep details of that out of our relationship. We can keep anything to do with my family out of our relationship. I just want you and me, not all the other stuff and people around us."

"Alright," Daisy said meekly.

When she received no response, she looked up and found herself absorbed in his eyes. His look of intensity drove through her body and straight to her core. She felt a familiar throbbing. She almost felt like she was on fire.

Phillip watched her face. Although she sounded timid and almost defeated, her body was emanating something powerful. He grew hard as he knew the times he'd seen her face look like it did.

"When can I see you again?" he asked, his voice definitely sounding huskier than it had minutes earlier.

The question broke the tension as Daisy laughed.

"Umm ... now?" she said and saw him smile at her.

A little bit of her relaxed self began to emerge again. She looked at him, and after a while, she became quiet. His eyes sparkled with amusement, but they also continued to hold the intensity that was affecting her. "Come home with me?" she said in almost a whisper.

Immediately Phillip nodded. He had to have her. His body was screaming out in arousal. He ate the remainder of his pasta but didn't take his eyes off her. When she'd finished, she licked her lips. That was all he could take.

"Let's go," he said, standing up and holding out his hand.

Daisy stood and enclosed it in her own.

"I need you too," she whispered.

Phillip couldn't get out of there fast enough. After a quick walk to her apartment, finally they were alone and inside her main door. There he backed her up against the door and pressed hard against her. His lips on hers and his tongue pushing into her mouth made her groan.

Daisy was past hungry. She was starving for him. She pulled away and walked to the bedroom with him following closely behind. Hastily they removed their clothing before she moved onto the bed and positioned herself on all fours, right on the edge.

With her ass in the air facing him, Phillip felt like he was in heaven. From any angle, he would have been in heaven. He watched as she reached for and passed a condom back to him.

"I want you now. Don't be gentle," she said, the authority back in her voice.

Phillip was so flustered and crazed with wanting that he dropped the foil packet. When he picked it up, he fumbled in an effort to open the thing. By the second, he needed her more, but he also fumbled more. Finally, he used his teeth to rip it open and quickly enclosed himself.

The view of her from where he stood was gorgeous. He felt he could look at her all night. From her folds, he saw wetness appearing - lots of it. He couldn't wait any longer. He stepped forward and eased into her. Slowly but firmly at first, he then picked up tempo and force.

"Hmm, yeah, that's it," he heard her moan. It pushed him on more. "Give it to me harder, Phillip! You feel really good."

Hearing her words, he knew he might not be able to keep up the tempo for much longer. When he got the first inkling that an orgasm might be starting, he pulled out of her and knelt on the ground. Ignoring her protest, he began licking her clit quickly. Almost immediately she climaxed against his tongue. He stood and resumed thrusting, finally letting himself reach the finish line. The power of his orgasm was incredible. Feeling his knees go weak, he had to hold her hips to steady himself as his body convulsed.

Daisy eased forward slowly, lowering her body down onto the bed. Phillip moved with her so that they were both lying down, still connected, with him on her back. To her, it felt secure, like he was shielding her from any dangers out in the world. To him, it felt like home, being able to physically touch the full length of her.

After a long while, he moved off her. They lay down beside each other and faced one another. No words were said. Each of them just looked, and subsequently fell asleep.

~~~~~

When Phillip woke, he saw the beginning of sunrise. The clock beside the bed revealed it was just after five in the morning. He was still on top of the bed, naked. When he turned his head the other way, he saw that Daisy was under the covers. Unsuccessfully he tried to creep under the covers without waking her.

"You must be cold," her sleepy voice said as she stirred. "Come closer to me. I'll warm you up."

Phillip smiled even though he could see her eyes were still closed. She wasn't quite awake yet. That didn't stop him from moving closer to her and into her hold. As he turned around and presented his back to her, she automatically curled around him. Being Friday, he had work on but not till nine. She would have work on too, earlier. He closed his eyes and waited for her alarm to go off. Lying in her arms felt far too good for him to even consider getting up simply because he'd happened to wake early.

~~~~~

"What are we doing, Phillip?" Daisy asked him an hour later after they had both woken to her regular alarm. She was lying against his chest, letting him use his strength and muscular body to envelop her.

"We are doing exactly what I want us to be

doing," he said gently. He felt a slight panic, like he thought she might bolt. "Aren't we doing what *you* want us to be doing?"

"Are we going to just forget everything in our lives apart from our own time together?" Daisy asked.

Phillip pondered that for a while before answering.

"I would like to think that we can find a balance between sharing what we can and both of us understanding that we will each keep from the other what we shouldn't share."

She lifted her head and looked at his face. He had fresh stubble that made him look even sexier. His suggestion didn't seem possible or even sane to her, but she didn't tell him that. Instead, she nodded and told herself not to worry anymore. What would be, would be.

"I have to get ready for work," she said and kissed him. When she pulled away, he nodded, having no desire to change her mind. "After work today, I'm meeting up with friends for dinner. When will I see you?"

"When would you like to?"

"Soon," she said and took him on a long period of kissing again. "Tomorrow? Brunch?"

"I'd like that," Phillip replied.

"And stay till Sunday night?"

"I'd like that even more."

CHAPTER 9

"*So*, when are we going to get to meet this masked mystery man?" Vinnie asked Daisy as the four friends sat around the solid wooden table. The location of their Friday night meal had been Emma's choice, and she'd chosen a pub that served good old-fashioned roasts. Each of them had a plate piled with roast lamb, roast vegetables, and gravy sitting before them.

Daisy laughed and lifted a mouthful of meat and gravy into her mouth. Vinnie suspected she'd timed it to avoid the question. He was right.

"Come *on*, Daisy!" Nicola said, sounding like a child who was being denied ice cream. "You can't have months and months of celibacy and then not even share details of the hot sex you're obviously having."

Daisy swallowed her food and grinned widely at all three faces before her. "*Seriously*? What would you want to know?"

"Well," Emma added in, holding up one hand and ensuring everyone could see she was about to begin a count-off on fingers of all the questions *she* wanted to ask. "First off, does he love or hate to use his tongue?" she asked and immediately heard everyone laugh out loud.

"Emma!" Nicola said as if she was about to tell her friend off. "That question isn't the first. It's the second. The *most* important one is how *big* is he?"

Daisy couldn't help but be equally disgusted and amused by the audacity of her friends. She said nothing and instead took another healthy mouthful.

"*I* heard he's rich and drives around in a Lamborghini," Vinnie pretended to whisper in Nicola's ear. "He's got *ten* ex-wives and is now looking for wife number eleven!"

Inside her mind, Daisy groaned. The efforts Vinnie would go to get details never ceased to amaze her. Eventually, he gave up and moved onto the more interesting topic of the new man in *his* life. It was a nice respite from her inner thoughts, getting to listen to him talk about his new boyfriend.

Her mind continued to drift back to Phillip. Of course, it did. He was beautiful. He was sexy. He was muscular and toned, *and* he had long eyelashes, but even removing all of those exterior things, he seemed to just be a good guy. Did it even matter what his family was like? Daisy argued with herself over that one. It shouldn't have mattered, but they *might* have been on the wrong side of the law - that being the same law that Daisy was on the *other* side of.

She caught herself out a few times, being enclosed in her own mind rather than listening to her friends. She kept trying to tune out to thoughts of him and refocus on what was being said, but truth be told, it was a relief when the evening ended. As much as she loved her friends, her heart and her head just weren't in it that night.

~~~~~

Phillip woke early Saturday morning but lay in bed as long as he could to prevent himself from having to get up to go to the bathroom. After that, he tried to go back to sleep. It was no use. He was far too awake - in all ways.

He made himself at least attempt to lie in bed, even if not for sleep. As he lay under the covers, he thought of the day and night to come. He'd loved spending the previous weekend with Daisy that he had. She had shown all sides of her then - her wit, her sarcasm, her laughter, and her seriousness. That was before they had known honestly who each other was. What would the weekend entail now that they had a couple of major facts out there in the open?

It was far too early in the morning for such serious thoughts. He lay back and let himself think about the more pleasurable aspects of their time together as his hand moved to where it needed to be. Then he leaned over, found a sock that would need to be washed anyway, and used it as a receiver for the incredible ejaculation that came from thinking about her body, her lips, and her hands.

~~~~~

"What are you up to?" Phillip asked his oldest sister, Sasha, when he finally readied himself for the day.

When he entered the kitchen to grab coffee and toast before he'd run out the door, she was absorbed in her mobile phone. It wasn't the device that put Phillip on alert, so much as the look on her face.

"None of your business," she threw back at him.

The tone stopped him in his tracks. She was obviously in one of her worse moods. With Sasha, there seemed to be two settings - slightly angry and very angry. It was an ongoing source of wonder to Phillip that his sister had the nature that she did. She was five years younger than him. In their childhood, they'd sometimes hung out and sometimes not, but for as long as he could remember, she'd had the worst temper he'd ever seen on anyone. She could be asked the time and want to rip someone's throat out for being bothered with the question. He'd seen her dragged into the cop station many times over the years. Usually, it was for violence or verbal abuse. Always she got away with either no charge or a minor charge. Sometimes Phillip saw her as a ticking time bomb. That thought scared him.

Sasha looked up from the screen in her hands. She didn't want to snap at her oldest brother. At times when she did it, she always regretted having reacted so quickly.

"Sorry. I'm going to head down to the bakery and pick up some munchies. I can get you something if you want," she said and saw surprise on Phillip's face. It was the look on his face that set her off again. Why did he have to look surprised? Why did he look like she never said or did nice things for people? That was why she gave up trying. People always looked at her like she was crap. "Actually, scrap that," she said as she stood up and started to walk out. "I'm not getting you anything."

Phillip stood still, wondering what had just happened. He was used to her tantrums that seemed to come out of nowhere, but as usual, he had no idea what was behind it. He heard the front door slam. It was a clear indicator that Sasha was no longer in the house.

"Who was that?" he heard his mother, Stacey, ask from behind him.

"Only one person exits the house that noisily - Sasha," Phillip replied. "What is going on with her, Ma? I know she's always been angry but is it my imagination, or is she getting worse?"

"She sings her own tune," Stacey replied. "You know that."

"I know," Phillip said and tried to push his sister out of his mind. He had far more pleasurable things to think about. "I'm making coffee. Do you want some?"

"Yes, please."

Phillip watched her sit down at the kitchen table as he made and carried their coffee cups over.

"Ma, are you okay? You look tired."

Stacey reached out and patted his hand. "I'm fine, but thank you for asking. It means a lot," she said.

The sadness of her smile wasn't lost on Phillip. Something was up, and no-one was telling him about it.

Once his mother had ventured into the shower, he sought out his father, Mark.

"Dad," Phillip said as he poked his head into the office that his father seemed to live in.

"Yep. Come in," Mark said and saw his oldest son walk in. "What's up?"

Phillip closed the door behind him.

"Is Ma okay? She looks … something."

Mark felt a sliver of pride. All his kids did what they were told - generally - but so few of them seemed to be able to see past themselves and really see others. Phillip had proven himself different on many occasions. He was perceptive. Sometimes he was the only one that seemed to care about his mother or his father.

"Come and sit down," he said and waited until Phillip was seated in front of him. "I think your mother has had a real scare with what Rex just went through. This way of living, Phillip, is how I was raised. Where you are now, I was at when I was growing up. My father lived like this when he was a kid too. Generation after generation of Leadbetter families instill this same way of life in their kids, and we keep doing it. Your mother wasn't like that when I met her. She was such a good girl," he said.

Phillip could see real love openly expressed on his father's face. It was a rare thing to see.

"Why she wanted to date me, I will never know, but she did," Mark continued. "Then she wanted to marry me. She didn't care that I was a thug. She is an incredible woman."

Phillip nodded but remained silent. It was unheard of that his father would talk openly like he was, but it was welcome. It didn't seem like so much of a different scenario that Phillip had found himself in recently.

"I think your mother is over living like this, truth be told, and I am starting to agree with her," Mark said. "We aren't getting any younger. It would be nice to live out the rest of our years in peace. You kids are old enough to live your own lives however you want. Our time as criminals has to end though."

As Phillip heard the words, he felt his heart begin

to pound.

"You mean, we don't have to do those things anymore?" he asked for clarification. "If we want to, we can live our lives how we want to, away from crime?"

Mark laughed softly.

"I wish you *all* would live away from crime. I know *that* won't happen. Sasha and Rex took to the life too well. I don't think they will ever change, and that's their choice," said Mark. "But you and David - you two are good men. I have always seen the goodness in you two. If you want an honest life away from all of this, Phillip, have it. Life is too short to live in more stress than you need to. I'm only sorry that it's taken me all these years to see that. A part of me wishes I'd stood up to my father and moved away from him. Your lives could have been so much better…"

"Dad, we have a good life. You and Ma have given us all that we could want, and you are great parents," Phillip said, the honesty of the declaration very clear in his voice. "No matter what we've done, you've given us all a home, and you and Ma have never treated us badly. Please don't think that any of us wish we'd been raised differently…"

The door opened, and Stacey walked in, tears in her eyes. She moved straight to Phillip and opened her arms. He stood and happily hugged her.

"Thank you, Phillip," she said. "You don't know how much hearing your words means to me."

"It's just the truth," he replied quietly as he pulled back from their hug. "Ma, you and Dad should live how you want to live. We can all look after ourselves."

Stacey nodded.

"Soon," she said. "Anya is only fifteen. Your father and I will still be here until she is through her schooling. Then we will reassess our lives and what time we have left together. Don't worry about this now. Go out, and make good choices."

Phillip hugged her once more and then excused himself. As he walked out, he found himself emotional. They had never been a lovey-dovey family, doing all that heart to heart and hugging stuff. It was nice to see that side of his parents. He hoped that he'd find that with someone one day. Hell, he hoped he'd find it with Daisy, if only she could look past his family's criminal history.

CHAPTER 10

James Stonewarden decided it was a good morning to head back to his family home and see how everyone was. Since Max's recovery, James hadn't spent much time with any of them. The family business was quiet, and for him, life moved ahead with his regular job and his women loving, just as it always had before the shooting.

He decided to call into the local bakery on the way to the large house he'd grown up in. His father would appreciate some of those cinnamon buns he'd always loved. Maybe he'd pick up some chunky chocolate chip cookies while he was there and take them out to Charlie after the visit home. She was pregnant. She was probably really missing those cookies now that she didn't live just down the road from the bakery.

Charlie. Nineteen, married and pregnant. James shook his head whenever he thought of that. If anyone else had talked about a 19-year-old in that situation, he would have thought some asshole had taken advantage and knocked a girl up without any thought for consequences. His sister wasn't in that situation. Even James could see how Charlie and Ash were around one another. They'd fallen in love. It hadn't been just some kid crush or even some weird chemical thing driven by good sex. No, they had met and just clicked. It was that easy for her. James had never had that happen to him. He got on with women, sure - lots of women. But looking at one and thinking he'd want to spend the rest of his life with them, day in day out? Hell, no! That was just *insanity*.

~~~~~

He pulled into the carpark of the mall the bakery

was nestled into the side of. Walking in, he could see a few people waiting. It wasn't too busy, but it was busy enough that he'd have to wait a while to get to the counter. He was happy to wait- until he saw the last of the cinnamon buns being bought.

"Umm, is there any chance you might like to pass those up today so that *I* could buy them?" he asked the woman in front of him.

It was a cheeky request, but he lived pretty much every day as a 'what the hell' day. As he looked at her, she turned around with a look on her face that definitely wasn't friendly. James instantly took a step back.

"Seriously? You think *you* are more important than *me*?" she asked, moving right up to him and raising a finger to his face in anger.

James was partially pissed off with her, partially impressed with her, and hell if he wasn't instantly *aroused* by her.

"Whoa! Sassy!! I *like* it," he said, not sure how anything he could say might be taken by the force of nature in front of him.

She looked like she wanted to punch him, but as he looked closely at her, he could see she was trying real hard to hold back a smirk. She was as tough a looking chick as he'd ever seen. Her arms were bare beyond the short-sleeved t-shirt she had on, and up one arm was an image of a gothic scene. James found his eyes drawn to it. He wasn't thinking when he reached out to touch it, wanting to move the arm so that he could look at more of the picture ingrained into it.

"Touch me, and I'll knife you," he heard the sassy voice say.

This time there was no humor in it, and when he looked at her, there was no hidden smirk. She was angry - right down to the guts of her soul.

"What's your deal, sweet thing?" he asked. "Overdue for your sugar craving? I was only looking at your tattoo. If you don't want people looking at it, here's an idea. Wear clothes with *long sleeves*!"

"Hey! Who's buying these?" the counter assistant called out as they pointed to the bag holding all of the cinnamon buns.

The woman turned around to him and then looked back at James. He saw a softening on her face. He assumed that wasn't something many people saw when they looked at her - not too often anyway.

"Let him have them," the woman said. "I'll take five of those chocolate brownies instead."

James was astounded and speechless - for at least thirty seconds. Then he leaned over her from behind and whispered into her ear, "Thank you, sweet thing."

It was a mistake. As the woman whirled around, James found a small knife at his chest. Sheesh, was she confusing or *what*!

"Whoa! Calm down," he said, taking a step backward. "I was just thanking you. I don't think good manners are anything to pull *that* out for."

The woman looked at the knife as if she hadn't even realized she'd pulled it out. She said nothing to James, instead just turning around, paying, and then walking out.

James looked at her throughout the movement. He watched her walk out the door and out of view of the bakery window.

He felt like he'd just come face to face with a tornado.

~~~~~

Sasha Leadbetter walked out of the bakery, brownies in hand. She'd really wanted those cinnamon buns. She could have had them, but that guy ... fuck, he was a looker alright. Guys never affected her. They were wimps, all of them. They didn't like pain. They didn't like chicks who were tough. They wanted pretty princesses with perfect hair, perfect nails, a tiny waist, and big breasts. She'd never be one of those bitches, and she'd never take crap from any guy. She was 23 years old. She'd lost her virginity two years earlier. That had been a mistake. She was stupid in that. That asshole had worked her over just to take that. Then he'd taken off and never talked to her again. That was the last time she'd had sex, and she had no intention of having it again. It didn't even feel good. People who said it was something amazing were liars.

She walked a little way and then stopped and looked in the window of a second-hand bookstore. She did like to read, and hell, anywhere that was happy to sell books for 50c deserved to have customers. While she stood there and let her eyes peruse the multitude of books on display in the window, she heard that voice again. She'd only just forgotten about him, and his voice was once again emanating into her brain.

"So, if I promise to stand back at this distance, are you gonna tell me your name, sassy girl?" James dared to ask.

Sasha turned to him. Hell, he was good looking - not in a pretty-boy type of way, but a more refined-bad-boy type of way. She didn't want to be involved with anyone, but that didn't mean she couldn't look and admire. He stood where he was, seemingly determined to not dare come near her. He didn't look like he'd ever back down to a woman, and yet he was staying exactly where he was - just like she wanted him to.

"Why would I want to tell you my name?" she threw back.

James felt his heart pounding. It was like he was facing an animal in pain. It could lie down and let him approach. It could equally lunge at him and rip his throat out.

Sasha watched as he slowly reached into the bakery bag and held up one cinnamon bun.

"Because I have something you want..." he said

in a melodic sing-song fashion as his eyebrows raised, and he revealed a mock sexy suggestive look on his face.

Sasha held back her desire to laugh. Venturing closer to him, she saw his nervousness as she moved forward enough to almost touch his chest with hers. She looked at his lips, teasing him without any intention of following through with the kiss she was pretending to offer.

James watched her as her lips moved toward his. Her eyes were dark brown, to the point where they were almost black. He couldn't put his finger on what exactly, but there was something about the girl that his body was reacting to.

He was drawn in, just as she'd wanted him to be. As soon as he closed his eyes in anticipation of her lips meeting his, he felt the cinnamon bun disappear from his hand. He pulled back and looked at what had just happened. After a couple of seconds, he threw his head back and laughed. Oh, yeah. She'd gotten him good. How the hell had *that* happened? He never lost control of a situation that involved a woman.

A smile was on her face as she bit into the bun. Then she just turned and walked away.

"Hey! Wait!" James called out to her. When she turned around, he yelled more. "I still don't know your name."

She said nothing. She walked away from him and didn't look back anymore, and that never happened to James Stonewarden. Never. Ever.

~~~~~

Sasha walked away feeling like her mood was stable. That guy had flirted with her. She was sure of that. He was also a looker, but no guy was going to treat her like crap again. No, she was wised up to them now. She wasn't for anyone to just walk over.

As her mind took over and led her thinking, she became more and more morose and then more and more angry. Having finished the cinnamon bun, she let the hand not holding her bakery bag return to her pocket. There was safety with the blade in her pocket. Feeling it under her fingertips was like a comfort. Some kids liked the feel of 'blankies' or 'cuddlies'.

Sasha Leadbetter liked the feel of a knife.

Especially when she was angry.

And that was a lot.

~~~~~

"Hey! You got your car back in one piece," James said to Max as he entered the living room of the Stonewarden family home. "She's looking good, too."

"She is, but I'm thinking about selling her," Max replied just as his father walked into the room.

"You are?" Mitchell asked, surprised. "Why?"

"Dad, someone tried to steal it," Max replied. "Hell, they *did* steal it. I don't want a car that people want to steal, and besides, me and Optimus are getting on just fine."

James laughed out loud.

"Optimus?!" He went to his baby brother and tousled his hair in affection. "You are one of a kind, Maximus."

"What are you doing here, James?" their father asked, wondering if there was some new trouble brewing somewhere.

"I just came to say hello," James said. "I haven't been here for a while. I brought you some cinnamon buns. I got some of the cookies that Charlie loves too. I'm gonna take them out to her soon."

"Can I come?" Max asked, missing his sister at the mention of her name.

"Sure thing," James called out as he ventured from the living room to the kitchen. He hadn't lived at home for a long while. That was no excuse for not appreciating the well-stocked cupboards and refrigerator.

"Thanks for the cinnamon buns. Is everything

okay with you?" he heard his father ask quietly from behind him.

"Yeah, of course," said James. "Why?"

"I'm just asking. We hardly ever see you…"

"I know. I'm sorry. I wanted a break after all that time in the hospital, seeing Max like that," James said quietly, not wanting his brother to hear his words. "I just needed to take some time to breathe again."

Mitchell looked at him. It was well past time that James and his older brother, Vic, each settled down and started a family. Mitchell knew it was pointless having a discussion along those lines. With James, women were for sexual pleasure and nothing else. He'd been taught to respect them, and Mitchell believed he did in his own way, but whether he would ever see more in a woman than he'd ever seen before was a mystery.

"Alright. I'm heading out," he said. "If you make a mess in here, clean it up!"

James smiled and saluted his father before resuming his search of the cupboards. There had to be something worth eating in the large kitchen that was about the same size as his entire apartment.

~~~~~

"Hey, Sis," Max said as he found himself later enveloped in Charlie's arms.

When she hugged him, he could definitely feel the baby bump. It kind of freaked him out that she was pregnant and going to become a mother, but he was happy for her.

"Hey, Ash," he said to his brother-in-law. He was still getting used to that term too. As if he hadn't already had enough brothers, now he had one more.

"Oh, Max, it is so good to see you," Charlie said. "And you, James, but what brings you out here?"

James lifted the bakery bag and instantly saw his sister's eyes shine as she giggled. "For me?"

He couldn't help but laugh at her enthusiasm.

"Chunky chocolate chip, baked fresh this morning."

Charlie looked at her brothers, then looked at her bag, then looked at her husband. It felt like a great day. She ushered them inside to make lunch for them all.

"Tom and Molly are away today, so it's just us," she said.

"How are you doing, Charlie? Is everything okay with the baby?" Max asked, not knowing anything about pregnancy but feeling like he should at least pretend he was interested.

"I'm fine. *We're* fine," she said, holding Ash's hand.

Max and James both looked on. Anyone seeing Ash and Charlie together could clearly see how they felt about each other. Both brothers silently wondered if something like that would ever happen in their own lives. It didn't seem such a great thing, the loving someone and settling down idea - except when Charlie and Ash were in the room. Then it looked like something that was very attractive indeed. They made it look easy. They made it look seamless.

James knew that he could have any woman he wanted - for sex, anyway. His mind cast fleetingly back to the woman he'd encountered at the bakery. She hadn't been bowled over by him at all. He still wasn't sure how he felt about that. He made a mental note to look in the mirror when he got back to his apartment. He wanted to check if perhaps his hair had started to go grey.

After eating, Ash took James out to the stables to see the horses so that Charlie could have some time alone with Max. They'd been closest to each other before the shooting. She saw much less of Max now that she was on the ranch. Ash didn't want her to feel isolated. He encouraged her to spend time with her family, even though what they did still was not good in Ash's eyes. No matter what, they were her family. They were important, regardless of what they did.

"How are things with you, Max? Really?" Charlie asked him as they settled on a small two-seat sofa in a tiny living room. When she compared the room to the healthy size of the house, she suspected that what was now a compact living room had probably been something unimportant when it had been built, like a coat closet. The size of the house she now resided in never ceased to amaze her - or Ash, who often joked that the 'small bathroom' he and Charlie shared was bigger than the entirety of his old apartment.

"I'm doing okay," Max replied. "The house doesn't seem the same without you there, though."

"Perhaps it's time you found someone special, huh?" Charlie asked. Immediately she read something on her brother's face.

"What?" she asked, grinning. "There's something there that you haven't told me."

Max laughed.

"No, it's nothing," he said. "Well, I met this girl, and I do really like her."

"Okay. That sounds good. Why don't you sound enthusiastic about it, if you do like her?"

"She isn't … she's not … she's…" he started to say but didn't feel right saying anything about Christy at all.

Charlie laughed.

"Okay, well, I am glad that she isn't and she's not," she teased him. She didn't press for more details. When Max wanted to talk, he always talked. "You know I'm here for you - always."

"You've got a lot going on…"

"No!" Charlie exclaimed. "I mean, we are running the ranch, yes, but I will always have time for you. No matter what."

"Soon, you'll have a little lady or little man running around your feet…"

"Yes, and they will need their Uncle Max as much as I need you," said Charlie. "Please, Max, I mean it. Keep talking to me. It helps me feel less detached from you guys."

Max looked at her. She looked tired but happy.

"Okay, but right now everything is fine in my world," he said, nodding. "It's uneventful. I am going to start looking for work, though. I'm thinking of looking for an entry-level mechanic's job somewhere."

"That's a great idea! You spent so much time on the Mustang and the ute. I bet you have as much knowledge as anyone who's studied for that kind of work."

"Maybe. We'll see."

"And you really don't want to tell me about the girl who's got your attention?" Charlie pushed.

Max chuckled softly.

"No. To be honest, I'm not sure how I feel. I want to move slowly there and just see how things pan out. But I promise that if I have any proper gossip, I'll keep you informed."

Charlie smiled and pulled him into a hug.

~~~~~

Out in the stables, Ash made small talk with James. It was hard for him to try and have lighthearted conversations with the Stonewarden men. He didn't want it to be difficult, but it was. They'd broken into his parent's apartment. His mother had ended up in hospital because of the stress that had flowed on from that. Regardless, they were Charlie's family, and he did want to make the effort and have some kind of neutral ground.

As far as he knew, the brothers themselves didn't know they'd robbed his parents. Charlie's dad knew - he'd been the one to go and get the ring back that his mother had been so distraught over. Other than that, as far as Ash believed, the boys themselves were oblivious.

"Is she really healthy, Ash?" James asked him,

taking him by surprise. "Really?"

Ash looked at him. When he'd first met the Stonewarden brothers, he'd been scared of each of them. Now that he was married to their sister and becoming a father, he felt an inner strength he hadn't felt before. They didn't intimidate him anymore.

"She is," he replied. "She has regular medical appointments, and everything is fine with her and the baby."

"She looks happy. I know that you are to be thanked for that," James said.

Surprised by the words, Ash kept quiet, sensing there was more coming that would surprise him.

"I'm envious of you, Ash," James continued. "I've never had any trouble dating women but finding someone to love - that must be amazing."

"It *is* amazing," Ash said. "I love your sister. I don't ever want to be apart from her."

James looked at his brother in law. He was a good kid.

"I know, and I'm glad that she found you. No-one else would have been good enough for our Charlie, I can promise you that."

CHAPTER 11

Phillip felt good. Showered, shaved, and looking and smelling as best he could, he started to walk out of his family home. Before he made it to the front door, he heard Anya's teenage voice behind him.

"You smell good. You must have a date," she said, starting the tease that he knew so well.

She was almost half his age, but she'd sussed him out early on. She knew how to charm her oldest brother and make him laugh. For a master pickpocket and small-time thief, Anya was surprisingly chirpy as a person. She couldn't have been any more different from her sister.

"Who is she?" she asked, grinning.

Phillip turned to her, smirked, winked, and then opened the door.

"That is for only me to know, baby sister," he said, teasing her back.

"Hey! I'm no baby!" she exclaimed.

Phillip laughed and closed the door behind him. Anya was okay. She'd come along when he was a teenager, so there was a different relationship between them than what he had with his other siblings. He'd seen her as a baby, then a toddler, and then beginning her school years. He'd helped her with homework when she'd needed it earlier on. Where she got her cheerful nature from had always been a curiosity of Phillip's, but he much preferred that to the constant anger and seriousness of his other sister.

As he made his way to the café where he was meeting Daisy, he thought about the conversation he'd had with his father. Phillip was 29 years old and the oldest in the family. For 29 years, his father, Mark Leadbetter, had lived his life and raised his children a certain way. Now he'd decided he didn't want to live that way anymore. Phillip wished his father had considered another option much, much earlier. Still, at least Anya would escape much of what her older siblings had done in their early 20s. She was a thief at heart - and a good one - but she was young enough to get that out of her system if their parents could work hard on reversing what they'd already drummed into her. It seemed an impossible and unlikely task, but in his heart, Phillip didn't worry about Anya so much. She got on with people, and she was likable. That would take her far, and she would probably grow out of her passion for theft as she broadened her social circle. Phillip was less certain about Rex and Sasha.

~~~~~

"Hey," he heard Daisy call out to him as he entered the small café.

Seeing she was already seated and waiting for him, Phillip took in the sight of her. She was in casual gear, but even in that, she looked immaculate and poised. With her blonde hair contrasting the black leather jacket she had on, she was stunning. If he hadn't already spent one weekend with her and seen her hair tousled and messy for most of it, he might believe that she was so well polished every minute of every day. He quickly turned his mind off to that thought. Remembering her hair messy was connected to remembering her naked in a wide variety of positions around her apartment…

"Hey!" he replied as he leaned down to kiss her softly. He sat opposite her at the tiny table she'd chosen near the rear of the café. "I hope you haven't been waiting long."

"No, you're all good, and you look *really* good," Daisy replied.

Phillip chuckled softly. When she stepped away from worrying about who she was and who he was, she was so easy going.

"And you look delectable," he replied, grinning.

Daisy laughed out loud.

"Delectable? Do you wish to eat me?" she teased him, whispering.

"Oh, yes. I very much do," Phillip whispered back and saw her blush. He took a deep breath and sat back, willing his body to relax at the suggestiveness passing between them. "How was dinner with your friends last night?"

"They were giving me a hard time about a masked mystery man."

"Were they now? And who would this masked mystery man be?"

"Some guy I met a while ago who has a beautiful body, and a beautiful smile, and beautiful eyes…"

"He sounds like quite the man. Will he get to meet your friends, do you think?"

Daisy pondered the question. Every man she'd been involved with, she had rushed into introducing them to her friends. They were like trophy men who she wanted to show off. Even Pete had started out that way, although he had grown on her as more likable for the long haul than her previous beaus had. But Phillip? Did she want to rush to introduce him?

"Perhaps in time," she replied. "For now, I feel selfish about my time with him. I want to enjoy brunch with him today, and then I want to take him back to my apartment and touch him everywhere."

Phillip couldn't help but grin excessively. He hoped they could eat quickly.

Very quickly.

~~~~~

"When we get inside, I want you to undress me," Daisy said as she put the key in her door.

Phillip heard the words and eagerly followed her through the door. She'd hardly closed it when she walked up to him and kissed him passionately. He heard her drop her bag and leather jacket on the floor and then felt her height change as she stepped out of her shoes, all the while maintaining her lips on his. He pulled away from her and looked at her attire. She was wearing a well-fitting v-neck long sleeve t-shirt. On her lower half were jeans. He hadn't seen her dressed in anything apart from her corporate gear before. She suited jeans and a t-shirt, although even in them, she looked incredibly well-groomed.

Not interested in not doing what she'd told him to do, he carefully lifted and removed her t-shirt. Underneath, she wore a red bra that was lacy. Through the lace, he could clearly see her nipples. It was a beautiful sight. He took his time, alternating between looking at her breasts, kissing her softly on the lips, and letting his lips caress the side of her neck. He didn't want to rush. They had all day, all night, and all the next day.

He heard her moaning as he let his tongue caress the skin in the small spot between her shoulder and her ear. He thought he could stay there for hours, caressing her in such a way if it meant listening to the desire he could clearly hear in her voice.

Daisy guided his lips back to hers and pulled herself tight against his chest as her arms wrapped around him.

Phillip felt her hands on his butt. He liked her hands being there. It felt like she was gripping him in a way that shouted, 'this is mine'. After a long while, he pulled back from her and reached down to undo her jeans.

Daisy closed her eyes and felt her legs slowly exposed to the air. He was gentle in pulling her jeans down, and he was thoughtful as he provided her with support while he removed them as she stepped out of them.

When they were clear, Phillip could see that the

briefs she had on were a match for her bra. Through the sheer lace, he could see her natural hair. Seeing it made him remember how glorious it was to taste her.

He stood up and kissed her passionately. Inside his jeans, he was stretched and hard. His body felt desperate to be inside hers, but he didn't want to rush.

Daisy generally moved things along at a fairly fast pace when it came to sex, not because she wanted it over with, but rather because she loved it so much that she just wanted to dive into it. It was like when she wanted to taste chocolate - she could take one tiny square at a time and make it last for ages, or she could dive right in and eat the block. Mostly she wished for the former but actually indulged in the latter. That was what sex was like with her, but for the moment, she wanted to go at his pace. So far she'd taken control of all the sexual pleasure they'd shared. Ahead of them meeting for brunch, she'd already decided that over the weekend, she wanted things more equal. In the moment they were currently in, she wanted him to take control.

Phillip guided her to the sofa and encouraged her to lie down along the length of it. Looking down at her for a long while, he drank in the sight of her body and the red see-through lingerie.

"You are so beautiful, Daisy," he said quietly.

She was used to complements but rarely believed them. The way he'd told her she was beautiful made her feel like he was being honest. She felt a little piece of the ice around her heart melt a tiny bit more at that moment.

As Phillip pulled his t-shirt off, he saw Daisy's eyes fall to the eagle tattoo on his chest. She'd said she loved looking at it, and he loved her looking at him. He'd never considered himself attractive. He just wasn't a guy who thought about things like that, but he felt it in her presence.

She watched as he removed his socks and shoes, then undid his jeans and slid them off. His gorgeous erection was highly visible under the boxer shorts he had on. She was eager to touch and see him fully naked, but instead of indulging her in that, Phillip lay down on top of her and just kissed her. His lips caressed hers, over and over, with a softness that melted her heart another tiny bit. She could feel his hardness rubbing against her subtly, and loved the feelings coming from the movement. The combination of that and the way he was kissing her and looking into her eyes between kisses, played with her senses *and* her emotions.

After a long while, she slid her hands inside his boxers and caressed his buttocks. The skin touching him there made him moan in pleasure. It wasn't a usual spot for erotic feelings to stem from, but she was increasingly affecting him the more she touched him in the simple way she was.

"I want to spread you out on your bed," he said quietly and saw her nod.

Phillip stood up, helped her up, and led her by the hand to her bedroom. There he pulled his boxers off and stood before her. He was at full attention, and Daisy felt her arousal pushed up a notch at the sight. His hands found their way to her body and gently removed her bra and panties, leaving her naked before him.

"Lie down," he said in almost a whisper.

Daisy did as she was told. As a general rule, she didn't like being told what to do, but something about him made her trust him that little bit more than others she'd been with. She felt him lie on top of her again, keeping his erection back as a way of being in control. She closed her eyes and focused on the way his body was moving over hers. His lips were everywhere, kissing her neck, her nipples, her inner thigh, her clit, and then teasingly moving down her leg until he kissed her ankles. It was a blissful massage of kisses. Every kiss felt invigorating, not only the ones directly on her core.

"Roll onto your tummy," she heard him whisper.

Following his instruction, she immediately felt his lips at the back of her neck. The sensation made her moan loudly. It was the exact point she'd always loved to be touched.

Hearing her react to it so much, Phillip stayed there for a long while, as he lay down on her back. From that position, he slid his hands around the side of her, encouraging her to lift herself enough to enable his fingers to lightly squeeze her nipples.

The combination of his fingers moving, and his lips on her most sensual point of her neck, pushed Daisy close to climax. She started to move her hips so that she was rubbing her clit on the bed. The four points of pleasure felt incredible.

Phillip became aware of what she was doing. The thought of her driving herself crazy by rubbing against the bedcover, in turn, drove him crazy. He saw the condoms on the bedside table and removed himself for a moment to grab one and slip it on. Once encased, he resumed his position where he'd been.

Daisy felt his hands once again start caressing her nipples as his lips moved over her neck. She then felt him push her thighs apart before she was engulfed in the feeling of him moving into her.

"Yes!" she said out loud.

The two of them moved slowly at first so that she could still rub against the bed while he moved in and out of her. After a while, he felt her raise her hips a little and move her hand to begin rubbing herself. The effect on Phillip was incredible. He could feel little twitches inside of her. Each one felt like a little squeeze on him.

"Phillip, please. I'm going to come any mo…"

He felt her grip him tightly as her body convulsed. He instantly started to thrust into her more quickly, until he also exploded in sweet orgasm. He made no attempt to move in a hurry. Her breasts were still cupped in his hands, and his torso was entirely covering hers. It felt good to be with her, not just sexually but entirely.

When he pulled off her, he lay down on his side and saw her turn to face him. Daisy kissed him in a way that made him think she had plenty more fuel in her yet. Her eagerness made him smile.

"You don't look like you need or want rest time," he said quietly.

Straight away, Daisy's look of intensity was replaced by a grin and a slight blush.

"Maybe," she said as she moved her body in a way that encouraged him to roll onto his back and pull her against him in an embrace. "But we have all weekend. I don't want to wear you out."

He chuckled while kissing her forehead.

"I'm just glad to be here with you. Thank you for asking me."

Daisy heard the seriousness in the tone of his voice. She raised her head and kissed his lips softly.

"There's no doubt that I want to be with you, Phillip."

"Maybe, when we're in a tight little bubble like we are right now," he replied. "But all those things on the outside of us are still there, Daisy. They aren't gone just because we're hiding away in your apartment."

Daisy heard the words and knew he was right, but since she'd first seen him at the café that morning, she'd tried to just focus on him as a man and not as a part of his family. That had helped her to feel more relaxed.

"I know," she said. "I know in the long run those other things will always be hanging over us, but can't we have moments like this where we pretend we aren't who we are?"

Phillip looked at her intently. She wanted a perfect world where there was no conflict and no drama. A part of him wished he could give her that.

"I know we hardly know each other, but from the

little time we've spent together, I already love who you are," he said. "Don't pretend you're not that person - not with me. Your job is your job. No matter how much you love it, it isn't *you*. You are beautiful and sexy and loving…"

"Loving?" she asked, giggling slightly. "How can you judge that just by the hot sex we've had so far?"

"I can tell by the way you keep cuddling into me," he said. "People who have sex for the sake of having sex don't usually stay around for cuddles. *I* think you have a loving nature inside of you, no matter how strong and independent you try to appear."

Daisy said nothing. She believed his words to be true, especially as she moved against him further still and felt him hold her tighter. She did love being an independent woman, but she also loved the security that she felt in his arms. His body was muscular and solid, and his arms around her were like a force field, keeping her safe. She shifted her head slightly so she could look again at the large eagle over his heart. She kissed his lips, kissed the eagle, and then rested her head down.

She didn't want to think anymore.

CHAPTER 12

As Sunday afternoon arrived, Daisy huddled against Phillip while they sat on her sofa. They had shared another incredible weekend together. Soon he would leave and return to his home. The thought was one that Daisy found she wasn't enthusiastic about.

"You seem tense. Do you want me to go now?" Phillip asked, reading something in her body.

"No," she replied quietly. "I was thinking the opposite, actually. It would be nice to have another day with you..." she said before her voice trailed off.

Phillip pulled back from her, forcing her to raise her head from his chest. When she faced him, he slipped his hand firmly into her hair and pulled her toward him.

Daisy welcomed it. Everything he did she welcomed, if she was honest with herself.

Lovingly Phillip moved his lips against hers for a long while. He felt the same way. He didn't want to leave. A part of him worried that once he walked out, that might be it. She might decide again she couldn't handle who he was and where he came from.

"Do you have to work tomorrow?" she asked with a sound of shyness in her voice.

Phillip smiled at her. Her blend of woman power and woman subtlety was incredible.

"No," he said. "I only work on a casual basis when Enrique needs me. As far as I know, he has nothing for me to work on this week at all."

Daisy sat quietly, her mind working. It seemed so easy to make the decision to take one day to spend with him. It would only be one day. She'd never taken a day off work. It wasn't an easy decision to make. Could she? Should she?

Phillip watched her face and smiled further.

"Do you want to share?" he asked, teasing her. She seemed confused, as if not sure what he was referring to. "You asked if I'm working tomorrow. Why?"

"I'd really like to spend more time with you, but to do that, I'd have to take a day off work."

"Daisy, I'd never ask you to…"

"Oh no, I wasn't meaning that you did," she said. "No, I mean, I was thinking that I would like to take a day off work and spend it with *you*."

Phillip said nothing in reply. The thought was welcome, but it was something she'd have to decide for herself. As if in answer to her own question, she stood slightly and then straddled him. As her arms moved around his neck, he moved his hands so that he cupped her butt. He loved the shape of her curves. Everything fitted him perfectly.

"You know what? I'm going to take the day off tomorrow. I've never done that. I think I'm long overdue. What do you think?" she asked and saw him laugh at her.

"I think you need to do what you need to do, Daisy," said Phillip.

"Can you be tempted to staying another night with me?" she asked.

His reply led them right back to her bedroom.

~~~~~

Across town, Sasha was walking along the waterside when she heard *that* voice again.

"Hey! Sassy girl!"

When she turned, she saw that guy running toward her - the same guy she'd seen at the bakery the day before.

James had seen her walking as he'd been driving. He hadn't even thought before pulling his car over, jumping out, and running to her.

"What do you want?" she asked him when he got closer.

James looked at her. Silently he asked himself the same thing. What did he want from the tough thing in front of him?

"I just saw you when I was driving past…"

"And?"

"And…" he started to say but couldn't even find an answer to that himself. "And I just wanted to say hi."

"Okay," Sasha replied before turning and just walking away from him.

"Are you ever going to tell me your name?" James called out.

Sasha didn't look back. He was a guy. He probably wanted sex. He probably thought she was an easy score. He was wrong. She was never going to be any asshole's bitch again. In need of comfort, she slipped her hand into her pocket and softly caressed her only friend - her knife.

James watched her for a minute longer before remembering he really couldn't be parked where he'd stopped. Seeing no reaction from her, he turned and began walking back to his car. His head was shaking from side to side. Only one word was evident in his thoughts. *Unbelievable!*

~~~~~

Monday morning, Daisy made her phone call to say she wouldn't be working that day. It was the first such phone call she'd made in her lifetime. It was unheard of to anyone who knew her that she would ever do such a thing. As she hung up from the phone call, she felt like a naughty schoolgirl, telling a tale as an excuse to do naughty things all day instead of what she should be doing.

As the morning passed, Phillip lovingly lay on top of her, moving in and out of her slowly. He'd lost count of the number of orgasms he'd had, and she'd had. It had been an incredible long weekend. Still they continued to explore and learn more about each other's bodies. Lying, sitting, standing, kneeling - even he'd never had as much sex as they were having in such a short period of time.

As lunchtime Monday arrived, both lay on their backs in her bed, sated.

"I think you're dehydrating me," he teased her and heard her giggle. "No, honestly, I have no more liquid inside of me. I need to replenish hydration."

Daisy knew he was teasing her, but moved out of the bed and walked to the kitchen to grab them each a drink. While out there, she couldn't help it - she had to pick her phone up and check nothing important had happened.

When she saw three calls from her boss, she panicked. Immediately she forgot Phillip and their drinks. She dialed her work number. When she got through, she heard urgency in the voice at the other end of the line.

"Daisy, I'm so sorry to have called you. I was in a panic, but really, it's nothing you need to come in for."

"What is it? What's happened?" Daisy asked, wondering what could have caused such a reaction in her normally-steady boss.

"There's been a stabbing of a young girl," her boss said. "We'll represent the victim, but at the moment, both girls are in hospital. The one who used the knife is under police guard."

"Oh, but what was the urgency with it all then?" Daisy asked, intrigued about what could have caused her normally-steady boss to be so excited.

"Oh! Sorry! I didn't mention, did I? The one being accused of using the knife is the sister of the kid who was accused of the shootout. Leadbetter. His older sister…"

Daisy felt her heart move from beating to downright pounding.

"His sister … she was the one who used the knife?"

"Apparently. Sasha's her name. Apparently, she attacked someone but was stabbed in return. Both of them are in hospital…"

Daisy cut her employer off mid-sentence.

"Okay," she said. "Thanks for letting me know. I'll be back in the office tomorrow."

She heard her employer mumble a surprised goodbye and then hang up. When she did so, Daisy stood still for a moment to just think.

Phillip had moved out of the bedroom and approached her. He'd heard the end of the conversation but not the most important aspect of it.

"Are you alright, Daisy?" he asked softly. Despite the quietness of the question, he startled her. "Sorry. I didn't mean to scare you."

"No," Daisy started to say, preparing the words she needed to say to him. "Phillip, we need to get dressed," she said when it suddenly seemed ludicrous that they were naked, but she needed to sit him down to break news to him.

Phillip had a feeling of dread inside of him. Whatever she was about to say, it wasn't good. He said nothing as he quietly dressed and watched her do the same.

Finally, she guided him to the sofa.

"You need to get to the hospital," she said quietly. "That was my boss. She was trying to get hold of me because of a stabbing between two girls." She saw him sit quietly with a look of confusion on his face. "Phillip, do you have a sister? Sasha?"

Phillip heard the question come from Daisy's lips, but his mind refused to put the two things together. Stabbing. Sasha. The two couldn't be related.

"Phillip!" he heard her say with more force in her voice. "Is Sasha Leadbetter your sister?"

"Yes," he said quietly. Daisy saw him shake his head as if his mind were finally clearing. "Yes, Sasha is my sister."

"Right. Listen to me. She's been in a stabbing. She's at the hospital. She and the victim are both in the hospital. Sasha's apparently under police guard."

Phillip continued to sit still as if he just wasn't hearing her.

"Come with me," Daisy said as she stood up and reached out her hand to pull him up. Words weren't working. "Come on. We're going in my car."

Phillip followed her, but even he could sense he was in shock. He felt numb as he got into Daisy's car and she drove. Soon they were in front of the hospital.

"I can't come in with you, Phillip, but you need to go inside and go and find Sasha. Now!"

Phillip nodded. He could hear the instruction, even if he wasn't quite functioning correctly. He looked at Daisy and gave her a kiss before silently getting out of the car, closing the door, and walking into the large hospital entry.

Daisy pulled away. Because of her job, she couldn't support him in whatever he was going to find inside. As she drove back to her apartment, she felt deep regret in that.

~~~~~

As soon as he walked through the large sliding doors at the front entrance to the hospital, Phillip finally found his mind return to normal. Daisy was only in the peripheral of his thoughts. He was thankful she'd told him what she knew, and she'd dropped him off at the hospital so quickly. Now he needed to focus on his family.

He ran to the front desk and got the information he needed. Sasha was on the fourth floor, room 412. She was also being restricted from having visitors. Phillip didn't care about that. He made his way steadily to the ward she was in.

As soon as he exited the elevator, his mother and father came into view. They were in a standing embrace. Phillip could tell by the shaking of his mother's shoulders that she was crying heavily.

"Phillip," he heard his father Mark call out to him as the two men viewed each other. Immediately Stacey pulled away from her husband and turned to face her oldest son.

Phillip moved forward quickly. As soon as he reached his parents, he felt his mother pull him into an embrace. He gladly wrapped his arms around her. He could feel tears start to threaten in his own eyes. Fear encroached on him. Was Sasha still alive?

"What's happened?" he asked his father quietly.

Mark watched his son holding Stacey. It was a rare thing to see, his kids giving their mother the affection she was due. It wasn't their fault. They had all been raised to be independent and strong. Part of that had been them being told to get over things rather than feel sorry for themselves and cry about it. Part of that had been their family as a whole not sharing affectionate moments. Mark once again felt regret at the way he'd followed the Leadbetter recipe for raising children.

"Sasha's been stabbed," he said. "The girl she apparently attacked is in here too. Both of them are still out to it, but the cops are watching Sasha."

Phillip nodded. He knew his sister's temper. For years, he'd watched as it got her into trouble again and again. He had no reason to suspect that whatever had gone down, she hadn't started.

Stacey pulled away from her son and wiped her eyes. She'd raised her kids to be strong. She needed to be strong herself. Lead by example - that was the Leadbetter way.

"They won't let us go in there. They won't let us see her," she said quietly, disbelief evident in her voice.

"They're acting like she's some kind of threat to everyone - like when she wakes up, she's gonna run around knifing people."

Phillip watched his mother speak and shake her head. Even to him, that idea sounded ridiculous. Sasha was bad-tempered, yes. She sometimes got violent, yes. But she'd hurt large numbers of people? Highly unlikely.

The three of them sat down together.

"Do the others know?" Phillip asked quietly and saw his father shake his head.

"We only got the phone call a while ago and just got here ourselves," Mark replied, then looked at his son with curiosity evident in his eyes. "How did *you* know to come here?"

Phillip gulped. If he told that story, he'd have to say Daisy was a lawyer - a lawyer who it seemed not only had been involved in Rex's trial but now might also be involved in Sasha's trial if one was going to happen. He couldn't even think of any words he could use to sideswipe the question by answering while at the same time *not* answering.

"I'd rather not say," he said quietly.

Mark nodded. He knew full well that sometimes it was best to not know things. To keep loved ones safe, sometimes that meant not telling them things that might later incriminate them.

"I can call the others if you want," Phillip said.

"Yes, please, Phillip," his mother replied. She had moved into her husband's arms again. She looked comfortable. She looked loved. Phillip realized, looking at the two of them holding one another, that even though it was new for him to see, there was no way it was a new thing for them to share. He found peace in the belief that although his parents had always presented a tough unloving front to him and his siblings, his mother probably *had* experienced love and affection all of the years that she'd been married to his father.

He nodded at them, stood, and moved away a little to make calls to his two brothers and his youngest sister, Anya. She was only 15. How was she going to handle what had happened to her only sister? Silently Phillip hoped the incident might serve as something to jolt Anya out of her criminal ways before she got any deeper into that lifestyle.

Mark held his wife tightly. His mind was working non-stop. Sasha had always worried him. He had no idea where her temper came from. Yes, she'd been raised to be tough, but she had a level of anger in her that had never shown in his other kids. Right through her school years he and Stacey had fairly regularly been called into school offices after Sasha had hit another kid or swore at them, calling them extreme names. She'd seen counselors and social workers. Sometimes she'd seemed to find a period of time where she could keep her temper level and maintained. Those periods never lasted long.

Despite the trouble that Sasha got herself into now and then, Mark knew she had good points. She'd never so much as spoken back to him or her mother. He knew that some parents had trouble in their own homes, with teenagers that treated them viciously. Sasha had never been like that. She did her own thing, and she always presented a tough image, but to her mother and father, she'd never shown disrespect. Mark had to believe that said something and *meant* something.

Phillip returned to where his parents sat. "David's working for another hour, and then he'll come down. I left a message for Rex, and I'm just going to head out to meet up with Anya. She's at the mall but is going to leave in a few minutes. I'll talk to her on the way back here."

Mark and Stacey both looked at him and nodded. He was a good son. In his teenage years, he'd given them a few moments of grief too, but nothing serious. He'd always done what they told him to do. He'd always done the criminal jobs he'd received instructions for. He'd equally outgrown his rebellious times pretty quickly. Mark and Stacey had both been real glad about that.

~~~~~

"Hey, baby sister," Phillip greeted Anya when she came into view.

"Don't call me *baby*!" she replied.

She was trying to look tough as she said it, but Phillip grinned at her. As far as siblings went, she was definitely the most likable. She smiled at him but then became serious.

"What's happened?" she asked. "Is it Rex?"

Phillip could hear the fear in her voice.

"No, not Rex," he replied. "I don't know the details about what's happened yet, but it's Sasha. She's been stabbed, and she's in hospital."

Anya stopped walking and looked at him in disbelief.

"But nothing ever happens to Sasha. She'd *kill* someone before they could hurt her."

Phillip heard the words and understood what she meant, but the choice of words did make him cringe. He didn't want to think of Sasha killing anyone. She had a tough exterior and knew how to project that. He'd never thought she had a tendency toward killing.

"We don't know what happened," he said. "Come on. Dad and Ma are at the hospital waiting for us."

"How are they?" Anya asked softly, sounding like she might begin to cry.

"They're fine. Both of them are fine, but I think Ma's really upset, so we need to support her," Phillip replied. "She might be needing your hugs when we get there."

Neither said anything more till they arrived at the ward. Immediately upon entering, Anya walked to her mother. Stacey, in return, stood and wrapped her arms tightly around her youngest child.

Two girls. Stacey had given birth to three girls, but only two had lived. They should have been close as sisters. In reality, they couldn't have been more different or more further apart than Anya and Sasha were. They were like polar opposites in every single way. It was only the oddly chirpy personality of Anya that helped keep the peace there. She had a good instinct. She knew she had to stay out of her sister's way and her sister's business. If she'd been any different, Stacey knew that she and Mark would have had sister scraps in their house of the physical nature.

"Is there any news?" Phillip asked, directing the question at his father.

Mark shook his head.

"All we can do is sit and wait for someone to tell us how she is and when we can see her."

CHAPTER 13

Inside the hospital room, Sasha opened her eyes. Immediately she could feel a sharp pain in her side. She reached down with one hand and felt something over the area that was sore. A bandage or some kind of padding? What the *fuck* was going on?

She turned her head and looked around. She wasn't at home, that was for sure. And the *smell*. It hit her hard. It was like some weird extreme cleaning fluid or something. Finally, she understood that she was in the hospital. She tried to clear her mind and figure out what she was doing there. She couldn't remember anything that had happened. She could remember being at the bakery. She could remember the guy from that day. He had called out to her the day after, too. *He* was in her memory. She couldn't remember anything else since then.

At the doorway, she could see a cop. She didn't want to talk to him, but she wanted answers. She was about to call out to him when a nurse entered the room.

"What's going on?" Sasha asked quietly. She could feel her regular mood threatening, but she tried hard to hold it at bay. She needed answers. She wouldn't get them if she showed anger. "Why am I here?"

The nurse looked at her. For a moment, Sasha saw some form of alarm - or perhaps fear. Then the woman seemed to push aside whatever that emotion had been.

"You're in the hospital, Sasha," the nurse said softly while grabbing and looking at the chart at the end of the bed. "How are you feeling? Are you in pain?"

Sasha nodded slightly.

"Yeah, but it's okay. I can handle it. I just want to

know how I got here. I don't remember…"

The nurse watched as the young woman before her seemed to fall asleep mid-sentence.

"We need to question her," the police officer said from the doorway.

"Well, that might be so, but for now, she's asleep. I don't think she presently has much to say."

~~~~~

Hours later, after police had entered and then left Sasha's room, Mark and Stacey were allowed to see their daughter.

"They're saying I tried to kill someone," Sasha said as she saw her parents enter. "I didn't."

"What happened, Sasha?" Mark asked. "Just tell us what happened."

Sasha felt panicked. She didn't even know.

"I can't remember, but I know I wouldn't have tried to kill someone, Dad," she replied. "I'd *never* do that."

Mark looked closely at her. She was good at lying. She always had been. But he agreed with her self-assessment. She was a tough young woman. She wasn't a murderer.

"I believe you," he reassured her.

"Just rest, Sasha. Your dad and I will stay right here," Stacey said to her daughter.

She automatically raised a hand and softly caressed Sasha's forehead. It had been a long time since Sasha had allowed people to touch her in any way. It was nice to see that for once, she didn't object.

Mark walked out and along to the waiting room.

"Phillip, take Anya home. Your mother and I are going to stay here…"

"But we want to see…" Anya started to say. She instantly cut her words short when she saw the look on her father's face.

"Okay," Phillip replied.

He wanted to know more. He wanted answers, but he'd always done what his father asked of him. Today was no exception. He guided his sister away so the two of them could return home and wait.

When they arrived, Anya went to the living room and put on a DVD. Phillip didn't stop her. She had her own ways of dealing with things that went on in their family. Escapism via movies was one of them. He was glad she could find some peace from such an easy activity.

He searched the kitchen and began to cook a meal for the two of them. As he did, his thoughts returned to Daisy. He'd have loved to have been able to be in her arms. He knew he couldn't be. The current situation was one of those times she'd warned him about. It was one of those times where something would happen in his family, and she'd somehow be involved in the other side of that same happening. He didn't know for sure she was going to have anything to do with anything about Sasha, but she *had* received that phone call.

"Here, kiddo," he said once he'd finished cooking and handed a bowl of cheesy pasta to Anya.

She looked at him and smiled as she received the food. She wasn't hungry, but he was trying to be supportive. She welcomed him sitting down on the sofa next to her.

"Thanks," she said quietly. For a few minutes, she tried to focus on the screen in front of them. Her mind wasn't in it. She turned her body so that she was facing Phillip. "Does it feel to you like bad things are starting to happen more regularly? To all of us, I mean."

Phillip looked closely at his youngest sister. She was past the age of him being able to tell her a story and have her easily believe it. She was fifteen, but she was fairly mature. It was time to talk to her as an adult.

"I think we live a life that makes it likely that we'll get in trouble with the law."

"Oh, yeah, I get that, but Rex getting accused of shooting at people. Now Sasha getting accused of knifing someone..."

"We don't know the details about that yet, Anya," Phillip said. "She might have..."

"No, she wouldn't," Anya instantly replied. "She might threaten something stupid like that, but she's never hurt anyone, Phillip. I just don't believe she'd do that."

Phillip put his arm around her, pulled her to him, and kissed her forehead.

"We just have to wait and see. Now eat before this culinary masterpiece gets cold."

Anya knew it was a signal to change the subject. She didn't argue. She turned her head toward the TV screen and began to eat.

CHAPTER 14

Daisy sat in her office, looking out the large glass window. From there, she could see masses of buildings. It was raining. She found herself focusing less on the buildings and more on the individual raindrops hitting and settling on the window. It had been two weeks since she'd dropped Phillip off at the hospital. He hadn't tried to see her or contact her. She hadn't tried to see or contact him. While his sister was suspected of being the initiator of the stabbing, Daisy knew she shouldn't have anything to do with him.

She missed him so much. It made no sense. He hadn't even been in her life for very long. That logic didn't stop the reality.

The police were building a case. From the sounds of it, they wanted Sasha to be found guilty of attempted murder. She could be the first Leadbetter who was found guilty of something that would put them away for a long time. In the eyes of the cops, that was long overdue.

Daisy followed the instructions of senior partners at the law firm. She'd always loved the feeling that came from helping to put criminals away. It gave her a sense of contributing in some small way to making the world a safer place. But she did feel for Phillip, being in the situation he must be in. Having read Sasha's extensive police file, Daisy knew that Phillip's sister must be one tough chick. Notes on her went back years and years. Briefly, Daisy found herself wondering if Phillip was the same in nature as his sister. Was he also angry and violent? Maybe he just hid it well...

She couldn't believe that. Her gut wouldn't let her. Her instinct reassured her that he was a good man, right through to the depths of his soul. He might follow his family's ways, but he had a goodness inside of him. She was sure of it.

"How's everything going?" Daisy heard the voice of her supervisor ask from the doorway.

Hastily, Daisy turned away from the large windows and smiled. "Good. There's a lot to read, but I think I'm getting to know Sasha Leadbetter quite well."

Her supervisor nodded.

"Good. The first Leadbetter is going to jail. Everyone's pretty sure of that. We need to make sure that does happen."

Daisy watched as her supervisor moved away and disappeared from view. It was her job to help put Phillip's sister in jail. Despite such a case being good for her legal experience, it only left a sour taste in her mouth.

~~~~~

When she got home that night, she did as she'd been doing a lot in previous weeks, tossing off her shoes then lying down along the length of her sofa. Her eyes closed, and she rubbed them. It was a soothing way of dismissing the day's work. Every day, she learned more and more about Sasha Leadbetter. A part of her felt sorry for the young woman. She'd been in trouble since she was in her early school years. Had everything that could have been done, really *been* done, for someone with such anger issues? Or had a system ignored some kind of explanation and let a young woman just live in her own angry world?

Daisy had to turn off that thinking. She was a lawyer. She had a job to do. She knew the police had located and sourced different video footage. It might be the last nail in the coffin, as far as the case went.

Her phone started to ring. She leaned down and pulled it out of her handbag. Emma's name flashed on the screen.

"Yo," Daisy said in her usual determined-to-not-sound-like-a-lawyer-to-friends voice.

"We're meeting at Bobby Blue's tomorrow for dinner," Emma said, excitement in her voice.

Daisy smiled. Emma had been talking about the new restaurant since it had opened a month earlier.

"You remember to make a reservation this time?" she teased her friend.

"*Yes*!" Emma replied with mock exasperation in her voice. "Six o'clock. Don't be late. They have two set-time sittings, so we'll be kicked out at seven-thirty."

"Okay."

"Hey. You okay?" Emma asked, hearing something missing in her friend's voice.

"Yeah, I'm all good," Daisy responded as she rubbed her eyes with the other hand.

"Still missing hot man, huh?"

Daisy chuckled softly.

"Yeah, a bit, but I'm about to go and have a long soak in the tub. I'll see you guys tomorrow at six. Are we meeting inside or outside?"

"Six, inside the door, so they know we're there."

Daisy heard the call disconnect. They always hung up on one another. It was just their way.

She let the phone drop from her hand onto the floor. She couldn't turn her thoughts off to the fact that she was helping to put away the sister of the man she loved spending time with. Why had fate brought him to her if she had to do such a thing to him and his family? Where was the fairness in that? And it wasn't even just the one time. She'd already worked on the trial for his *brother*. Silently she wondered if, over time, fate was going to test her by making her work on legal cases against every single person in his family.

The bath beckoned. Her shoulders revealed the tenseness of her work. She could feel stiffness as she undressed and waited for the bath to fill with the bubbles and scent of the bath soak she'd put in. As she waited, she looked in the mirror. She'd never minded her body, but Phillip had made her feel beautiful in every way. She loved the way he kissed her skin in different places. As she reached up and touched her nipples, she remembered the way she loved him flicking his tongue over them. She loved the way he used his tongue on her, bringing her to climax, and how he felt when he thrust into her...

"Fuck," she said to no-one listening as she remembered the bath and saw how full it was getting.

After turning off the taps, she lowered herself into the water, soaped up her hands, and closed her eyes. Indulging in the scent of the bath soak, she let her hands move over herself. It was easy to imagine Phillip touching her. They'd spent such a small amount of time together, but each occasion had been intense. He'd learned how to please her quickly. Hell, he'd done more than learn - he'd *mastered* how to please her. She'd always received attention from men. No-one had worked so hard in pleasing her as he did. He was beautiful.

Her finger found its final target as she visualized in her mind a replay of their last weekend together. The image that sent her over the edge was one of him on top of her, moving in and out of her while kissing her softly and lovingly.

She didn't want things to be over.

She wanted him.

She *needed* him.

~~~~~

"Sasha's coming home tomorrow," Stacey informed her family. She glanced around the large kitchen table. Four of her five kids were there - even Rex. He was still a worry, but he'd been quiet since his arrest. Stacey hoped he'd make a decision on his own to change the way he lived his life. It wasn't his fault he was the way he was, but it was up to him to change. No-one else could do that for him.

"And? What's happening as far as the cops are

concerned?" David asked.

Being the sibling who hardly ever spoke, everyone was surprised whenever he did.

"We'll just have to wait and see," Stacey said. "There's no court date set yet. I think they've been waiting for her to be well enough so it could happen this week."

"They're coming after us, aren't they?" Anya asked and saw her father look at her sharply. "They've tried to arrest all of us at some point. Sasha's finally given them a reason to."

Mark controlled his thoughts. He'd been thinking the same thing, but he didn't want to voice that.

"We don't know for sure what has happened or what is going to happen, but you all know Sasha," he said. "You know she has a temper. When she gets back, she'll be stressed and possibly still in pain. Don't make things worse. Ignore her if you have to, but don't any of you say anything that will anger her. The last thing she needs is losing her temper and doing something to make things look worse for her."

Each person around the table nodded and said nothing. They all knew Sasha. They also knew their father's advice was very sound.

~~~~~

Sasha lay in the hospital. She was sick of having to lie around so much. She wanted to get out. She wanted to walk and breathe fresh air. They'd told her she could go home the next morning and she couldn't wait. Not that going home was any great thing, but it was sure better than being in hospital.

She looked out the window. Her side still ached, but she'd had a lecture from the doctor. He'd told her how lucky she was.

"Two inches to the right," he'd said as if to stress she'd be dead now if she hadn't accepted the knife to where it had gone in.

"Finally I found you!" she heard a woman's voice say, breaking her out of her thoughts.

When she turned, she saw a face she didn't recognize.

"I've been looking for you for days," the woman said.

Sasha sat up, thinking some crazy person was on the loose.

"I'm sorry. I don't think…"

"You don't remember, do you?" the woman asked as she moved closer to the bed. "You don't remember the night you saved me and my daughter?"

Sasha was confused. For a moment, she really did think she was in the presence of a crazy person.

"I … I don't think…" she mumbled again. It was the most she could muster.

She was relieved when she saw a nurse enter the room.

"I have been looking for this young lady for a long time," the woman said to the nurse. "My daughter and I were heading home a couple of weeks ago, and some woman jumped us…"

"Oh my Lord," the nurse said. "I'll call the police at once. You don't need to be around this one…"

The woman looked confused. She could see the nurse had misunderstood what she was going to say.

"No, you don't understand," she said. "*This* isn't the woman who jumped us. This is the young woman who *saved* us."

The nurse asked for clarification and got it. Quickly, as she'd been instructed, she called the detective who'd been in and out of the ward since the Leadbetter patient had arrived. Within thirty minutes, the detective walked into Sasha's hospital room. He introduced himself to the woman in the room and then began to question her.

"I think you might be mistaken," he said. "Ms

Leadbetter here stabbed someone. She assaulted them…"

"No," the woman said. "I'm sorry, Detective, but *you're* wrong. We were attacked - my daughter and I - and this young woman stepped in. I saw that other girl's knife sink into her. This young woman here told us to run, right as I saw the blade go in. All I could think about was the safety of my daughter, so we ran. When I looked back, she was falling to the ground." She paused and looked at Sasha. "I'm so sorry. I just needed to get my daughter safe…"

Sasha was overwhelmed. She couldn't remember anything so couldn't agree or disagree, but she could be gracious. She hardly ever was, but that didn't mean she didn't know *how* to be.

"It's okay," she said. "Really. I'm okay."

The woman turned her attention back to the detective.

"I hope this young woman isn't in any kind of trouble. She's a hero…"

"She stabbed someone…"

"I didn't see that, but if she did, it must have been later. When we ran away, that other girl was standing over her as if gloating about what she'd done. She was laughing. It was such a…" she said and visibly shuddered. "It was such an *evil* laugh. Like stabbing someone was the funniest thing she'd ever seen … or done."

The detective looked thoughtful.

"What did the other girl look like?" he asked.

The woman went on to describe what she could remember of the horrible woman she'd seen that night. After she finished, the detective nodded then excused himself.

The woman turned back to Sasha.

"I really am sorry. If I'd been on my own…"

"I'm cool. Don't worry," Sasha said, feeling a

small smile appear on her face. It was something even she wasn't used to. "Thanks for coming in, though. Hopefully, it'll help make the cops leave me alone." She lay still, her mind flowing back and forth between wanting to think and *not* wanting to think. Suddenly she thought of someone other than herself. "Is your daughter okay?"

"Yes! Thanks to you."

"Is she freaked by what she saw? How old is she?"

The woman smiled.

"She's ten," she said. "She was scared that night, but she seems okay now. She didn't see the attack on you. I made sure she just faced forward as we ran away."

"That's cool," Sasha replied. "Ten … everything seems so easy at ten, right? Then life starts just getting harder and harder…"

The woman looked at her.

"Her name is Nicky. She'd like to thank you sometime if you'd agree to see her."

"Yeah, sure, but she doesn't have to do that," said Sasha. "I can't even remember…"

"*I* remember, and I want my daughter to have good manners and know how to thank people who help her."

"Okay."

~~~~~

The next morning Sasha saw the woman return, this time with a child next to her. Sasha didn't mind young kids. They were innocent. They never meant to hurt - not the way adults always seemed to mean to hurt.

"Hey, hey! This must be little Nicky," Sasha said, determined to not let her usual mood rear its head.

"I'm not little! I'm ten!" the tiny voice said back to her, making Sasha laugh softly.

"Oh yeah, I can see now. It's cool to meet you, Nicky," she said, holding out her hand.

Slowly the child approached before smiling and shaking Sasha's hand.

"I'm pleased to meet you. My mum's been looking for you for ages. Thank you for saving us."

Sasha fought back a tear that threatened.

"That's cool, Nicky," she said. "You and your mum are special. Anyone can see that."

"Can I sit on your bed?" the small voice asked.

Sasha smiled. The kid was likable.

"Sure thing. Climb up here."

~~~~~

Phillip was tasked with going to pick up his sister from the hospital. Although she was usually either a little angry or really angry, he had to admit he'd missed seeing and hearing her boisterousness around the house.

When he walked into her hospital room, he couldn't have been more surprised than he was. His sister had a kid sitting on her bed, talking, and laughing with her. He'd never even seen Sasha talk to Anya like that. He felt completely blown away.

"Hey, Phillip," Sasha said when she saw him in the hallway. "This is Nicky, and her mother, Susan. This is my brother, Phillip."

Phillip looked at the young girl and smiled uncertainly.

"Your sister is a hero," he heard the woman say. When he turned to look at her, she smiled brilliantly at him.

"She is?"

After seeing her motion to him to move a little distance away from her daughter, she spoke to him in a hushed tone.

"She is. She prevented an attack on Nicky and me. She literally took a knife for us."

"But … the cops…"

"I know. They got the story wrong. I've told them what really happened…"

"Is that the end then?" asked Phillip.

Susan shrugged her shoulders.

"I don't know, sorry," she said. "They asked me questions, and I answered, but I don't know anything about whatever they're trying to charge your sister with."

"Well, thanks for speaking up anyway. None of us know what happened that night - including Sasha apparently. It hasn't made things easy."

"I'd like to stay in contact with her ... your sister," Susan said. "Nicky rarely takes to strangers but look at them."

Phillip did so and then turned back, nodding and smiling.

"Yeah, well, Sasha rarely takes to *anyone,* so maybe it could be a good friendship for both of them."

~~~~~

"Come on. Let's get you home," Phillip said to Sasha a long time later, after Susan and Nicky had left. "I'm warning you, though. Ma is going to fuss over you and hug you, and bake you mountains of cookies..." he teased her.

He expected her to bite. She always did. Surprisingly, he just saw her smile shyly at him and say nothing. He took the cue of silence and didn't tease her anymore. He'd wait for her anger setting to kick in, then he'd know she was back to normal.

On entering the house, Phillip watched as their mother engulfed his sister in her arms.

"Ma!" Sasha exclaimed, chastising her mother. "I'm still sore, and you're making the pain worse."

Stacey wasn't offended. She laughed a little, as did Phillip. The wise comment meant that Sasha was on the mend. No-one said anything as she quietly walked off to go to her room.

~~~~~

"Case is off, Daisy," a voice said as it entered her office doorway. "I don't have details yet, but some witness has provided a statement that has been supported by CCTV in the area. The Leadbetter girl is in the clear - again. How they keep doing it..." Daisy's supervisor said as she shook her head and left the room.

Daisy sat in silence, her mind full of thoughts. What did that mean for her and Phillip? Did it mean *anything* for her and Phillip? How did she feel about his sister being cleared of what she'd been accused of?

She wondered how *he* was feeling. She suspected he must have been overjoyed, of course. He'd never have wanted his sister to go to prison. Even if they weren't a close family, he didn't seem the type of man who would gain any joy from something like that happening. But then, how well did she truly know him? She felt like they'd known each other for years. In reality, it had been hardly any time at all. She felt like she knew him. In reality, she knew that she didn't.

The feeling was growing. She wanted to see him. She missed him. Maybe it was crazy to miss him so much so soon when she hardly knew him, but she couldn't help it. She wanted to feel his lips on hers and his arms around her.

Taking a moment to think, she considered that it was possible - probable, even - that their family had a lot to think about and deal with. Even if they'd received the same news she had, the sister had still been stabbed. There would likely be things they'd probably want to be left alone to get on with.

Daisy found resolution. She wanted to see Phillip, but she would wait for him to come to her.

~~~~~

Phillip stayed at home while Sasha settled back into her normal self. She wasn't as angry as she had been. He wondered if it might be building inside, preparing for one large lash out in the future. He hoped not. He didn't think his mother could take any more bad news regarding her kids.

He took on work around their home, giving the yard the best clean up it'd had in years. It was good to keep his mind and body active. He also knew it would help his mother out, having less to stress about.

At night, though, when he lay in his bed, Daisy always returned to his thoughts. He'd kept away from her while a threat of charge and trial loomed. They had finally received word that Sasha wasn't being charged with anything. She'd been a victim. Footage showed there was no way she could have been the one who stabbed the other woman who'd initially cried victim in the hospital. Everything was back to normal. He could relax once more.

The problem was that they, as a family, still kept getting into trouble. Even if Daisy could look past that, would they have to keep repeating the process? Having time out from one another every time Daisy's law firm happened to be the one called upon to prosecute a member of his family? It was a cruel card that fate had played, that one. How many legal firms were there in the city? And hers was the one that was selected to do this particular job, now not once but twice?

Where could he and Daisy go in a relationship? He'd never ask someone to give up their career, and he couldn't give up his family. As a couple, where could the two of them ever go?

There was no answer. Night after night, he asked the question but found no answer that worked. Night after night, he lay in his bed, thinking about her until he finally found sleep.

~~~~~

Mark quietly watched all of his kids. David was hardly ever at home, staying more often at his girlfriend's house than staying with his family. Rex was … Rex. Anya was slowly returning to going out with her friends again after a few days of just being at home. She had always steered clear of her big sister so her resolve to be in the house so much when Sasha had come home had been surprising but sweet to watch.

Then there was Phillip. Something was definitely going on with him, but whatever it was, Mark knew his son didn't want to talk about it.

Stacey held her husband tightly each night. Sometimes she needed his arms around her, but more often than not, she loved to put her arms around him. He was such a loving man, even though he'd been raised to be almost heartless. He'd never been anything but kind to her in all their years together.

As she lay with her chest against his back, she felt his hand tug her arm slightly, as if wrapping himself that little bit more in her. She chuckled softly against the back of his neck.

"Yes?" he asked, affection in his voice. "Did you want your hand to be somewhere else?" he asked, teasing her with suggestiveness.

Stacey laughed quietly against the solidness of his back.

"Where else *would* I put my hand?"

She could almost feel him smiling as she found her hand moved down over his chest and then onto him. They'd already made love earlier. She still wasn't surprised to find him hard again.

"Oh!" she exclaimed, already feeling her familiar throbbing begin. She loved the feel of all of his body. She *really* loved the feeling of him hard in her hand. She began to stroke him and instantly felt his hand move back to nestle between her legs. "Hmm."

They both lay still for a long while, feeling each other's fingers caressing.

"Straddle my face, my gorgeous woman," she heard Mark say, his voice deep.

She moved aside to let him lie on his back before she kissed his lips.

"I thought I'd worn you out earlier," she teased

him.

Mark laughed softly and kissed her back.

"I'm not going to exert myself. I'm going to relax and lie right here." He kissed her again, passionately. "Let me taste you."

"Only if you let me taste *you*," Stacey whispered before moving around. She felt his hands clamp down on her thighs and guide her into position before she felt his tongue begin its blissful playfulness. She indulged in the feeling before lying down and taking him in her mouth. Instantly she heard him moan.

They remained like that for a long while. He enjoyed the juices running down over his tongue and lips. She enjoyed the wonder of his hardness inside her mouth. They'd long ago learned synchronicity. It didn't take long before she started to feel her muscles shimmer. Mark let go at the same time as she reached her climax.

Only one thought went through his mind at that moment.

'God, I love this woman.'

CHAPTER 15

Daisy settled back into her regular routines. Work Monday to Friday. Dinner with friends Friday night. Sometimes work in weekends, sometimes relax in weekends. All the while, she tried hard to forget the rugged man who had played her body so well.

Eventually, she gave in to the fight. Trying to not think about him just wasn't working. He hadn't called her or tried to see her. What did that mean? Had he given up on them completely?

She started to do as he'd done weeks before. Every lunchtime, she went to the café and then sat in the park, next to the fountain. She looked out for him, but she didn't see him. Every day, she had a little bit of hope. Every afternoon, she went home and wondered what he was doing. She reached a point where she couldn't wait any longer. She wanted him.

Plain and simple.

~~~~~

Phillip had secured a whole week of work at Enrique's. To many, it wouldn't have been a lot, or anything to celebrate, but Phillip appreciated every hour he got to earn an honest wage.

As he lay beneath a car he was currently working on, he heard a familiar voice in the distance.

"That's him?" the voice purred in a blissful tone. Even hearing that made Phillip's blood warm.

He slid out from under the vehicle, just far enough so that he could raise his head and see if he was right in assessing who the person was.

Just as he slid out far enough to do that, Daisy saw him. He was in overalls that were almost black all over, and his face had smears on it. Even in that state, to

158

her, he looked like the most beautiful man she'd ever spent time with.

Phillip lay still and looked up at her. He didn't mind the view of her standing beside him in her corporate gear at all - especially the view from where he was, level with her ankles, looking up. Just seeing that skirt got him heated in memories.

"Hey, stranger," she said to him.

She smiled when she said it, but Phillip could hear the uncertainty in her voice.

"Hey, yourself," he replied.

"Are you going to make me bend over like this all day?" she teased him and saw him smile without moving.

"The view is quite outstanding from down here," he said.

"Perhaps I should come down to your level then," Daisy replied, grinning.

Phillip laughed out loud and finally pulled himself up to a sitting position before standing.

"Ah, no!" He stood before her and absorbed the enjoyment that came from simply being close to her. "What's up?"

Daisy's face moved from laughter to seriousness.

"Phillip, I miss you," she said. "I know we had to have time apart with what happened to your sister, but when can I see you again? *Can* I see you again?"

Phillip admired her at that moment. She knew what she wanted, and she just came right out and said it and then asked the questions she wanted to be answered. There was no pretense and no beating around the bush, asking in a roundabout way. She was straight to the point. He couldn't help but appreciate the ease of that.

"I've missed you, too," he said quietly. "Tell me when and where you want to get together, and I'll be there."

Daisy wanted to hug him but knew she couldn't.

She would have to wait. "Tonight?"

Phillip nodded. "Where?"

"My place?"

"Okay," he replied. "I have to head home after work but I can be there about six-thirty?"

Daisy nodded. Relief flowed through her veins. She'd worried he wouldn't want to see her. At that moment, she was glad she'd been wrong.

She continued to look at him. Even covered in grease, he looked kissable. She wanted to kiss him. It was hell that she couldn't. Finally, she found the strength to turn and walk away. She'd gone to his work to see if he wanted to see her. He did. Now she could smile again.

Phillip stood still for a long time, watching her leave. He never tired of looking at her in any position, clothed or not, but he still really loved the view of her from behind in that skirt.

"Stop perving and get back to work!" he heard Enrique call out to him with fondness in his voice.

Phillip laughed and returned to his spot under the car. He smiled, even though no-one could see him.

~~~~~

As he stood under the shower and washed the day's grime and grease from his hair, face, and body, he still smiled. He was going to see Daisy again. She hadn't given up on him. She had even gone so far as to seek him out at his work. That made him smile even more.

He groomed himself as well as he could. When he stepped out of the bathroom, he almost walked into Anya.

"Another date, big bro?" she teased him as they crossed paths in the hallway.

He smirked at her.

"Nothing you need to know about, baby sister."

"I'm not a *baby*!" she threw back at him, right on cue.

Phillip couldn't help but laugh out loud. It was the same joking every time they were together, but he never tired of it. Anya was always like a wave of sunshine flowing past.

Mark heard the interaction from where he sat in his office. He smiled to himself. His oldest son hadn't been himself for weeks. Suddenly he sounded vibrant and alive again. The word 'date' had leaped out at Mark, making him certain about what had been going on. Phillip had a woman. She must be someone who he was having drama with now and then. That would explain his mood changes. Mark felt relief. If that was all that was bothering his oldest son, that was fine enough. It was a normal part of life to worry about sometimes, but more than that, Mark knew it was well past time that Phillip found love and settled down to start his own family. Perhaps that time had finally arrived.

~~~~~

Daisy felt nervous. She'd rushed home after work and spent an hour trying to find satisfaction in how she looked. She knew, at a logical level, it was pointless. Usually, they ended up in bed, and her hair would become more than messed up anyway. What was the point of going to all that effort, only to have it destroyed in five minutes when in the company of a man she couldn't help but want to be naked with?

As she looked in the mirror again, she considered if she did want to get naked with him. Her body shouted out, *'yes'*! Her heart and her mind wondered if it might be time for her to push that aside for a moment and suggest the two of them sit and talk instead.

Weeks earlier, he'd said that the outside aspects of their lives didn't just disappear when they were in the bubble of her apartment. She knew he'd been right when he'd said that. She also considered that in recent weeks they'd both quietly stayed away from each other while his sister was under the watchful eye of the police.

Couldn't they just keep doing that? Couldn't they just stay clear of one another when they needed to, then rejoin when things evened out again?

She was still looking at herself and pondering options when she heard the buzzer to her apartment sound. She walked to the security screen near the door and pushed the enter button to allow him into the building. While waiting for him to walk up the two flights of stairs, she forced herself to take deep breaths. She was nervous. In her view, ridiculously so.

A few minutes later, she heard him knocking on her apartment door. When she opened the door, all thoughts of conversation were temporarily halted. He not only looked fine, but he smelt like he'd just had a shower. Daisy could smell the lovely musky smell of men's body wash and deodorant. For a moment, she felt like she was facing a god.

Phillip watched her face and grinned broadly at her.

"Did you want me to come *into* your apartment, or shall we talk here?" he teased her, seeing she'd become glued to the spot, right in the doorway.

Daisy blushed slightly and laughed softly at herself while moving aside and inviting him in.

"Sorry," she mumbled as she closed the door behind him.

When she turned around, he was standing near her, looking at her in anticipation of whatever she had planned. Usually, she wanted to be in control, but it unnerved her slightly that at that moment, she felt like she had to decide what she truly wanted.

Phillip could sense the nervousness in her. It surprised him, but he welcomed it. It meant he wasn't the only one uncertain about what was happening between them. When it didn't look like she was going to do anything, he stepped toward her slowly and eased his arms around her waist.

Daisy felt herself enclosed and relaxed instantly. They didn't kiss. They just held each other tightly for a long time, saying and doing nothing.

"Are you alright?" he finally asked as he pulled back from her slightly. When she nodded but said nothing, he held her hand and guided her to the sofa. He didn't try and kiss her. He also wanted them to talk and gain clarity about what they were to one another, and where they each wanted them to go. "Come and sit down with me."

Once settled, sitting and facing one another, Phillip continued to hold her hand.

"What has got you so silent?" he asked as he gently pushed away a stray hair that had fallen across her eye.

Daisy smiled at him, surprised herself at her sudden lack of confidence.

"I feel nervous," she admitted quietly and instantly saw him smile at her.

"Why?"

"I want us to be together," she continued. "I want to keep getting to know you and spending time with you…"

"And you can."

"But," she started to say.

Looking right into his eyes, she liked that he always gave her his full attention. For a fleeting moment, she thought back to her time with Pete. During their years together, he'd usually acknowledged what she'd said when she told him something, but it had been different from what she felt with Phillip. When she spoke now, it felt like Phillip wasn't listening because he was somehow obliged to, but because he did want to hear what she had to say.

"What do *you* want, Phillip?" she finally asked.

"Daisy, I'm here with you right now because I want to be with you - now and tomorrow, and the days after that," Phillip replied. "I have loved every minute I've spent with you. I want us to keep moving forward too." He paused and could see the confusion on her face. "What is really worrying you? Is it still my family?"

"No! Well, yes, and no," she said. "I'm not worried about your family's … lifestyle. It was hard at first, knowing I'm kind of on the other side of the law to … them." She stopped and looked at him. She hated saying things that could offend him, but she did want to be honest. She didn't see any reaction in him that said he took what she'd said as anything offensive. "It's more these issues with your family going through the court process…"

He chuckled softly, trying to lighten the mood. "Believe it or not, that hardly ever happens. I know you probably think differently because Rex and Sasha have both been in trouble in such a short period of time, but this isn't *usual* for us."

Daisy still felt uncertain. She wanted with all her heart to not have anything standing in the way. She wanted no barriers between them. She wanted to see where they could go without so many outside influences.

"What are you doing this weekend?" he asked, breaking into her thoughts.

"I … um … Friday night I usually go out with friends for dinner, and then nothing else is planned. Why?" she asked.

"Let's go away," Phillip suggested. "You and me, together, alone."

"Well, we could just hang out here for a weekend…"

"A week then," he said, getting visibly excited by the idea. "Is that possible?"

Daisy warmed to the idea more quickly than anyone who knew her would've been able to imagine. "Where would we go?"

"I don't care," Phillip said. "Let's go up the coast

and find a cheap motel on the waterfront. I really don't care where. You choose. I want to spend time with you somewhere where my family and your work can't reach us. I want us to have some time where we are unreachable."

Daisy nodded and smiled.

"I'll have to clear it with my boss first…"

"I know," Phillip replied, nodding. "I know that it might not be able to happen, and that's okay. Just tell me now if you would *like* to do something like that … with me."

"You know I would…"

"Tell me," he said softly as he moved closer to her. "If it is what you want, *tell* me you want to go away with me and be alone with me with our phones off and no-one being able to interrupt us."

His lips were close to hers. As they'd moved closer, Daisy found that she was less able to think, but she did hear the question. She nodded.

"I do want to spend time with you, Phillip - just you."

Finally, he kissed her. It took only seconds for Daisy to feel her body react, and her need to be closer to him increase. Finding her strength and confidence again, she pushed him back so that he was sitting with his back and neck against the back of the sofa. Quickly she straddled him. She hardly looked at him before she plunged her lips on his again and pushed her tongue into his mouth to begin caressing his. Through her own excitement, she heard him moan.

When she started to move her hips against his, grinding down on him, Phillip could hardly bear it. It felt so good that he didn't want her to stop either. It seemed like in only an instant, she'd transformed from being a quiet and timid woman, uncertain of anything, to jumping on him and alighting his body like it was suddenly on fire.

"Naked. Bed. Now," she said in accentuated words.

Phillip was amused as he watched her climb off him and stand up.

"Yes, Ma'am," he said, grinning broadly as he stood.

At him laughing softly at her forcefulness, he finally saw her relax and smile with almost a blush on her face. He took her hand in his and kissed her softly before the two of them walked to her bedroom.

There, Daisy didn't give any more orders. She let him take the lead, spending a long time lying with her on the bed, kissing her over and over, before he started to remove any clothing from her or himself. It wasn't the same speed at which she'd felt she needed to have him in her when they'd been in the living room, but once she felt him kissing her so lovingly, she indulged in it.

After he'd undressed her and pleasured her to climax, Daisy watched as he stood and removed his clothing. As always, her eyes fell to the eagle that graced his chest. In its entirety, she loved Phillip's body. He was muscular and toned but had a relaxed shape to him at the same time. When he moved onto the bed again and lay down on top of her, she welcomed him into her arms. He kissed her softly, over and over, not rushing to the final stretch.

"I've missed you," he said quietly as she pulled him closer to her.

"I've missed you too."

After taking a moment to slide on a condom, Daisy felt him ease into her. He did it with surprising smoothness and slowness. She could feel every tiny piece of progress he made as he slid in deeper and deeper until she knew he was as far into her as he could be. For a long time, he lay still, completely enclosed in her, while kissing her lips over and over.

Phillip could feel her hands on his back, moving

up and down over his skin. He loved that she touched him. Not every woman he'd been with had done that. Daisy's hands on him were magical. He kissed her for a long time, loving the softness of her lips against his. She'd dropped her aggressive desperation of earlier and had fallen back into loving mode. He loved both, but he knew that among the most passionate sexual times, there had to be some moments of softness. He needed it. It evened everything out.

Daisy removed her arms from his back and raised them above her head. The movement stretched her breasts upward, and the sight captured Phillip's eyes as he pulled back slightly from her to let her move. She looked magnificent with her arms up and her lips intensely red from their kissing. It was enough to push him on. His arousal was driven up as he started to move in her. It felt like it had been months since he'd last been connected with her. At the same time, it felt like no time had passed at all.

"Don't hold back," she whispered to him.

That was enough to push Phillip on that little bit more. He finally pulled his torso up slightly and concentrated all effort on his hips. Thrusting into her harder and harder each time he sunk into her, he looked down at her and watched her face. The way she looked into his eyes, combined with her mouth opening in extreme arousal and the way she began to moan, took him to the edge. He pushed into her harder and finally felt the blissful and long-overdue release come. Instantly he felt her arms come down and hold him tightly as he felt the muscles throughout his entire body do their merry dance.

He rested on her. It felt incredible to be connected with her again. It felt even better to lie on her and feel her arms holding him. He hardly felt any desire to move, but eventually did.

As he pulled off her and then lay back, Daisy

moved so that she could huddle against his body as they lay facing one another.

"I'm not sure if I could handle a whole week with you," Daisy teased him. "I might explode."

Phillip laughed as he tightened his arm around her.

"Maybe we should try something new, like a no-sex holiday."

"No way!" she said, making him laugh harder. "Besides, I don't think I could keep my hands off you, even if I did want to try." She paused and leaned in to kiss him. "I'll talk to my boss tomorrow about taking a week off."

"Are you sure? I don't want you to do something that you don't want to…"

"I never do anything I don't want to, Phillip."

Phillip wrapped his hand in her hair and pulled her to him to kiss her passionately.

"I believe that."

"Want me to show you what I do want to do now?" she asked, the tone of her voice running through his body and making him instantly alert.

"Go for it."

He just got the words out before she moved her head down and he felt the warmth of her mouth engulf him. Then he thought about nothing else.

~~~~~

Saturday morning, Daisy woke early. Phillip hadn't stayed over since before their break apart, so she desperately looked forward to the night to come. It was a simple plan for the morning. Breakfast, shower, pack, and then head off in her car to pick Phillip up. After that, they were going to drive up the coast and stop wherever they felt like it. They had no set place to stay, and no set route to follow. Phones turned off. Bodies turned on.

As she sat in her apartment, enjoying her usual morning coffee and cereal, she felt her nerves kick in.

She knew it was silly. They had spent entire weekends together before. There was nothing to be nervous about, but she was. Since their break and that first evening together, they'd seen each other a few times but only for a few hours at a time. They had both agreed to ease back day to day but then spend the week away together to reconnect. It was a sound plan.

Daisy knew she'd rushed with Pete to a degree. She'd gotten caught up in him meeting a long list of criteria she'd formulated in her mind about what the perfect man was. The list had been stupid, she now realized. Who cared if a man was good looking, had a nice car, and held a high paid job? Since meeting Phillip, she had come to believe that perhaps other aspects of someone were more important than their social standing, their job, or the size of their bank account. Something had to be said for kindness, support, friendliness, and simple respect.

After taking some time to close her eyes and breathe deeply, she finished her breakfast and headed to the shower. As she stood under the warm water and lathered herself with her favorite scented body wash, she knew her body was on high alert. Always when she was near Phillip and even when she just thought about him, her body responded. She wondered briefly if it was normal. She'd always felt fairly sexual with past boyfriends, but her libido had definitely heightened since she'd met him. She loved that he was willing to try different things as she wanted to. Different positions she'd always wanted to try but had been too shy to, she knew she could suggest to him, and he would give it a go. Nothing was ever a bother to him. He really was, when she thought about it, the most easy-going guy she'd ever spent time with.

Under the flow of water, she was turned on. It was easy to consider running her fingers over her own body and indulge in that feeling. Instead, she rinsed off, dried herself, and applied light makeup. She didn't often not take time to work over her long blonde hair. For their week away, she was going to relax and forget about it. In fact, she might not even dress up. She remembered the gym gear she'd spent a heap of money on when Pete had split from her. She'd had full intention of going to the gym to work off frustrations. She still had the intention of going there … one day. In the meantime, she had some pretty nice activewear that would be more comfortable in the car.

She rummaged through her drawers and pulled out track pants. They were as sporty as anyone else would wear, being black with a slight flare at the bottom of the legs and a white stripe down each side. She slipped them on and looked in the mirror. As a general rule, she never went anywhere in track pants. Hell, she never even *wore* track pants. She was always in corporate gear of skirt and blouse, or a dress, or she was in jeans and her leather jacket. Why not do as other people do for once?

Seeing the warm sunshine outside, she topped it off with a long-sleeved hooded t-shirt and slipped on some sandals. She could do casual. She *could!* Besides, it would be another test of Phillip's personality. She could still clearly remember the battering Pete used to give her just because she'd put on a pair of jeans. He was definitely of the view that casual was equal to sloppy. Her jeans had been the first thing she'd started wearing more often as soon as he walked out on her.

After looking in the mirror one more time, she threw some tidier gear into her bag, slipped on her sunglasses, and then walked out. Phillip could accept her or not accept her. What would be, would be.

~~~~~

Phillip took a long shower, trying to hold back from indulging in what his body wanted his hand to do. The times he'd seen Daisy since their break had been few and far between, but each time had been amazing. They didn't need to spend a long time together for it to be a good time, but he was looking forward to spending some serious time with her. The fact that she'd gone ahead with asking her boss for the time off spoke volumes to him. It told him just how much she did like being with him, just as he liked being with her.

He looked in the mirror and made sure he was looking as good as he thought he could before packing a backpack and heading toward the front door to wait.

"Where are you going?" Anya's voice called out just as he thought he was going to be able to escape unnoticed.

"I'm heading out ... for a week," he replied.

"What? Where are you going then? How come I don't know about this?" Anya asked in her classic pretend-whine in her voice.

Phillip laughed at her.

"I'm going *somewhere,* and you don't know because you don't *need* to know. Do you tell me where you're going every day, baby sister?"

"I'm not a baby!" she said, holding back a laugh. "Seriously, though, do Dad and Ma know you're going away for a week?"

"Who's going away for a week?" Phillip heard his father ask as he appeared.

"Phillip, *apparently.*"

"Oh?" Mark asked.

Phillip looked at his father, wondering if he was ever going to be able to get out the door.

"Dad, I'm just heading away for a few days. Don't worry. I won't be getting into trouble."

Mark looked at his son. He could almost see a blush over his face.

"Who is this woman who's made such an impact on you?" he dared to ask.

Phillip, at that moment, considered the horror of

his parents finding out who Daisy was. They should have noticed her in the courtroom on the day of Rex's trial. Perhaps they hadn't - perhaps fate might have been kind and not let them notice her since she wasn't the main lawyer talking that day. For a fleeting moment, Phillip wondered if introducing Daisy to his parents could ever be a reality.

"I don't want to talk about her, Dad. She's picking me up soon, so I'm going to head out to the porch and wait there. I'll see you guys next week," he said and moved to the front door before anyone else could confront him.

Mark saw the flustered state his son was in. It wasn't normal for Phillip, but perhaps that just said how important the woman was, whoever she was. He knew Phillip had had his share of girlfriends since he was a teenager, but none of them ever seemed to be around for long.

Perhaps this one would become *the* one.

CHAPTER 16

"Hey," Phillip said as he jumped into the passenger seat of Daisy's car when she pulled up. Immediately he saw her unlatch her seatbelt and lean over to kiss him … deeply.

"Hmm. Yum," he followed up, making her grin brilliantly at him.

Daisy's nerves were on edge. She was excited to the brim and kept surprising herself at how excited she really was.

"Are you ready?" she asked and saw him smile suggestively.

"I'm always ready," he said. "You should know that by now."

The comment made Daisy burst out laughing. It was the right thing to relax her and let the stress and anxiety flow out of her body.

"Right you are," she said quietly as she glanced over his body, from head to toe and back again. Even in his usual attire of jeans and t-shirt, he was beautiful. Especially his shapely upper arms… "Best we get going then."

Finally, she turned her eyes forward, started the car, and began to drive.

"Which direction?" she asked.

"The coast," Phillip said, grinning.

Daisy laughed at him.

"I'm assuming we'll have to either go up the coast or down the coast. I don't have one of those cars that turn into a submarine."

"Haha, cheeky. I'm quite fond of going up … and going down…"

She laughed again.

"Stop being rude and give me a direction!"

Phillip loved seeing her like she was. Coming off her was such an aura of simple *joy*. It was something he hadn't seen in such a degree on her before.

"Okay. North," he said. "Let's go north up the coast. I think there are a few small towns there that have B&Bs."

Phillip saw her glance at him and smile. Her eyes were shining. He couldn't help but grin.

"North it is," Daisy replied, smiling and nodding.

As they settled into the drive, Phillip looked at her. She wasn't wearing corporate gear. He hadn't expected her to, of course, but she also wasn't wearing her usual casual gear of jeans. He was surprised to see her in track pants and a hoodie. With her sunglasses settled on her nose and her long blonde hair up in a simple ponytail, she looked *hot*.

"You aren't going to look at me the whole time I'm driving, are you?" she asked him with a slight blush on her face. She hoped he wasn't being offended or horrified that she hadn't made any effort in her appearance.

"Sorry," Phillip replied, blushing at having been caught staring. "You look beautiful. I'll *try* not to look at you so much, but I'm not promising anything."

Once again, he managed to relax her.

"Are your family … going … to miss you?" she dared to ask. His family was generally off-limits, but there had to be a way they could talk about them without him being offended or concerned about what they were talking about.

"It's okay to ask about them, Daisy," he said quietly. "They're just normal people. I have a mother and a father and brothers and sisters."

"I know. I worry about asking something I shouldn't…"

"Thank you, but don't worry. And no, they won't

miss me. They'll hardly notice I'm not there. The only noticeable people in my house are my sisters - one for her eternal happiness and the other for her eternal sourness. I'm the quiet one," he said and immediately heard her chuckle slightly.

"I know for a fact that you aren't quiet, Phillip," Daisy teased him. "I've heard the level of sounds *you* make…"

Phillip burst out laughing.

"Now who's being rude?!"

~~~~~

"Hey, do you want to pull over there and walk along the beach? That looks like some kind of café too. Are you hungry?" Phillip asked as a small group of buildings on the beachfront came into view.

"Yep," Daisy replied as she entered the carpark overlooking the water.

As she grabbed her handbag and got out of the car, the smell of the ocean hit her. She raised her face to the sun and breathed it in.

After getting out of the car, Phillip went to approach her but stopped when he saw her face. She looked so peaceful that he had no desire to interrupt her. Slowly he saw her open her eyes and focus on him. When she did, he moved forward and edged her back until she was up against the car door.

"Kiss me," she said with noticeable urgency in her voice.

Phillip gladly obeyed. His jeans instantly tightened, but he couldn't help but push up against her as he kissed her, tongue and all.

Daisy suddenly felt the advantage of track pants. She could easily feel him hard against her. She let her hands drop to his lower back and tried to pull him closer. The friction of him rubbing his pelvis against her was delicious.

"We're in public," he whispered in her ear while

still holding her tightly.

"We need to *not* be in public … soon," she replied, smiling against his cheek.

Phillip pulled away, trying hard to will his discomfort away.

"Food!" he said as he purposely looked away from her and toward the buildings.

Daisy happily moved toward him and placed her hand in his when he held it out for her.

"Those clouds are quickly starting to look ominous. Do you want to walk along the beach while that tiny bit of sun's out?" Daisy asked and instantly saw Phillip turn and smile at her.

"Okay," he said simply as they turned away from the buildings and toward the sand.

As they took off their shoes and ran onto the beach, Daisy immediately felt a level of freedom she hadn't felt literally for years. On the sand, feeling invigorated, she ran. Breathing in the sea air and listening to the gulls overhead, she felt incredibly alive.

Phillip watched her and laughed to himself. They'd shared fun moments, but as he watched her, she seemed almost childish in her playfulness and happiness. It was a side of her he hadn't seen before. He liked it.

He stood still while she ran further and further away from him. He didn't want to run with her. She was enjoying her moment, and he wanted her to indulge in it. Besides, it was too much fun just watching her.

Daisy ran around, feeling as if she was intoxicated. When she became out of breath, she made a mental note to start going to the gym. As she turned around, she saw Phillip back where they'd entered the beach. She smiled and waved at him before beginning to walk back to him. As she started her return journey, she felt the first raindrop hit her face. Then another.

Within seconds, it was raining - *really* raining. Despite her lack of breath, she ran back toward where he still stood, not making any move toward the shelter of the nearby buildings.

"Why are you standing in the rain still?" she called out to him as she neared him.

"I'm not going anywhere until you come back here," he said cheekily, his grin huge as he teased her. "Besides, I want to see your top get wet."

Daisy burst out laughing as she closed the gap between them. Seeing his arms outstretched, she happily jumped into them to give him the biggest, juiciest kiss she could muster.

"Okay, now we need to get inside," Phillip eventually said as he felt drops of rain beginning their way down the neckline of his t-shirt and onto his back.

They dashed into a small doorway and found themselves in a café. No-one else was there, making it blissfully quiet.

"You got inside just in time," a voice said from behind the counter. "That storm's been coming for a while. It ain't going away anytime soon." Phillip and Daisy turned and saw a rugged old guy looking at them with amusement in his eyes. "We've got a mighty fine beef stew as our special today. It'll warm you up, if you're hungry."

After ordering and paying, Daisy led the way to a table by the window. In the distance, they could see lightning bolts lighting up the sky. It was like being in a front-row seat to a lighting spectacular. Neither said anything as they waited for their food to arrive, both content to just watch what was happening outside.

"Here you go," the older man said as he placed their meals down on the table in front of them. "That'll have you feeling toasty warm in no time."

"Thanks. Actually, we were hoping to find somewhere to stay up the coast. Is there anywhere around here?" Daisy asked, already enjoying the heavenly smell wafting up from the plate in front of her.

"Oh, yes. Next door. My missus runs a bed and breakfast in the next building over. It ain't much and it ain't glamorous, but head over there when you finish your meals. Maybe it'll suit your needs. I don't think this weather's going to shift anytime soon, so take your time enjoying your meal."

He left them in peace to enjoy the warmth of the food while watching the lightning spectacular outside.

~~~~~

"Daisy?" she and Phillip heard after they'd finished their meal and were enjoying sitting and watching the rain hit the window. Although less frequently, they were still entranced by an occasional lightning strike in the distance.

Daisy heard the voice and turned in disbelief. She'd hoped it wasn't him. When she focused on the face, her heart dropped. It *was* him. Pete.

"Um, hi."

Phillip watched the man move toward them. He was in a suit, and not a cheap one. Even Phillip knew that. The guy was immaculate. He was as polished as Daisy was day to day in her corporate and casual gear.

Daisy saw Pete's eyes move over her as he neared their table. Seeing her wearing sporty gear was enough to bring a look of distaste to his face. Looking past him, Daisy saw a woman in a designer dress. She didn't look friendly. If anything, she looked downright *pissed*.

"We are getting something to eat," Pete said, doing some kind of assessment that was evident to all three people in his company. "Shall we join you?"

"Ahh, no, sorry. We already ate, and now we are leaving," Daisy said, starting to stand.

Months had passed since she'd seen last him. When she looked at him, she felt absolutely nothing. No regret. No sadness. Just a void of nothingness.

Phillip took the cue, glad at her suggestion that they were going to walk out.

"Daisy, we should talk…" Pete called out when they'd moved a couple of meters away.

"No, I don't think we need to do that," Daisy called back. "Enjoy your meal. Eat the stew. It's amazing!"

Daisy opened the outer door and walked out, knowing Phillip was right behind her. It was still raining heavily, but the feeling of that was far more preferable to the discomfort from seeing her ex inside.

Phillip moved to her and guided her to the car. They got inside quickly and sat quietly for a long while. As he looked at her, he thought she almost looked like she was in some kind of shock. He wanted to ask about the guy. He opted not to.

Finally, Daisy turned to him.

"That guy said there was a B&B on the other side, right? Do you think we should drive around and see if we can park closer?" she asked, not wanting to dwell on Pete.

"Yeah, it feels like this storm is getting worse, too," Phillip replied, nodding. "It might be better to see if you can park behind the buildings rather than here on the waterfront."

Daisy agreed and silently drove until they found the B&B frontage and carpark. Quickly they grabbed their bags and ventured inside, both desperately hoping that there was a room available.

"Oh dear, you two look like you've walked a *mile* in the rain!" a woman called out to them as she appeared behind the front desk.

Daisy laughed softly.

"It feels like it, too, but we just came from our car!"

"You were recommended to us by the gentleman next door…" Phillip started to say before he saw the older woman burst out laughing.

"Gentleman?! Oh, Lord, that husband of mine

ain't no gentleman, but he is good at bringing me business so I have to keep loving him," she said with a wink and a distinctive tease in her voice that made Daisy and Phillip both warm to her. "So you're looking for a room then? One or two?"

"Just one," Phillip said, smiling.

"I can do that for you. How many nights were you thinking of staying?" she asked and saw Phillip and Daisy look uncertain. "If you're not sure now, you can let me know in the morning. Just so I don't accept another booking and leave you homeless."

"Thank you."

The woman proceeded to explain rules and take their details before grabbing a key.

"Follow me," she said. "I have a lovely room that looks right over the beach."

They followed her and were led to a large room that was decorated in an old English style. A four-poster bed was curtained, and off to the side were a wall of large double-hung sash windows, each with a window seat below. Daisy moved toward them and looked out. Still, there was lightning in the distance.

"It's beautiful!" she exclaimed, making the woman smile.

"Lovely. Well, you have a little ensuite through that door," the woman said. "It ain't much, but it has what you'll need. Come and see me before ten tomorrow morning and let me know then if you'll be staying another night or moving on, please."

"Of course," Phillip said, nodding. "Thank you."

The door closed, leaving Daisy and Phillip alone - in wet clothes.

"You are going to get sick if you stay in those," Phillip said. "I must insist you take them all off at once, to prevent any chance of you getting ill," he teased her in a mock voice of authority.

Daisy laughed softly.

"Well, you are wet too. *I* insist you take *those* off," she said, pointing at his attire.

Without taking their eyes off one another, each individually stripped. For the first time in a long while, Daisy felt timid, standing naked. She rushed to the ensuite and grabbed a large bath towel to wrap around herself.

"Are you shy all of a sudden?" Phillip asked as he approached her.

Completely naked and completely at attention, he was a sight to see.

After a minute of pretending to be confident, he also went to the ensuite. He came out with one towel around his hips and another smaller one in his hand.

"Come and sit on the bed."

Daisy followed his instruction and felt him raise the towel in his hands and begin drying her hair. He was so gentle. She closed her eyes and enjoyed the softness of his caresses. From drying her hair, he moved to kiss her bare shoulder … and neck … and back…

"Wait! We need to hang up those clothes," Daisy said as she jumped up. Phillip laughed at her but joined her.

Finally, after putting their wet clothes on hangers in the bathroom, they returned and climbed into bed. With the curtains left open, for a long while they cuddled while watching the wild weather outside. With his chest warm against her back, Daisy felt secure and safe.

"Thank you, Phillip," she said, feeling emotional.

"For what?"

"For not giving up," she said as she moved onto her back so she could partially face him.

"I don't want to go anywhere, Daisy," Phillip said. "I want to just be with you - however - whenever."

Daisy turned onto her side again and resumed her stare out the window. She smiled as she felt him once again mold his front around her back. It was the first night that both were happy in just that. No more was needed. Where they were and what they were doing was perfect enough. It was still early in the afternoon but cuddling in a nice warm bed together while a storm lashed outside seemed the most perfect thing of all to do.

Soon both were fast asleep.

~~~~~

When Daisy woke in the morning, she could see the weather outside was still stormy. She felt like she was still in the same position she could remember being in the evening before. Phillip still huddled against her back while his arm draped securely over her. She could hear a faint purr coming from him - not silence but not quite a snore. She smiled and stayed still. It was a beautiful way to wake up, being in his arms.

While she lay still, she remembered having seen her ex the evening before. She tried to summon some kind of emotion about that, but there was just nothing there. What did that say about their relationship? She'd felt saddened and upset at the time. If she'd truly loved Pete, wouldn't she have grieved for the loss of their relationship for longer? Wouldn't she have felt something when she saw him again, with a woman by his side no less?

She wondered briefly how long she might get to spend with Phillip. It wasn't a happy thought. There were so many variables that could leap in at any time and make it uncomfortable to be together, if not unbearable. It wasn't forgotten to her that even though she'd only taken a seated role in the courtroom when Rex was on trial, there was a chance that Phillip's mother and father had seen her. That inspired the question - could there be any time in the future when she would be able to meet his family? Even if their parents hadn't seen her there, there was still Rex. *He* must remember her, if not from court, then perhaps from the night in the carpark.

The ways things could go horribly wrong and end

whatever it was that she had with Phillip seemed endless. She had to remind herself that things went wrong in relationships every single day. There didn't need to be situations like they were in for that to happen. There was no point in worrying about it.

Unconsciously she huddled backward as if to move her back even closer against Phillip's chest.

"I don't think there's any gap there," she heard him say sleepily, making her smile at the sound of his sleepy voice. "But lift your head..."

She did as he said and felt his other arm come around and rest under her neck. With both of his arms tight around her, she felt beautifully calm and quite simply at home. She gracefully ignored the hard-on pressing firmly against her thighs, resolving instead to let herself fall back into slumber, just as the purr indicated he'd done.

~~~~~

"Hey, sleepyhead," Daisy heard his voice say gently as she slowly opened her eyes for a second time.

She loved the feeling of him being so close to her, holding her. She wanted to turn toward him, but his chest against her back was beautiful. She felt warm and safe enclosed in his arms like she was.

"Hey, yourself," she said in almost a whisper. "The day doesn't look any brighter than last night," she continued as she watched the rain pounding the glass of the windows.

"It feels like a good day to lie in bed," Phillip said as he purposefully moved his hands in a wander down her body.

He was gentle. He never wanted to force any woman into anything. His touch was tentative, like testing the temperature.

Daisy smiled and finally turned toward him.

"I think you're right," she said. "I'm not against the idea of lying right here and watching the rain outside."

"Watching the rain outside?" he asked, laughing slightly. "I was thinking more along the lines of you looking this way rather than that way."

Daisy grinned widely before moving closer to him and kissing him. The hard-on wasn't gone. May as well make use of it. She continued to kiss him as she rolled on top of him, encased him in a condom, and slid right down. She needed no foreplay. She just wanted *him*.

Phillip watched her. She'd stayed back from being an initiator in their recent times together. He was very happy to let her take the lead and do whatever the hell she wanted to him.

~~~~~

"We need to make a decision about whether we're staying here another night or not," Phillip said a long time later as they lay together in each other's arms once more. "We need to let the owner know."

"I know," Daisy responded quietly, thinking. "I'd quite like to. What do you think?"

"I think I can get out of bed long enough to walk downstairs and check that's still okay."

"Alright. You go. I'll keep the bed warm," she said cheekily, making him smile as he reluctantly pulled himself out of bed and dressed.

When he'd left, Daisy remained in bed and watched the drops on the window again. She felt thoughtful, or emotional, or … *something*. She didn't know. She just knew she didn't feel like moving or thinking or doing anything. At a logical level, she couldn't even really determine if that was because she'd seen Pete the night before or if it was because she was with Phillip in a new place for a decent length of time. For all she knew, it could have been due to something entirely different.

A part of her wanted to rouse herself and get out

of bed. The other half of her wanted to lie where she was and not move for the day. Her head had been full of conflicting feelings and thoughts for so long that she considered everything might simply be catching up on her now that she was taking an actual break from day to day life.

Reluctantly she felt the need to use the bathroom. It would mean getting out of the nice warm bed, but it had to be done. Once in the ensuite, she looked at the quaint claw foot bathtub. That was an idea that did wake her up. She closed the door and quickly used the toilet while she ran the water. Looking in the mirror, she considered that she looked tired. She wondered if the stresses of her work were showing on her face. She'd never seen anything remotely wonderful about her face, but she wasn't someone to spend too much time thinking about it either.

After pulling her long blonde hair up into a loose bun on top of her head, she dumped the complimentary body wash into the water. Bubbles began to fill, and it smelled glorious. She'd always bathed alone. No guy had ever really wanted to bathe with her. She wondered what it was like to share such a thing.

Once the water level was as high as she wanted it to be, she turned to the door, wondering if Phillip liked baths. She opened the door wide and then eased herself down into the warm water. There was only one sure way to find out.

~~~~~

Phillip talked with the B&B owner and confirmed their stay for one more night. When he turned to begin to walk back to the room, he heard the same male voice call out that he'd heard the night before in the building next door.

"Hey!" it said.

Phillip considered pretending not to have heard it, but he wasn't going to be intimidated. The guy obviously had money and lots of it. Phillip had never been at ease around money, but he wasn't rude. Whatever the dude wanted to say, Phillip could hear and then move on.

When he turned right around, he saw the man walking up to him. He looked angry. Phillip remained still and remained silent, waiting to see what would happen. Behind the guy, he could see the woman he'd been with the night before. She stood back as if afraid of what might be about to go down.

"What do you think you are doing, spending time with Daisy? She's taken…"

"She's *taken?*" Phillip asked in disbelief. "Are you in some way implying she's with *you?*"

"Yes…" the guy started to say before going quiet. He appeared to be quickly rethinking whatever strategy he'd had.

"Really? And what of this lovely woman behind you? Does she agree that you are *Daisy's* man?" Phillip asked.

He wouldn't have brought her into any other conversation the guy might have broached on, but implying he was still involved with Daisy infuriated Phillip.

Pete looked uncomfortable and apologetic as he half turned toward the woman behind him.

"I … we're engaged…"

"Ahh, you're *Pete,*" Phillip said as he confirmed in his mind where this guy fitted into Daisy's life. She'd told him a little about Pete, although she hadn't given a physical description and she hadn't mentioned him since their meeting the evening before. "The same Pete who she *was* engaged to. The same Pete who dumped her months ago?"

Pete looked embarrassed. He was still wearing expensive clothing, but he appeared to be almost shrinking in front of Phillip and whoever the woman was.

"I want her back," he dared to say.

In that instant, Phillip saw the woman turn and walk out. Rightly so, in his view.

"Are you kidding me? Could you have insulted that beautiful woman who just walked out any more than you just did? You … fucking … *idiot*. If Daisy wants to see you…"

"Let me guess. You'll make sure that doesn't happen…" Phillip heard him say in the cockiest voice of sarcasm.

"If Daisy wants to *see* you," Phillip said again, moving right up to Pete. "Then I have no doubt she will call you and tell you. She is a beautiful, strong, independent woman who knows how to go after what she wants. If what she wants is *you*, I am sure she'll certainly let you know."

The response wasn't what Pete had expected, and it silenced him. For months he'd wondered if he'd done the right thing, walking away from Daisy. Sherri had been a time filler really. She'd caressed his ego and provided company while he built up the courage to consider going after Daisy again. Seeing her the night before with the thug that was currently in front of him had hastened his determination greatly. What the hell would she be doing with a guy like that anyway? He had tattoos right up his arms. He wore jeans and a t-shirt that definitely hadn't ever seen a professional dry cleaner. On top of all that, he looked like a common criminal. There was no way that Daisy could be with a guy like that. She *couldn't!*

Phillip turned and walked away. He expected the guy to yell or scream or follow him. It seemed none of those things were going to happen. Phillip still took a long way back to the room. The fact that Daisy's ex had turned up where he had when he had made Phillip slightly nervous. What were the chances? He purposely backtracked where he could to be sure that the creep wasn't following him to find out where Daisy was.

As he opened the door, he was transported in his senses. Through his nose, he could smell something flowery, fresh, and clean. Through his ears, he could hear the slight swish of water being moved. When he moved to the doorway of the ensuite, his eyes were filled with the most beautiful sight. Lying in the bath with bubble foam covering her entire body except for her head and her breasts, Daisy looked incredible. Phillip could hardly move from where he stood. He was enraptured. She was beautiful and sexy as hell.

"Hi," she said simply as if they were just doing some mundane thing on any given day.

"Hi," Phillip replied quietly, his throat dry all of a sudden.

"Do you like baths?" she asked, appearing shy and timid.

Phillip smiled and wondered if he was in heaven.

"Right now, I do."

Daisy laughed and flicked some foam at him. Phillip considered moving forward. The sight before him was so sexy that he felt glued to the spot. He'd also grown instantly in his jeans. Something about all those bubbles with her breasts poking through them and her nipples hard - she could be a pinup girl looking like that!

"Are you speechless?" she teased him.

"Yes," he responded, grinning so much his face was starting to ache.

"I think we could position ourselves so that both of us could fit in here … if you wanted to join me, that is."

Phillip needed no more words of encouragement. His shoes and socks were off straight away, followed by jeans, boxers, and t-shirt. He was hard, but he wasn't going to hide that. Let her know what she did to him - that was his philosophy as he moved forward toward the tub.

They both giggled like children as they tried to find a way to fit and relax together in the small tub. Finally, it was easiest if he sat back, and she straddled him and relaxed her chest on his.

"I take it all was okay with us staying another night?" Daisy asked quietly between soft kisses she laid on his lips. She could feel Phillip's hands caressing her back. It was soothing to her body and her mind.

"Yeah, I just asked for one more night," he replied. "The storm is due to pass tonight, apparently. I didn't know if you'd like to continue up the coast or not. We can decide that tomorrow morning if you're okay with that?"

She kissed him again.

"Sounds good," she said before letting out a deep sigh. "But that leaves a very long day today. What shall we do?"

Phillip laughed at her. He liked it when she was suggestively cheeky.

"I'm sure we'll find a way to fill in the day."

Pulling her closer to him, he kissed her passionately. He wasn't sure whether to mention her ex or not. He certainly didn't want to ruin the moment they were currently experiencing. If he said anything at all, it would probably be best to wait for a far less romantic moment.

"I am getting hungry," Daisy said. "Do you think they might do breakfast next door?"

Phillip chuckled. "You know we're in a bed and *breakfast*, right?"

Daisy rolled her eyes at him.

"Yes! But where is breakfast then?!"

Phillip laughed at her. She was funny when she was trying to be funny.

"It's downstairs. I saw a small dining room. They only have breakfast on for another half hour, though, so we might have missed our opportunity there unless you want to run there now."

Daisy weighed up food versus lying in the bath with the gorgeously tattooed man with a beautiful physique.

"No, I'm not that hungry."

Phillip smiled as he felt her rest her head on his chest. He was glad of her decision. It felt warm, snug, safe, and comfortable lying as they were. He was in no hurry to move either.

As they lay together, relaxed, and at peace, his mind wandered to possibilities of his future. He was almost thirty years old. He'd given everything to doing what his father and mother had wanted him to do all of his life. At what point was he allowed to stop living under their rule and start living his own life? At what point *should* he stop living under their instruction and make his life his own?

His father had gently insinuated that the criminal side of their lives was going to stop, but he was surrounded still by people his age who had grown up as he had. Rhett and Greg had grown up in the same house as his father. They'd been teenagers together and had known crime every day of their lives since. Would *they* accept it if Phillip's father were to walk away from the entire lifestyle he had helped create for so many people? Phillip knew that although there weren't always lots of people in his family home, close acquaintances of the Leadbetters spread far and wide. Generations of his family had pulled in random people who hadn't even been related. Those people had kids who'd been pulled in by the next generation of his family - and so on, and so on. Was his father even being realistic when he indicated that he wanted to walk away from it all?

"I like this," he heard Daisy say even though she didn't look at him. Her cheek was still resting on his chest as he held her close to him. "Being with you like this ... being with you *any* way is nice."

Phillip kissed the top of her head.

"I love being with you, too," he said quietly.

For a brief moment, he tried to remember what had happened in past relationships that had resulted in them ending. It was no use. He could hardly remember the girls, let alone that moment when he'd gone his separate ways from any of them. He hoped that whenever everything came crashing down, and he had to walk away from Daisy, he wouldn't forget her. She was amazing. She was beautiful. She was staunch, but soft and loving at the same time. He'd never met anyone like her before and he didn't think he'd ever meet anyone like her again.

He was resolved. He just had to make it work - even if that meant causing disharmony among the wide Leadbetter clan.

As the water cooled, Daisy started to feel hunger kick in. It had been her first experience sharing a bathtub with someone else. She'd liked it. With him, everything seemed simple - except for all the outer aspects surrounding him. For a moment, she visualized the two of them jumping into a bubble and being inaccessible to everything and everyone else like they had a shield around them that was completely impenetrable. It was a folly of an idea, but it was still a nice one to think about for a moment.

"I'm ready to get out. Are you hungry?" she asked him as she sat up.

Phillip nodded as his eyes looked securely up and down her torso. She had soapy bubbles on her even though most of the bubbles had disappeared from the water.

"How about we stand and turn on the shower, and I rinse all of those off you? I have full intention of kissing every beautiful inch of you today, and I don't wanna be tasting soap!"

Daisy smiled, and they giggled again at trying to

coordinate moving from lying down to standing in the small tub. The shower comprised a shower head that could be taken off the wall bracket and held in hand. She watched as Phillip turned it on and then began moving it all over her body. With his free hand, he caressed and rubbed, determined to get every minuscule of soapiness away from her skin. The longer he ran the shower spray over different parts of her body, the more she seemed to melt into it.

As she turned this way and that, she looked phenomenal in Phillip's eyes. When he rinsed and caressed her breasts, he saw her eyes close and her lips part. It was only natural that he would then lower the shower head and direct the spray upward. Her legs spreading wider told him clearly that she fully wanted him to keep doing what he was doing. He knelt before her and looked upward. In response, Daisy lifted one foot and placed it on a higher edge of the bath.

A long time passed with Phillip alternating between pointing the water pressure at her clit and hearing her moan in response, and him pointing the water away while he reached up and ran his tongue over her. Eventually, he put the shower head down and concentrated only on the caresses of his tongue. It wasn't long before she moaned heavily, and her body shook all over.

"Hmm, I guess you had your breakfast then," she said cheekily when her body had relaxed after the peak of the orgasm. She saw Phillip look up at her with almost a blush on his face, intermingled with the broadest grin. "But if we're playing kiss-each-other-all-over today, then it would be best that I now rinse *you* off completely."

Phillip stood and let her do to him what he'd done to her. Feeling her hand moving over his skin while the water blasted him was incredible.

"Shall I?" she asked him, looking directly into his

eyes as she held the shower head up. He didn't need any clarification.

"I don't know. Should you?" he teased her and saw her smile as she lowered the water flow to just hit the side of his erection. She looked into his eyes to see how it might feel on him.

Phillip felt a slight jolt with the water hitting him. Even he hadn't experimented with water that way, and he'd found a lot of things to try with his private bits over the years he'd been familiar with them!

"Keep moving it," he said to encourage her to move the flow further onto him.

As she moved it at different angles, he became aware of a whole range of sensations. He wasn't going to need any other stimulation. He felt like he'd been hard for hours. His body was at bursting point. He was just thinking that when the eruption happened, creeping up on him with speed and force.

Daisy saw it happen and was entranced. She hadn't watched his ejaculation before. She didn't think she'd ever watched *any* guy's ejaculation before. It was intriguing. She could see little micro ejaculations moving along under the skin before bursting out after the initial main gush.

She carefully moved the water flow right away. One thing she did know about him already was that he got sensitive for at least a few minutes after orgasm. She wasn't going to point a strong water flow at him when he was like that. Instead, she looked up and rinsed his chest again before beginning to rinse away his juice from the side of the tub. When she'd done that, she became aware that he was watching her intently. He took the showerhead from her, placed it back on its wall bracket, and pulled her close to him for a standing embrace. Naked and wet, it was beautiful. Daisy happily kissed him and welcomed the kiss deepen. They stood like that for a very long time.

"Come on, beautiful woman," he finally said, aware that the room was cooling down. "I am going to towel you off, let you get wrapped up nice and warm, and then whisk you away for food before I ravish your gorgeous body again."

Daisy could only smile. Nothing needed to be said to that. It was a sentiment that was beautifully complete in itself.

~~~~~

After dressing and wrapping up in warm jackets and jeans, they finally left the safe confines of their room. As they stepped outside, they immediately felt the impact of the storm that was still definitely happening. The force of the wind made them hold hands firmly as they fought the wind blowing into their faces and made a slow journey to the next building over. Once inside, it felt blissfully warm and peaceful again.

"Oh, good afternoon to you!" the same old guy called out when he saw them. "You're just in time for an excellent brew of freshly made soup, if I can tempt you. I have either a seafood chowder made from fresh local fish, mussels, and squid, or, if that doesn't tickle your fancy, I have a beautiful vegetable broth."

Daisy almost sighed out loud at the glorious aromas already reaching her from the kitchen.

"Definitely the seafood chowder for me, thanks," she said, feeling her stomach start to growl. "It sounds divine."

"Yeah, I'll have the same, thanks," Phillip said.

When all was settled, the two of them returned to the same table they'd sat at the evening before. Once again, there were no other patrons when they got there.

Phillip felt nervous. He still hadn't mentioned Daisy's ex to her. He didn't know if he should. They were having such a perfect day already. Did he want to poison their time together? The whole idea of getting away was to get away together, alone, without any distractions, but it was her ex. Should she know? He considered options…

"Daisy!" they both heard again. Phillip closed his eyes, partially in disbelief, and partially because he wasn't surprised. All he dreaded was that he hadn't told her something that she very possibly was going to believe he should have. He had no choice but to hope she would be understanding if Pete was going to tell her about the conversation he'd had with Phillip earlier.

Daisy looked at Pete.

"What do you want, Pete? We are over, and you're with someone … new … where's your girlfriend?" she asked.

"She isn't my girlfriend," her ex replied awkwardly. "Well, not now, anyway."

Phillip tried hard to keep the smirk to himself about that one. Was the guy so clueless to not have even considered how his girlfriend would feel if he openly declared he wanted his ex back? He must have inherited his extremely apparent wealth. There was no way he could be a successful businessman with that kind of ignorance.

"I don't care anyway," Daisy said. "Please leave me alone."

"No. As I already told *him*," he started to say, indicating Phillip with some kind of nod and hand flick. "I want you back."

Daisy heard the sentence and looked briefly at Phillip. He hadn't mentioned having had any kind of conversation with Pete. When the hell had *that* happened? She let her mind flick back through the previous evening and the current morning. The only time he'd been away from her had been when he'd gone down to reception. He hadn't come back and mentioned anything.

She smiled at him. Of course, he didn't say anything. He came back and saw her in the bath. She could have been angry at him, but she wasn't, and she wouldn't be. She didn't care about Pete enough to consider it even worth mentioning, and if Phillip had said something as soon as he'd come into the room, they wouldn't have enjoyed such a beautiful morning in the bath.

"I don't care what you want," she said, resuming her glance at Pete. "Not anymore. Move on. I have."

Pete had hoped him suggesting he and that guy had spoken would infuriate her and question the asshole's honesty. Instead, she showed nothing. There was no emotion at all behind her eyes as she looked at him. Pete felt incredibly sad and angry all at the same time.

Right then, the owner brought two bowls of chowder to the table and carefully placed them down.

"Are you joining these two?" he asked.

Instantly he received a loud, "No!" from Phillip and Daisy.

The synchronicity of their response made them laugh softly. Pete hated seeing that. Right in front of him, they began to eat their meals, having dismissed him entirely. He felt like he was invisible and nothing to be acknowledged. He turned and walked out. If he was going to win her back, he was going to have to take a far more subtle approach. He wasn't too stupid to see that.

Daisy said nothing as she began gulping down her soup. Thick and creamy with incredible flavor, she just wanted to devour the taste. She didn't want to think about anything.

Phillip silently watched her while he also began enjoying their meal. When they'd both finished, he finally spoke. He had to. He felt like he'd kept something major from her.

"I'm sorry I didn't mention I saw him earlier. I didn't want to ruin our incredible morning..." he started to say before being cut off by Daisy reaching out and taking his hand in hers.

"I know," Daisy said. "I'm not angry about you keeping to yourself whatever happened between you two. I'm *glad*. I don't want to know anything about him any more. I want to just focus on you … and me … together. That was what this time was about, right? The two of us enjoying each other without any other people invading us."

Phillip turned his hand over and lifted hers to his lips.

"I know it's not a long term solution to … *things* happening…"

"I know," Daisy said, nodding with a sad smile on her face. "I just want to make the most of every moment we can have now."

"Me too," Phillip said, smiling. "Now, do you think we might be able to buy something here now to eat later? Once I get you alone again, I might not want to leave again for the rest of the afternoon."

Daisy gave him a grin that did hold happiness in it. She felt exactly the same way.

CHAPTER 17

Mark Leadbetter sat in his home office and contemplated options for the remainder of his life. He knew he and Stacey had always lived a little on the edge with the ongoing expectation to raise their kids 'the Leadbetter way', but now things felt different. Perhaps it was that he was getting older. It was a nice argument but didn't hold very well since his own father had lived and remained active in his criminal lifestyle right up till the day he'd died at the ripe old age of 83.

"Am I just becoming more aware of your facial expressions these days, or are you actually becoming more and more thoughtful in your old age?" he heard his cousin Greg ask teasingly.

Mark half laughed. "I *am* thinking about our lifestyle, more and more. Sometimes I wonder if this way of living really is any way to live."

Greg looked at his cousin. They were close in age and had grown up in the same household. In addition to being related by blood, they'd also been good friends their entire lives.

"It's the way our family has always lived," Greg said, not giving any indication of what he truly thought about that.

"I know, but … I don't know," Mark said. "I think you're right. I *am* getting old."

Greg smiled but said nothing. He'd lived a good life. He had never married, but certainly, a great many women had crossed his path.

"When are you going to settle down and have some kids? Shit, *you* are getting old!" Mark teased his cousin.

The comment made Greg laugh out loud.

"I've probably got a heap of kids out there, as you well know. I think I stopped counting women after number fifty or so … and *that* was a long time ago!"

Mark chuckled. He couldn't argue. Greg had been quite the womanizer in his twenties … and thirties.

"Yeah, you always caught their eye easily enough."

"So did *you*!" Greg exclaimed. "The only difference is that Stacey secured your heart, and no other woman ever succeeded in their efforts to get you in the sack."

"I don't think there's another woman out there like her, Greg. Not for me. I hate to think about what life would be like if anything happened…"

"Don't go there," Greg said. "We live this lifestyle, but we're all okay. No-one's gotten sick or had any major accidents for ages…"

"Except for Sasha getting stabbed, you mean."

"Well, yeah, that was unfortunate, but she got through it okay, and look at what's come out of that. She's great with that kid. I've never seen her take to anyone like she has with that little girl."

Mark nodded. He agreed. His always-angry daughter was starting to have moments where she wasn't angry at all. They were still few and far between, and they did only seem to happen when she had little Nicky with her, but it was a start.

"I know," he said. "We are fortunate in not being a family who get sick with major disease. And we get away with a lot. I just wonder if I want to do this till the day I stop breathing. Don't you want more?"

Greg pondered the question for a long while as he looked at the flame in the open fireplace.

"Sometimes," he said, nodding. "Sometimes I wish I'd chosen one of those many women and made her my wife like you did. I've always been envious of what you and Stacey have. I don't even know why I've kept myself distanced for so long. We get told when we're kids that we have to be tough. That's great for not getting hurt. It's not so great for learning to feel your own heart, though."

"Well, everyone seems quiet right now," said Mark. "No-one's come forward with anything for us to talk about or do. I'm thinking everyone is out there just doing their own thing, and I don't care. There's supposed to be this stupid pecking order where people come to me and discuss things like potential burglaries and stuff, but why? *Why* do I need to hear all about those things and give permission for stuff like that to happen?"

"Because it's always been that way," replied Greg.

"Why can't it change? Why can't *we* change it?"

Inside, Greg agreed with what his cousin was expressing. It was an established way of life, but *why* was it? Who was the Leadbetter who laid down the grounding for all the rules and regulations they apparently had to live by in order to live by the family name?

"I don't know."

~~~~~

Stacey sat in the swing seat on the front porch of their large home. She'd been sitting there a lot since Rex had come home. Even the current weather state of heavy rain and wind didn't stop her from being out there when she wanted to think. It meant wearing layer upon layer like she was currently wearing, but that was okay. She knew Greg was inside talking with Mark. They were both a couple of the good ones as far as the Leadbetter family went.

Having been the official head of the family since his father had left this world, Mark had led everyone in a similar way to how his predecessor had. But Stacey knew Mark's heart. It wasn't like the older generations'. In addition to being thieves, they'd been violent people. They'd believed in abusing women, murdering, and taking whatever they wanted without any care for what they were doing to others. Mark still followed the family ways as much as he could, but he'd stomped out violence as far as Stacey could see.

Their 'family' spread wide, most by blood, but a huge number weren't in any way related. The couples she did get to see, she did believe were happy together. They weren't together for the sake of raising more criminals, like generations before, and no man could have treated any woman better than how Mark had always treated her. For a guy who looked like he could murder without blinking, toward her, he was loving and supportive. He loved her. She'd never doubted that. She'd seen women throw themselves at him over their decades together, but always he'd stayed by her side. Not once had she questioned if he'd been faithful to her. She knew he always had been. He didn't express love in front of their kids, but he sure did when their bedroom door was closed.

As she thought about that aspect of their life together, a smirk unknowingly crept onto her face. Except for each time she'd been heavily pregnant, she and Mark had always kept up their marital loving. It was something that bound them, and they both equally loved. They fitted together so well. Even now, more than thirty years on, just thinking about his body made her own body alert and aroused.

"What are *you* thinking about, I wonder?" she heard Greg ask as he approached from the front door, pulling on a woolly hat and zipping up the warm jacket he wore.

Stacey laughed softly.

"And you can *keep* wondering, Greg," she replied, instantly receiving a grin from him. "What's happening in your world?"

"Nothing," he said as he sat next to her. "Absolutely nothing."

"You sound like you're regretting something or missing something."

Greg looked at her. He was Mark's likable cousin. She was Mark's likable wife. They'd always gotten on well.

"I don't know. Mark sounds a bit wistful, like he's rethinking some things. I guess hearing him speak has made me look at my own life too."

"It's not a bad life, is it?" asked Stacey.

"No."

"You've had a fair few good shags in your lifetime," she said cheekily, making him laugh out loud.

"Fuck, yes," he said, smiling widely. "I cannot deny that."

"Not one to catch your heart, though."

She saw his face relax as he turned his gaze out to the street.

"No," he said quietly.

Stacey didn't question him any more. He was one of the few people she'd found over the years that she could sit with without any need for ongoing conversation. They were alike in that way. They both understood that silence wasn't a bad thing. Sometimes two people sitting in silence was actually just really nice.

After a long while, he stood.

"You should go inside before you get sick in this weather. I better head off and leave you guys in peace," he said, still in contemplation.

"We just *were* in peace," Stacey replied, teasing him.

"Haha. I'll catch you later, Stacey Bear," he said, using the fond name he'd given her when they were teenagers, and Mark had first started bringing her to the house.

"See ya, Greggy Bear," she called out to him and was treated to him turning back from his walk down the path for long enough to give her a smile and a wave.

~~~~~

Greg walked to his home. It was rainy and windy as hell, but he didn't care about that. It was nice to have fresh air and the opportunity to think. Walking was always good for thinking.

He'd moved out of the Leadbetter family home when he'd reached his twenties, and he'd never gone back. In truth, it had never really felt like his home. He'd spent the first decade of his life in a different house, with his parents and sister. It was only the three of them being killed in a gang shootout that had resulted in Greg having to go and live with his cousins. He'd been just a kid, but he could still remember how it had felt to be moving into a different house as everything and everyone he'd known before then had just disappeared.

It had taken him till he got into his thirties before he'd saved enough to buy his own home, but with the spoils of the extensive criminal activity he'd been caught up in over the years, he'd been able to find a cheap home that he could pay cash for without having to rack up debt. He was one of the lucky ones like that. People had come and gone in the house he'd bought. Now he was back to living alone. He didn't mind it. He had things inside of him that he liked to keep to himself. It was easier to do that when he was on his own.

He knew that years earlier, he should have proactively sought out love. He should have given it a chance. Now his life was passing him by. He had feelings inside, but they were ones he knew he could never voice - not being a part of the family and lifestyle he was.

~~~~~

Stacey continued to sit on the front porch. Two of her kids were inside, but both were quiet. It was normal for Anya to be almost unheard from. Sasha - not so much. She'd changed since the stabbing. Stacey could see it clearly. She hadn't talked to Sasha much since she'd come home from the hospital. Her oldest daughter was sometimes like a stranger.

Stacey had often wondered where Sasha would end up going in life. Her strong anti-social behaviors had always rubbed people the wrong way. When Stacey was honest with herself, she knew that was how Sasha liked it. For some reason, she'd never really wanted people to like her, but she had strength and qualities. Not everyone saw them, but they were there. She was independent and strong-willed, but she was respectful. She'd never intentionally hurt Stacey or Mark. Even Anya, who Stacey had always expected would drive Sasha nuts with her ever-happy mood, generally got nothing from Sasha. It didn't take much for people outside of their family to be intimidated by her, but she'd never turned on anyone inside their home.

"What are you thinking about with such a serious look on your face, my beautiful wife?" she heard Mark ask as he quietly came and sat beside her.

Automatically his arm came out, and she nestled against his chest as the arm enclosed her shoulder and held her firmly.

"I was just thinking about Sasha," she replied, speaking in a hushed tone. "How did your talk with Greg go?" she then asked, not wanting to talk about her daughter when Sasha was so close by.

Mark kissed her softly before answering. Sometimes those lips just had to be kissed.

"He's fine," he said. "Everyone's fine. I don't really think I'm needed, to be honest. Everyone's doing their own thing, and I haven't got the energy to go out and seek intel on any possible jobs."

Stacey put her lips to his and enjoyed more of his kisses.

"You're needed by *me*."

Mark could hear the husky tone of her voice that told him she was in an emotional mood.

"I know. That is part of what makes me the luckiest man on the planet," he said softly before indulging in giving her a proper kiss, tongue and all. If the weather hadn't been so horrid, he could have sat there, kissing her like that for hours. "Will you come inside? This weather's freaking me out."

Stacey nodded and stood with him, happily placing her hand in his as they ventured into the warmth and dryness of their home.

"I hope Phillip's okay, wherever he is," she said. "It's not normal to not hear from him like this."

Mark laughed as he closed the front door behind them.

"Stace, he's off with a woman," he said. "I don't know where he is, but I bet he hasn't even *noticed* what's happening outside!"

The thought of her oldest son with a woman he liked enough to go away with made Stacey smile. If any of her children were going to give her a grandchild, surely Phillip would be the one. He was the one with the biggest heart. He just needed to find the right person who wanted it. Maybe the new mystery woman was the one - the right one that he'd stay with and finally enjoy love with.

CHAPTER 18

Max Stonewarden lay on his bed in the large Stonewarden family home. Since returning home after his time in the hospital, he'd been drifting. His father and brothers had done only one big job since then and it had almost ended in disaster. They'd gotten away with the jewels without being caught but it was close enough to have shaken them all up. His father hadn't suggested any other jobs since.

It had now been months since they'd done anything for the family business. It had never been a full-time thing but it had equally never been as quiet as it was. The time Max found to think about everything drove him on in the consideration of going out and getting a proper job. It wasn't something any of the Stonewardens needed to do. The family business kept everyone well off enough financially, even after all the donations they made to charities. But James and Vic, Max's older brothers, both had part-time jobs and even Charlie, pregnant as she was, was learning to take over management of the ranch she and Ash lived on. The only one who didn't seem to do anything honest was their brother Fitz. Max didn't even consider him in the calculations. In sibling order, he sat between Max and Charlie but for some unknown reason he just didn't fit. He never had. Max was polite to his younger brother but would never go out of his way to find him or talk to him.

As he lay on his bed with his mind thinking, eventually it returned to Christy. He'd seen her twice and he'd asked her for her number. He had thought she would call him. Girls *always* called him, even when he didn't even want them to. He really wanted *her* to.

He pictured her face. It was easy to remember her

face, he realized. Her eyes. Her eyelashes. Her very kissable lips. He had no problem at all being able to visualize her features. He could also visualize her body shape. That was his biggest conflict. Not because he couldn't like her the size she was, but because he *could*. Not only that, but he *did*. It was the fact that he liked her so much that made him feel like he must be missing something. It just made no logical sense that he would be attracted to someone that big. How could he logically question his reasoning but at the same time feel the attraction? He feared he would hurt her if he kept chasing her. He worried that she'd end up really liking him and then finally one day he'd realize he couldn't be with her because he no longer found her attractive. Of course, that was always the way - people liked someone and then one day they didn't so they ended things and both moved on. It was a normal course of life. But he didn't want to have that easy-going thinking with her. He felt slightly protective of her, if he thought about it. He didn't want to see her hurt, and he suspected that he could hurt her. It made jumping off the edge and pursuing her all the more difficult.

He made a decision. He sat up and grabbed his phone.

No more waiting for her to ring. *He* was going to call *her*.

~~~~~

When her mobile started vibrating in her handbag, Christy picked it up and thought she must be imagining things. The screen said 'Max'. She'd only met one guy by that name. There couldn't be any doubt who it was that was calling. There *wasn't* any doubt. She just wanted there to be.

"Hello?" she said as she answered the call.

"Christy, it's me, Max," he said, sounding like he might be as nervous as she was at that moment. "How are you?"

"Oh, hey, Max," she replied, attempting to sound relaxed as her heart boomed in her chest. "I'm good. How are you?"

"I'm doing okay. Can I see you?" Max asked, deciding to just jump right in instead of lurking around the sidelines like he'd been doing.

"You can," Christy pushed out. Her throat was dry and she could hardly think, she was so unused to having guys call her.

Max laughed softly at her. He knew she was nervous enough in person. She was probably dying inside with nervousness talking to him now. He had no desire to prolong any agony for her. "What are you doing after work?"

"Oh, tonight I do the meals for the homeless. But tomorrow night I have no plans if you want to do something then."

"I do. But tonight - can I come and help you?"

Christy was surprised into silence. Temporarily. "Max, you said you don't feel comfortable around people who live on the streets. I can meet you tomorrow…"

"Christy, there are heaps of things about me that I'd like to change. This is one of them. I'm not going to pressure you but please consider letting me help you out tonight. Just tonight. I might hate it. I might love it. Help me to find out."

The speech was confident and it was well structured. That was something Christy could always appreciate. "Alright, well they can always use more volunteers, that's for sure. I usually go home after work and then I head down there after I've had a bite to eat so that I don't eat there."

"Great. What if I pick you up from work and we go grab something together?"

Christy smiled. She couldn't help it. She had no idea what he was up to, ringing her and asking to see her, but she did like his enthusiasm. Even if … when …

he turned out to be a jerk who was just intending to make her look like a fool, she did have to concede that Max Stonewarden was extremely easy to like.

"Okay. I finish at five."

"Great. See you then, Christy."

She smiled to herself and put her phone back in her handbag. She wouldn't see him at five and that was okay. That was the way her mind always worked. Except this time she considered that maybe her mind was wrong on this occasion. Maybe - just maybe - she *would* see him at five.

~~~~~

Max jumped off his bed, feeling energized. He grabbed his phone, wallet, and keys and ran down the large staircase. He was smiling until he heard voices. They belonged to his father and his younger brother.

"Dad, it's a sure thing. You know my intel is always good. The owners of these jewels are going to be here for one month. That's it. Then the gems are heading off with the owners to some unknown place at the bottom of the world or something like that."

Max popped his head around the doorway to the living room. Fitz and their father were sitting on a sofa. Max could see the level of intense consideration on his father's face.

"What's going on?" he asked as he walked right into the room and sat on the sofa facing them.

"Fitz has found us a job to do. It sounds positive," Mitchell Stonewarden said as he looked at Max. Still, he could remember how it had been months earlier, watching Max lying still in a coma in hospital. That had shaken Mitchell up hugely. He'd never been so scared about anything as he was when he'd watched Max like that. Even as a soldier serving his country in war-torn regions of the world, nothing had affected him the way the fear of his son dying had.

"Oh, yeah? What is it?" Max asked. He wasn't

sure he wanted to do such crap anymore. Although it had been months since the shooting, the cops still didn't know who had pulled the trigger. That only kept Max in constant worry about whether he and Charlie had been actual targets or just in the wrong place at the wrong time. He knew there was another family of thieves who liked going after jewels too. They didn't usually hit the same types that Max's family did, but they were still out there. Somewhere.

Fitz spoke up and repeated to Max what he'd just told their father. Fitz had little time for any of his brothers. Hell, he hardly had time for his father. They were all like in a little team of their own. A clique of Stonewardens. His last name was Stonewarden but he'd never really felt like one. He much preferred to keep to himself and hang with other people. Officially he still lived in the family home. Unofficially he was hardly ever there. Except for jobs. Then he came home. He thrived on them and his father was a master at strategy. Fitz was excellent in what he did but he wasn't stupid. For the jobs to go as planned, his father's military strictness and quick thinking were required. Otherwise, Fitz would long ago have been planning and doing jobs without his family.

The three of them talked and lightly threw ideas of positives and negatives out there. It was how it always began. Once they'd talked for a long while, Mitchell got on his phone and summoned Vic, Regan, and James home. They had an idea. Now they needed a plan. That was something they all worked on together. Each had different ways of seeing things. That meant that each could view something different as a potential problem. Nothing anyone said in the planning process was ever disregarded. Every scenario and every tiny sliver of scenario was listened to, talked about, and pulled apart to minuscule proportions. Nothing could or would be taken for granted.

The last job had been a close call. This one wouldn't be. It *couldn't* be.

~~~~~

The Stonewarden boys talked for hours. All the while, Max watched the time. He knew it was highly likely he could get so engrossed in the present topic of conversation that he could forget all about heading out to pick Christy up at five. He was desperate to not let that happen.

When he saw the clock turn to four-thirty he spoke up. "Dad, I need to go," he said tentatively. He knew rules were rules. No-one went anywhere during planning.

"Where are you going?" Mitchell asked, surprised. He expected Fitz to challenge things. Never Max.

"Got a date, Maximus?" James teased his younger brother as he zoned into their conversation.

Max was embarrassed. Putting a woman before family was unheard of. He looked at his father and was relieved to see at least a look of relaxed *something*.

"Come with me," Mitchell said, standing and looking at Max. He led him to the kitchen, away from the other boys. "What's up?"

"Dad, I didn't know this meeting was taking place tonight. I made plans with someone…"

"And you can't unmake them?"

"I … this girl … I get the impression that she's used to people letting her down, Dad. If she was anyone else I wouldn't care but I really don't want to do this to this particular person. She…"

Mitchell understood. Sometimes one person stood out as simply being more important. He wouldn't tease his son or make him stick to family rules. Max was as much a playboy as his brothers were. If he liked some woman enough to put her above all else, Mitchell wasn't brave enough to do anything to upset that.

"She deserves better?" he asked and immediately saw Max nod.

"*I* think she does. I promise I will come home early but please don't make me stand her up or let her down."

"Alright, Max. We can keep talking about the job without you here. Let's go back. Before you go we'll organize another planning meeting, which I *will* expect you to be here for."

Max nodded in relief. "Of course. Thank you."

Mitchell pulled his son toward him and kissed him sloppily on the forehead. "Love is in the air…" he sang quietly, making Max laugh and blush at the same time. His dad was strict but as far as fathers went, he was alright.

~~~~~

Max made haste to the police station. He was determined to not let Christy down. When he arrived she wasn't there. He sent her a text message. 'I'm outside.' After a few minutes of no response, he saw her walk out, look up and down the street, and then start walking toward him. He leaped out of the car and moved around in time to open the door for her, but not before giving her a brilliant smile.

Christy smiled at him in return before she sat in the car. She watched him move around to the other side and climb in. His smile didn't waver.

"Where are we going?" he asked her as he put his seatbelt on. He felt the need to do something and look somewhere other than her face for a moment. There was a very definite pull to kiss her. He wanted to fight that. At least for the moment.

"Oh … I don't know. Where do you want to go?"

"What do you usually do before you go to the homeless meals place?"

She giggled slightly at his wording. "You know the *meals* aren't homeless, right?" Max loved the sound of that giggle and the look on her face as she laughed. "I cook something up at home..." she eventually said without thinking about what his follow on from that would be.

"Great. You'll have to guide me how to get there."

Christy was startled. Max Stonewarden coming to her apartment? Why oh why hadn't she thought that possibility through before she'd said she cooked something at home?!

"You want to ... come to my apartment?" she asked tentatively. She was asking if that was what he was implying. He took it as an invitation.

"Sure. That sounds good. How do we get there?"

"I don't know..." she responded vaguely, making him laugh.

"You don't know ... how to get to your own apartment?" he teased her and then toned it down a bit. "Christy, stop being all nervous and stuff. Come on. We'll do as you always do. Unless you *don't* usually cook something at home..."

When she focused and heard his uncertainty she chastised herself silently and resolved to at least act more confidently.

"No, I do, and I can cook for us both. It's no problem. So! You need to drive..."

She explained the way as he drove. It was a good thing as having to focus on something helped ease her worries and nervousness. She became fully relaxed ... until they stood at her door. Then she became aware that she was letting a guy she hardly knew into her apartment.

Max saw the change in her again. He liked it. It was refreshing. *She* was refreshing.

After a flustered moment, she opened the apartment door and welcomed him in. She'd never had a guy in her home before. It felt scary but exciting.

"Right, what are we cooking?" Max asked in an

attempt to distract her again. From the time he'd already spent with her he suspected that when she wasn't listening to her mind telling her insulting things, she found it easier to get on and deal with things. He moved toward the kitchen and opened the refrigerator, making himself right at home.

Christy watched him and eventually smiled. He had no qualms at all about being there and looking through her food supplies. It could have been offensive. She found it quite nice, being able to let him make decisions.

"Okay," she said, turning her brain off again and walking toward him. "I have a load of salad stuff here, and I was going to cook up some of these chicken drumsticks in the oven. They usually take about forty minutes though."

"Perfect," Max said, smiling broadly. That was a great amount of time she'd have to talk to him for. He pulled the things from the fridge and put them on the bench. "What do you cook these on?" he asked, engaging her again.

Between the two of them, they got the chicken in the oven and cooking. As they both began preparing and assembling salad ingredients on their plates, Max encouraged her to speak.

"So, tell me what I'm going to be doing when we get there tonight," he said and saw her gradually relax and become more confident the more she spoke. He was learning to read her and he was learning to help her relax. He already knew she'd never be a woman who would react well to a guy charging at her. She needed time to warm up. She needed space to ease into difficult situations. She would need to be coaxed gently if he was ever going to build up to kissing her.

As many knew, Max Stonewarden was often excitable and impatient.

For her though, he was going to be as patient and

wait as long as it would take.

~~~~~

Back at the Stonewarden family home the remaining boys and their father talked about different aspects of the job they had decided they were going to do. They would have another planning session in three days. At that session, they would start to formulate definite strategies. For the present moment, each felt adrenaline flowing.

Mitchell looked around at each of his sons that were present.

Fitz was in his element. He always was when it came to jobs. He was hardly ever seen at any other time but he was always reliable when it came to the family business. Mitchell didn't know what made his youngest son so different from the others. He'd always guessed that one day the reason would reveal itself. So far one day hadn't yet arrived.

James was his usual self. He could be a kidder, could James. And as far as womanizing went, he was top of the charts for the Stonewarden lads, Mitchell guessed. If he'd been born a hundred years earlier people would have openly talked about his 'swagger'. But when it came to work he did have the ability to focus and be serious.

Regan was quiet and serious, as usual. He was the only son who seemed to have an ongoing relationship. Most nights he stayed at his girlfriend's house. They'd been together for a couple of years. Mitchell wondered if at any time he might get a wedding invitation but so far nothing was happening there. He made a mental note to pull Regan aside and nudge him with a 'make an honest woman of her' speech.

His oldest, Vic, was the one Mitchell would hand the business to when it was time for him to retire. He felt like he'd wanted that for a while but at the same time, he wasn't sure if it was what he wanted or not. He wasn't going to think about that yet, but he knew he needed to start introducing Vic to all aspects of the business. Vic was always on-site for the heists and other jobs but he hadn't yet any idea where the gems went after their family stole them. There was a whole host of processes that Vic had to be trained in, and people he had yet to meet. That was the extent of what Mitchell knew about his oldest son. He'd left home years earlier. He never talked about relationships or friendships or anything else. He was the most private one of them all ... apart from Fitz.

"Can we go then, Dad?" James asked. "We'll talk more next meeting, right?"

"Where are you off to in such a hurry?" Mitchell asked, teasing him without really wanting to know the answer.

"I got places to be," James replied, his face revealing his huge smile. He didn't need to openly say he was going to see a woman and have a shag.

"Yes, you can go. All of you except Vic," he said, turning to his oldest son. "Can you stay a few more minutes?"

"Yep," Vic said in his usual good-natured monotone.

Mitchell watched James, Regan and Fitz all burst out the door and head off in their individual directions. After they'd gone, he turned to Vic.

"I want to talk to you about taking over the business," he said and saw the surprise on his son's face.

"Now?"

"Now ... now I want to *talk* to you about it. It isn't something that can happen instantly, Vic, but I want to start introducing you to some aspects of it that you haven't had to deal with yet. First, though, I need to know if you *want* to be head of the business in the future."

"Yes! Dad, I've been waiting for ages for you to *let* me."

Mitchell smiled. His oldest son hardly ever spoke with animation. It was a joy to see.

"Okay, well, let's focus on this job first, and then when it's over with, we'll spend some time together working through that."

"Thank you," Vic replied quietly. Inside he felt excited. He'd wanted to take over for so long. *Finally,* it was going to happen.

"Go now. We'll sort things out later."

Vic nodded, stood, and surprised his father by giving him a very brief but manly hug. Then he walked out. Mitchell sat in silence for a long while. There was nobody else in the house. There used to always be the certainty that Charlie was in the house. He missed her. The house wasn't the same without her. Sometimes he went and sat in her room. He knew she wasn't far away. A short car journey and he could see her anytime. But on nights when no-one else was home, he felt the lack of her presence. He didn't want to. She was in a good place at the ranch with Ash and a little one on the way. With her pregnancy, the family was going to be growing in size. It felt like the opposite. It felt like everyone was leaving.

Leaning back on the sofa and closing his eyes he began to feel a sliver of loneliness flow over him. He didn't want to acknowledge it. He didn't *want* it. He'd loved Caroline and dedicated his life to her. He wasn't ready to move on. Was he?

He looked at the clock on the wall. It wasn't late but he was drained. He took himself off to bed, lay under the covers, and remembered his wife. Then he let the tears come. In almost everything, he knew he was a strong man. He'd survived war. He'd seen things no human should ever see. He'd been a solo dad to a tribe of kids on his own for the past decade. But still, when he thought about Caroline, he was inclined to curl up into the fetal position and just cry. So he did.

CHAPTER 19

Rhett faced Mark and watched his expressions. Rhett had lived with Mark and the older generation of Leadbetters when he was young. There was no connection in blood, but there was a strong connection in loyalty.

"You think this jewelry is real?" Mark asked him, his voice alight with eagerness. "This isn't some prank by someone? It's not some costume jewelry or some story that's just been made up?"

Rhett shook his head.

"I believe it's real," he said. "We'll do lots more digging if you think we should try this. They're only here for a few weeks, from what I can make out of what the guy was saying. The security isn't meant to be so great, though. That's why I thought it could be good for us. We haven't done anything as a family for a really long time."

Mark pondered what he was being told. His family survived well enough on petty crime. Theft provided in one form or another. He'd always advised his kids to go for jewelry because it was so small and easy to grab and to hide. Many times he'd read about large-scale jewelry passing through the city. More than once, there had been a follow-up story telling that the same gems had been stolen, and the thieves were still at large. Mark envied whoever did that stuff. Not that he'd ever tell another living soul *that,* of course.

"What is your gut telling you about this?" Mark asked Rhett.

He trusted him implicitly and Rhett had never misinformed of anything. When he saw something that he believed could be done, the Leadbetters followed his lead, and it always ended up being great.

"It's telling me that this is a good score," Rhett replied. "Like I say, I'll keep digging. If you can get a few others on board to use their skills for what they do and double-check everything, I really do think we can do this."

"These won't be everyday gems, though. What are we going to do with them once we have them?" Mark asked.

He could almost see Rhett's mind churning over as he considered that.

"Leave that with me. I'll have an answer before we move forward. Just give me a yes or no, for now, so I know whether to dig or let things lie."

Mark could feel adrenaline flowing through his veins. Not having done any major burglary in recent times, he'd forgotten how exciting planning something was. Subconsciously he did an assessment of who all was in the house. If everyone except his wife was out, he knew what he was going to be suggesting to her once Rhett left.

"Do it," he said, nodding. "Find out what you can and let me know what your thoughts are then. I'll call around and talk to the others. How long till this stuff is in town?"

"Eight weeks."

Mark nodded.

"Okay," he said. "Let's catch up next week?"

Rhett smiled and nodded in return before turning and walking out. His adrenaline was also flowing. He'd always loved the thrill of being a thief. It was one reason he was eternally grateful for Mark's parents having accepted him into their home and their family when he was a teenager. Being a Leadbetter - even a pretend one - was downright thrilling when big things happened.

~~~~~

After Mark saw Rhett out, he walked through the house. Sasha and Anya were nowhere to be seen. Rex was presently hardly ever home and never during the day. Mark did a quick scour of their bedrooms and the living areas just in case. Finally, he heard the shower running. He did a double-take through the house and yard to see if Stacey was anywhere else.

Finally sure it was her in the bathroom, he knocked on the door.

"Yep?" she called out over the sound of the water.

"Can I come in?" Mark asked.

He knew what he wanted, but he'd never force it if she didn't.

"You can," she said in a sing-song tone of seductiveness.

Mark smiled to himself and slowly opened the door. When he entered, he could see the outline of her body through the white semi-sheer shower curtain. As if knowing he could see her, he watched as the silhouette's hands ran over the silhouette's breasts in a side-on view. He could then see one hand move downward.

Mark was hot in an instant. He gulped.

"Are you going to join me and help me get clean? I'm feeling a little dirty," she said in her playful teasing. The result was Mark laughing out loud whilst at the same time feeling his erection stretch to full strength.

"Are you just?" he teased her back as he removed his clothing.

Stacey poked her head around the edge of the curtain to see him approaching slowly, naked, and standing to glorious attention.

"I am when you look like that, my gorgeous husband," she said. "Come in here and let me soap you up."

"Fuck I love it when you talk dirty," Mark said, grinning.

He stepped into the bathtub and pulled the curtain around behind him. For the moment, it felt like they were in their own private little tent, hidden away from the rest of the world. He saw Stacey reach for the bar of soap that sat in a wall-mounted soap dish.

"Wait," he said, taking both of her hands in his. "First, let me put my arms around you and kiss you."

Stacey happily obliged. Wrapping her arms around him and clutching his ass in her hands, she felt him do the same to her. Despite his cock standing tall and proud between them, Mark pulled her as close to him as he could as he kissed her with deep passion. He never tired of kissing her. She always kissed with passion. She hardly ever had time for those little lips-only deals. No, when Stacey kissed, she did it full-on, and he loved it. He always had. He always would.

They stood together like that under the warmth of the water flow without any hurry to move. Even as aroused as he was, he was tentative to pull his lips and tongue away from hers.

"Hmm, will you sit on the edge of the bath for me?" he asked.

Stacey gladly obliged, spreading her legs wide as she sat down. They were so in sync. She knew he was going to lick her clit. She also knew it wasn't going to take long for her to climax.

Mark indulged in the taste of her. He was bursting, so he hurried. He was a master of making her last as long as they wanted her to last before she let loose in orgasm. Today was a hurry day. He needed to be inside of her *soon!*

It took only a few minutes before Stacey felt her muscles shimmer and then contract in blissful pleasure. When she was on the downside of the orgasm, she turned around and held onto the edge of the bath, presenting him with her ass.

Mark needed no explanation or invitation. Instantly he bent his knees to her height and slid into her. Fuck, yes, that was exactly what he needed. He was so turned on that he knew it would only take a few…

Unexpectedly his body reached its point of no return. The ejaculation rocked every muscle in his body as he firmly held her hips.

Gently he pulled out of her and supported her as she stood up and turned around to face him. Once more, he kissed her, again with passion. He was done. He'd had the orgasm he'd needed to have, but he wasn't going to rush anywhere. Kissing his wife was something he could do for hours.

~~~~~

"Mark, what's happened?" Stacey asked him after they'd left the bathroom and made their way to their bedroom to dry off and get dressed.

She saw him look at her as if confused. She tried not to laugh. Their years together had made her fully aware that post-orgasm, he often had a completely blank mind and wouldn't be focused on whatever he'd focused on *prior* to sexual pleasure. She walked up to him with towel in hand and lovingly rubbed his scalp with it to help dry off his hair.

"Something had you wound up earlier," she continued, nudging him a little.

Mark smiled. He cast his mind back.

"Rhett said there's a possibility of a job coming up," he said. "He thinks it could be a really good score if we could pull it off."

Stacey stopped her caresses, surprised. She had been thinking they weren't going to put their family in danger anymore.

"What?"

"There's some jewelry coming into town that won't have extreme security around it. Rhett thinks that with enough organization and the right plan, we could grab it…" He stopped talking when he saw the look on her face. "Stace, what is it?"

"I thought … I thought you didn't want to *do* that kind of stuff anymore."

His face changed. It revealed the level of confusion he felt in the moment.

"I know, but it's just one more job," he said.

Stacey felt saddened. She'd been a fool to believe he wanted out of the life they'd lived since they were teenagers. It was hardly ever that he surprised her or disappointed her. In that one moment of time, he'd done both.

Mark could feel the level of disappointment emanating from her. Never had she ever questioned or made any kind of opinion known of the things he and others associated with the family had done. He felt sick that she so was so visibly upset. He never wanted to upset her. He loved her. Sometimes he thought he loved her more than anything else he'd ever known.

Stacey stood still, her mind and heart consumed with concern as he stepped closer to her and gently caressed her upper arms with his hands.

"What are you worried about?" he asked.

"You! I want to live the rest of my life with you beside me - not behind bars, not injured, and certainly not dead. What has changed in you since you told me you weren't going to do anything like this again? What has made you so easily disregard what you said to me?"

Mark was speechless. Her questions were valid. He hadn't wanted to do any more jobs, but as soon as Rhett had put the idea in his head, it had felt like a drug flowing through his veins.

"I don't know," he said as he finished dressing and sat on the edge of the bed with his head down. He didn't look at her as she sat next to him. "I don't know what changed. For so long, I've wanted to be free of this life so you and I could have a *better* life…"

"We *do* have a better life, Mark!" Stacey exclaimed. "This life that we have is far better than what it will be if you go to prison or get yourself hurt or killed!"

"But maybe this is just who I am, Stace," Mark said. "I hear of an opportunity like this, and I feel alive for the first time in ages."

Stacey was resigned. She'd never spoken against him, and she wouldn't at that moment. All she could hope for was that this 'one more job' was going to be successful, and it wasn't going to be the 'one more job' that put her husband away for the rest of his life - or worse ... *took* his life.

She pulled him into her arms and said nothing more. He was her husband. He loved her. He'd given her five incredible kids and supported all of them throughout their lives. He'd never been violent or mean toward any of them. She loved him. Deeply. That just had to be enough.

CHAPTER 20

Phillip cuddled closer into Daisy. They were on their last night away together. They'd stayed in two different bed and breakfast inns up the coast. When the weather had finally cleared, they'd been able to indulge in some beautiful walks along the beach. Being able to hold hands, breathe in the incredibly fresh air, and listen to the sounds of the water and birds overhead felt like freedom in itself.

Neither had turned on their phones since the day they'd ventured on their journey. Both reluctantly admitted inside that they might be missing something important, but it was a decision they'd made together. It was a decision they both would see through.

"Tomorrow, we return to reality," he heard Daisy say quietly.

She was lying on her back with her arm around him while he half lay on her chest. He raised his head and kissed her softly.

"I know," he said quietly. "But this has been incredible, Daisy. Thank you for coming away with me."

Daisy pulled him to her and kissed him passionately.

"Thank you for suggesting it. No matter what, Phillip, please know and believe that I really do love being with you."

"I know," he replied, nodding. "I feel the same way. Everything will be okay."

Daisy didn't respond in words. She so much wanted to believe that everything *would* be okay between them, but fate had already established a pattern of throwing things in their way. It seemed unlikely that fate was going to give up any time soon.

Instead of speaking, she pushed Phillip onto his back and lay down on top of him.

"I know it's getting late, but I'm not tired yet. Are you?" she asked as she rubbed herself against his growing hardness.

"I don't think I could possibly relax when you are moving against me like that," Phillip said, chuckling.

Daisy continued to rub against him as he became harder and harder. The feeling of the movement, combined with kissing him deeply, was all it took for her to collapse in a powerful orgasm. She'd lost count of orgasms for the week. All she knew was that she was having enough for them to each be incredibly intense.

"I'm going to need a while when we get back to let my body recover from this time with you."

Phillip grinned and nudged her off him.

"Well, you just lie there and relax if you're worn out," he said as he slipped a condom on. "I'll take over the hard work from here."

Daisy raised her hands above her head and relaxed her legs wide as she watched him position himself. The feeling of being filled up by him was always beautiful. He didn't rush. He took his time, kissing her and enjoying looking into her eyes. As he used his hands and arms to raise his chest higher, Daisy's eyes fell to the eagle over his heart. She'd always associated tattoos with roughness because so many criminals she'd assisted in prosecuting in court had them. Her view on that was changing. In her eyes, the images over Phillip's arms and chest were magnificent, and he was a true image of beauty.

Phillip watched her eyes darting over his chest, arms, face, lips. He loved the way she looked at him. What she saw in him, he still had no idea, but he loved that whatever she was seeing, she *was* seeing it. He was a common guy. To many, he'd be considered a thug. When he saw her look at him like she was, he felt like he was okay. He must be. Why else would someone like her want to be anywhere near someone like him?

The feeling started to grow. He stopped moving, leaned down, and kissed her softly. Once the feeling eased off, he began to move again. There was no need to rush. It was their final night before returning to the real world. He was determined to make her smile well into the night.

~~~~~

The next morning, after their last moments of pleasure in their room, Daisy stood at the window of the small room they were in. Soon they would check out, but first, she just wanted to take a moment to look out at the view. She wanted the entire week to be implanted deeply into her mind so that whatever lay ahead of them, the time away with him would remain one of the best weeks she'd ever had. They'd been together pretty much every hour of every day for an entire week but not once had Daisy felt stifled or like she was suffocating. That said a lot. She'd enjoyed her independence since Pete had walked away from her. She liked being an independent woman who didn't need a man, but she had to concede that she liked being with him - a lot. Every minute of every day.

She felt him approach her from behind and weave his arms around her, joining her in taking in the view.

"Are you happy you came away?" he asked quietly before he pushed aside her long blonde hair and kissed the back of her neck gently.

"You know I am," she replied. "I needed this - to be away from everything for a while, and I've loved every minute of our week together."

"Me, too," Phillip said as she slowly turned around and moved her hands to around his neck. "You are an incredible woman, Daisy. I don't understand why you want to spend time with me, but I am so glad that you do."

Daisy looked at his face closely and saw a slight tear in his eye.

"You are a good man, Phillip. No matter what has happened in your life or with people around you, and no matter what happens in the future, I know that you have a huge amount of goodness in here," she said, lowering a hand and caressing his chest.

"I *want* to be a good man. For you."

Daisy chuckled softly.

"You already are," she said. "It's in the core of your soul. You are perfection."

Phillip laughed out loud. It was all getting far too soppy. It had to stop.

"*Perfection?*" he asked, teasing her. "You are gorgeous, and so cute with your big word speaking."

Daisy smiled and pulled away.

"Come on, you perfect man. Let's start heading home."

~~~~~

On the journey back, they talked. There were so many things they still didn't know about each other. It was becoming a mastered art, asking some questions but not others - saying some things but not saying other things. They were consistently becoming more in tune with each other as far as what shouldn't be asked because it wouldn't be a welcome question to answer. There was still a sadness in Daisy as she wondered if she'd ever be able to meet his family, let alone integrate into them, knowing what she did about them from the extensive files on them. But that was far out into the future if it were ever to happen. She had to keep pushing the thoughts into the back of her mind so she could keep smiling at him.

When she pulled the car up to the outside of his home, she wondered if he might invite her in. He didn't. Instead, he undid his seatbelt and turned to her.

"When will I see you again?" Phillip asked.

Daisy smiled at him.

"You ask that like I'm moving to another country," she said and saw him blush slightly.

"I think tonight and tomorrow are going to be strange without you there beside me," he said.

"I'm heading back into the office tomorrow but I might have a lot to catch up on," Daisy said. "Do you want to meet me for lunch, maybe on Wednesday? That'll give you a couple of days to settle back into things too."

"Okay," Phillip said, already feeling a gap beginning.

He leaned over and kissed her softly, grabbed his bag, and climbed out. By the time he reached the front door, she was already out of view.

"Hey! Big bro!" he heard Anya call as she ran toward him with her arms held out wide.

Phillip laughed at her overdramatic scene of enthusiasm.

"Hey, baby sister. How have you been?" he asked as he dropped his bag and met her in her overdramatic hug.

"I'm not a baby!" she said on cue, making them both laugh. "How was your week? Did you miss me? I bet you did, didn't you."

"Of course I did," he lied while grinning. "There was no sunshine where I went, Anya, and that was because you weren't there, I'm sure," he threw in for good measure, making her give him an eye roll of great proportion.

He grabbed his bag and made for his room. Once inside the door, he went straight to the window. Despite having had an incredible week, he felt a true sadness flow over him. Everything was so easy in a tight little bubble away from the world. Nothing would be so easy now that the bubble had burst, and everything from the world was able to invade them once more.

A knock on his bedroom door broke him out of his thoughts.

"Yeah," he called out and saw his mother enter tentatively.

She generally never entered his room. If they interacted, it was always in passing in the living room or kitchen. When he saw her, he went to her and put his arms around her. It was a new thing they were all doing, but he figured he'd risk being told to stay away for the possibility of making her smile and feel wanted as a mother.

"How are you, Ma?" he asked her when he pulled away from her. "Is everything okay? Did I miss anything?"

For a moment, Stacey considered telling him about the upcoming job his father was working out details for. She decided to let it go. If Mark wanted to do that, he could be the one to recruit the help for it.

"No, nothing has happened here. Are you okay?"

"Yep," he said as he started to pull clothes out of his overnight bag. "Did you guys get a storm here? It was wild where we were for those first couple of nights."

"It was a bit windy and rainy, but it was okay," Stacey said, wanting to question him more but not sure where the line sat now that he was the age he was. "And your ... friend..."

Phillip heard the pause and smiled. "Daisy."

"Ahh, Daisy. She had a good time?"

"I think so. It was nice, being away with her," Phillip said. "I really like her, Ma. We have a good time together."

"I'm glad. It's about time you settled down."

Phillip stopped what he was doing and looked at her sadly.

"Ma, I can't 'settle down' and you know it."

"Why not?" Stacey asked.

"Because of this life that we live. I can't ask

someone to accept the things I do, and even if I *could* do that, who would accept who I am?"

"She doesn't know anything about us?"

He considered lying. He definitely wasn't going to tell the whole truth. There had to be some middle ground that could satisfy that question. "She does know that we tend to cross paths with the law now and then."

"And yet she still went away with you. She can't think you're an ax murderer or man of a violent temper if she did that."

"No, I don't think she assumes our … *ways* … mean I'm violent," said Phillip. "But there are a few things that would always be challenges between us because of our different ways of living."

Stacey could tell he was being cryptic in an effort to not fully answer her question.

"You don't have to answer if you don't want to," she said. "Sometimes it's okay to just say, 'I can't answer that.'"

"I know. It's just a bit of a weird situation. I don't want to talk about it, but I do really like being with her."

"Will you bring her over so I can meet her?" Stacey asked.

"No, that definitely falls into part of it being a weird situation, unfortunately," he said, making his mother very curious by his words.

"Phillip, you know *I* wasn't of this world when I met your father," she said. "It was a surprise at first to hear about some of his antics, but over time, his character far outweighed his family's ways. Maybe me talking to her and telling my story…"

"No! Ma, thank you but no. The uncomfortable aspect of me being with her won't be improved by you talking to her, believe me."

"Alright. Well, I'm glad that you had a good week away. Do you have work at Enrique's this week?"

"I don't know. I've had my phone off all week. I'd

better put it on to charge..." he said vaguely as he pulled it out of his bag and connected the charger. "I'll check messages soon. Hopefully, there's something for me. I really want to start earning proper money."

Stacey looked at him. Once upon a time, he'd been a baby. Her firstborn. Her first son. It was hard to believe that the solid build man in front of her had come from her womb. He needed to be loved. He *should* be loved. She hoped he would find it, whether or not with his current 'Daisy'.

~~~~~

Daisy stepped into her apartment and breathed in the smell of greenery. After doing a quick check of moisture levels in all of her plant pots, she sat on her sofa and closed her eyes. She had heaps of things to do. She felt like doing nothing. She turned and lay along the length of it. As she did, her mind turned back to the week that had now ended. What a glorious week it had been. It had added somewhat of a fairy tale kind of chapter to the ongoing intrigue she shared with Phillip. He was like her knight in shining armor with his strength.

"Oh god, I can't keep thinking about you, Philip!" she called out to no-one as she quickly sat up. She needed to unpack and do laundry. She needed to get things ready for work the next day. She'd need to probably buy some milk and other things for the week. She needed to check her phone messages... "Shit, where's my phone?"

She jumped up and forced herself to get swept away in things on her invisible 'to do' list. Working through so many things, it was finally easy to push Phillip from her mind entirely.

~~~~~

After Phillip had sorted stuff out and received Enrique's message to go and see him first thing Monday if he wanted to work, he finally felt caught up and able to relax. He ventured into the kitchen to find food.

"Hey," he heard his father say. When he turned around, Mark was looking at him intently.

"Hey, Dad. I'm going to make something to eat," he started to say.

He intended to offer whatever he was going to prepare to his father as well, except he couldn't concentrate or see anything that he felt like eating.

"I need to talk to you," Mark said. Immediately he saw Phillip close the cupboard he'd been investigating and focus.

"What? What's happened?" Phillip asked, suddenly considering something had happened to one of his siblings. "Not Sasha…"

"No, no, nothing like that," Mark said as he took a step closer. "There's a possibility we have a decent sized job coming up."

Phillip felt an ache that resembled his heart drop out of his chest and slam into the floor. His week away with Daisy had left him resolved that he was going to make better choices. He was going to keep away from crime and live an honest life instead.

"Say something," Mark said, curious about why his oldest son wasn't at all enthusiastic about what he'd just said. "It's been a while since an opportunity like this came up…"

"Why?" Phillip asked without thought.

"Why what?"

"Why do you need to do it?"

"It isn't just me. We'll all play a part…"

"No!" Phillip said forcefully.

Mark was stunned into silence for a moment. That one word would easily come from Rex but never his other kids.

"What?" he asked, sure he couldn't have heard correctly.

"No," Phillip said. "Dad, we have a good enough

life. You don't need to go and do those things. You told me weeks ago that you didn't *want* to do those things, but if you are going to, you're going to have to do them without me beside you."

"You will do what I tell you..." Mark said, feeling a rare sliver of anger beginning in his veins.

"No! Not any more. Not when it comes to things like this. You told me that I could go and live a life away from crime if I wanted to, and I am going to do that. I won't be a part of any of it anymore." Both men were quiet for a minute before Phillip spoke again. "I have always done everything you ever asked of me but, Dad, I'm almost thirty. Think back to when you were my age. By then, you had already been married to Ma for years, and you had four kids together. Imagine if you had none of that at my age. I love you, and I love Ma, but I am saying no to you in this. I need to sort my life out and find a way to have a family myself, and I can't do that with the threat of cops knocking on my door all the time."

It was an impassioned speech. For a moment, Mark was impressed and completely understanding. Then his mood changed, and all he could see was that his son was being rebellious and not doing what he should.

"If you don't want to be a part of this family, pack your things, and get out," he said to his son.

Phillip looked at his father in disbelief. It was an extreme reaction from Mark, but in the depths of his heart, Phillip knew it was well overdue that he moved out of the family home. If he could find a job, he'd be okay. Enrique was a good guy. He'd probably say good things about him and help him to find regular work somewhere. He'd only need to get a roof over his head for a short time, surely.

He silently walked around his father, went directly to his room, and began to fill a large old backpack. He wouldn't need to take much. Clothes, phone, wallet, toiletries. Everything else from his life could stay. He needed none of it.

As he walked out of his room, he almost collided with his mother.

"Phillip? Where are you going? You only just got back," she said, thinking he must be heading over to his girlfriend's place. If he was missing his flower already, that was a great thing in Stacey's eyes.

Phillip put his backpack down and pulled his mother into an embrace. The strength and firmness of it told her clearly that something had gone down that she didn't know about.

"Ma, I love you. I know we don't use those words in this family, but I do. Never doubt you are the greatest mother any kid could have," he said before kissing her forehead, picking up his backpack, and walking out.

Stacey looked at the front door for a long time after it had closed. What the hell had that been all about? She turned and walked toward the kitchen. There she found her husband, standing and looking out the kitchen window into the back yard.

"Mark?"

He turned and looked at his wife. He was in a place of intense emotion. There was anger in his body, but it conflicted with regret and sadness. Everything was fighting within his brain.

"Has something happened with Phillip?" Stacey asked. She expected Mark to walk toward her as he always did when something serious happened. Instead, she saw him remain in the same spot, unmoving. She knew his facial expressions. Whatever had silently just happened, it was rocking him and not in a good way. "Where is he going?"

"I don't know," Mark answered, at least being able to be honest in that.

Stacey walked closer and stood in front of him,

forcing him to look at her. "Do you know *why* he is going?"

"I told him to go," he replied.

She didn't need to ask anything more. In all honesty, she had no desire to try and talk Mark into asking Phillip to come back. It was well overdue that their son established his own life. If his father kicking him out was what prompted such a thing to happen, Stacey knew it could only be to Phillip's benefit. In the meantime, though, how should she look at her husband? If he hadn't expressed to her in prior months his own desire to be out of the criminal world, she would have been happy and supporting him in the job he was excited about. But something about him having said that to her, and then turn around and want to do a robbery, just upset her.

Mark forced himself to look straight on into his wife's eyes. He could see that once more, he had let her down. He wanted to move and put his arms around her, but he wasn't so sure that would be welcome in that instant.

Footsteps approaching broke the moment.

"Hey," Anya said in her eternally cheerful voice. "What's happening?"

Stacey had her back to her daughter. While she could, she closed her eyes and considered how Anya was going to handle Phillip having left. Her youngest and her oldest. They were her two kids who had the closest relationship. After composing herself, she turned around.

"Hello, little one. What's new with you today?" Stacey asked, plastering on as much of a smile as she could. She didn't want to say anything about Phillip. That news could wait.

Mark stood where he was, listening to his youngest child talk about things she'd been doing, and something she'd 'acquired'. He felt sick knowing she stole things because he'd taught her to, and yet he was excited about doing a burglary job himself. It was all too much. The conflict in his body, his heart, and his head was starting to grow to epic proportions. He needed fresh air.

Once Anya had stopped talking for a moment, he excused himself to go through the back door and out into the yard. A new load of chopped trees had arrived the day before. Grabbing the axe and getting stuck into chopping firewood would be an ideal way to vent the intense frustration building in his soul.

~~~~~

Phillip walked out without any idea about where he would go. All he knew was that he wanted to be out of there. His father telling him to go had only made things easier for him, in all honesty. He should have stood up and said no to his father years ago. Maybe if he'd done that, he would already be settled and living a perfectly happy life.

When he was three blocks from his home, he heard his name called. When he looked up, he saw Greg approaching him.

"Hey, I'm just on my way to your place to see your dad," he said. "Are you alright?" he then asked as he noticed the seriousness of Phillip's facial expression.

"Yeah, I just have to find somewhere to live. Things are a bit tense at home," Phillip replied, trying to act with decorum and diplomacy rather than imply his father was being an asshole.

"I've got a couple of spare bedrooms," said Greg. "Do you want to crash there?"

"Seriously? I thought you were liking having your own space again."

Greg smiled shyly.

"Yeah, but hey, I've got the room, and you need somewhere to stay. Here," he said, taking one key off his keyring and handing it to Phillip. "You know the way. When you get there, you'll easily be able to see which

237

room is mine. Either of the others you're welcome to grab."

"But I don't know if I can afford…"

"Phillip, you're family," Greg said. "We'll sort out the details later. Just get yourself settled and safe before night closes in."

Phillip nodded and smiled sadly.

"Thanks, Greg."

"Anytime, kid. I'll see you later," Greg replied before turning and resuming his walk to the Leadbetter family home.

~~~~~

Phillip picked a room in his new home and lay down on the bed. He wondered what else could happen in a day after having such an incredible week away with Daisy. After she entered his mind, he thought about her for a long while. He longed to talk to her, but he didn't want to bug her. She'd said she'd have heaps to do over the coming days. That was okay. He looked forward to seeing her for lunch on Wednesday.

A darker thought crossed over his mind. He'd stood up to his father. He'd said 'no'. A part of him was scared. He didn't know how his father would react to that, let alone how anyone else in the extended circle would react - especially if they had a full-on robbery planned. Would they be pissed if he wasn't there to play his part? Thinking about that possibility, he was glad he wasn't expected to see Daisy for a couple of days. He didn't want her to be caught up in any crossfire. As far as he knew, people never walked away from the Leadbetter family. Not blood relatives or those who had joined them over the years. Not until they stopped breathing anyway.

For a while, he'd let himself pretend he was just part of a small family. He couldn't keep pretending. It was back in the forefront of his mind again that he'd been raised by more than a family. He was part of the Leadbetter gang, and if they had a job on, it most definitely would be expected that he would contribute to it.

He hoped he was overreacting. If he was, that was cool. Nothing would come of it, and only he would know the fear in his mind. If he wasn't, where was that going to put Greg? Phillip wouldn't say anything just yet. Greg was his father's right-hand man. If there was something that was going to be needed to be said, Greg would definitely let him know.

CHAPTER 21

Monday morning, Daisy woke to the sound of her alarm. It was a sound she hadn't heard for over a week. Despite that being one difference from her week away, she still found her arms automatically reaching out as if to find Phillip's warm body. It wasn't there. Of course, it wasn't. He was warm and safe in his bed in his family home.

Turning and rolling onto her back, she opened her eyes and looked at the ceiling. It had taken a long time to get to sleep the night before. She'd gone to bed tired, and sure she'd fall asleep straight away. The absence of his warmth and the security that came from being in his arms had left her feeling awake and alone.

She missed him. Already. It was crazy, but it was true. The tough-looking guy with tattoos and a look that would scare many had turned her heart, and she hated the thought of being away from him. It was a good thing that he lived at home among people Daisy was afraid to come face to face with. If he hadn't, she might have done something stupid like jump in her car and drive to his house to surprise him and entice him to pull her into his arms. But that was never going to happen. It never *could* happen given her perimeter association to Rex's case, and the night he'd tried to corner her with his mates.

As the second snooze alarm sounded, she pushed all Leadbetters from her mind as she deactivated woman mode and reactivated lawyer mode. For the first time in her life, she'd been away from the office for an entire week. She hoped her bosses weren't more annoyed with her for going away for the week than they'd sounded. They had seemed happy enough. She hoped they were.

She jumped in the shower and took her time making herself look perfect again. After a week of not caring what she looked like, it suddenly felt like hard work even though she'd always worked hard to maintain an exceptional appearance. She fondly remembered back to Phillip seeing her in her gym gear. He hadn't looked down on her. If anything, he'd reacted as if he really liked her in track pants. It was a contrast to how Pete had always responded to her putting on casual gear. Even when she'd seen him during her week away with Phillip, she hadn't missed the way Pete had assessed what she'd been wearing. His face had clearly said what he thought of that. No doubt about it.

Pete. She'd pushed him from her mind. As she stood in front of the mirror and tidied the last piece of hair to get it in place, she thought about him again. He'd declared he wanted her back. She regarded that as a reaction on his part, nothing more. He'd seen her with another man, and panic had hit him as he finally realized she was no longer his. She was with someone else.

Thinking about him from the distance of time that had passed, and now having spent such a glorious time with Phillip, Daisy couldn't remember what had attracted her to Pete in the first place. He was all about money. He exuded it every minute of every day. No-one could look at him and not see it. Once upon a time, a man with such a look of perfection was what she'd wanted and sought. Now she felt different.

She looked at the wall clock and turned off her mind. Men had to be kept at bay in her thoughts. Anything could be waiting for her at the office. She had to commit to giving her attention to it fully once she got there.

What she hoped most of all was that no Leadbetters were going to be in trouble with the law at present. If she turned up at the office and was told her firm was helping to go after them again, Daisy didn't know what she would do.

It was all up to fate.

~~~~~

Phillip wandered down to Enrique's after he woke Monday morning. He hadn't seen Greg, so had avoided any conversation that might have been on the agenda. He wasn't sure where he wanted things to stand between him and his father. He didn't want to have that conversation with Greg just yet.

"Hey, hey! My best mechanic is back," Enrique called out, as he always did when Phillip wandered in.

Phillip waited for Steve to argue the point, but all was quiet.

"Hey, Enrique," Phillip said as he shook the older man's hand. "Have you got some work on for me? Please tell me you have. I really need to start earning some regular cash."

Enrique patted Phillip on the back.

"You, my friend, have perfect timing. Come into my office."

Phillip followed, intrigued. Once Enrique motioned for him to sit and both men faced one another over the large wooden desk, Enrique continued.

"Steve left," he said.

"What?" Phillip asked, surprised. Steve had always been there, for as long as he could remember. "*Why?*"

"He was offered a better paying job," Enrique said. "It was a bit of a shock, but you know I couldn't afford to pay him any more to match the other offer. He was a good worker for all these years. I don't hold any grudge. He's got his lady and those little ones to look after. In his position, I probably would have done the same thing."

"I was only out of town a week! How could it happen so quickly?"

Enrique nodded in agreement.

"I know. He applied and was offered the job. They needed him straight away, and he went. He does have my blessing, and perhaps for you and me both, this is good news. How would you feel about taking on full-time hours? I know you only ever wanted to be casual..."

"*Hell*, yes!" Phillip almost shouted, excited, and disbelieving the timing of what was happening. He saw Enrique laugh. "I'll work as many hours as you want me to. Just say you'll give me regular hours each week so that I can afford a place of my own."

Enrique looked surprised.

"You're moving out of mummy and daddy's home? Finally?" he teased Phillip.

"Haha. You know I've had some stupid family obligation thing going on. Now I want to make a break. I wanna be on my own."

"Alright, well, if you want the job, it's yours. When can you start?"

Phillip smiled, reached down into his bag, and pulled out his overalls.

"Now?" he asked, excited.

Enrique stood and shook Phillip's hand. He'd never had any issue with Phillip. He came from a family who were known among certain circles to not be great to get on the wrong side of, but Enrique had never believed Phillip was really like them.

"Welcome aboard."

Phillip grinned broadly. Fate threw some weird things at him sometimes but the timing of being offered full-time work was extraordinary and welcome.

"Thank you," he said.

"Okay," Enrique said. "You're now on the clock, so get your ass out of my office and go see Tom. He's got the priority sheet for this week. He'll assign you your work."

Phillip nodded and walked out. He had a job - a real job. He finally had a full-time job that would enable him to earn his own money *honestly*.

That was something to smile about indeed.

~~~~~

Daisy's morning flew past. It seemed like a mountain of files she'd found on her desk when she'd arrived but sitting down, turning her phone off, and just focusing had enabled her to at least get a top-level background understanding of cases that had been assigned to her. She was pleased to note the name 'Leadbetter' didn't once pass in front of her eyes.

As she quickly ate a sandwich during the short break she was taking at lunchtime, she turned on her phone and immediately received a text.

'Just thinking about you, beautiful Daisy,' the words said below Phillip's name.

She smiled and responded immediately.

'And I'm thinking about you, gorgeous Phillip.'

She heard nothing more, but it was enough to make her smile for the rest of the afternoon. When she found her mind drifting back to her week away with Phillip, she let herself take a breather and indulge in the memory and the resulting feeling. She missed him. It had only been 24 hours since she'd seen him, but already it felt like there was a gap somewhere. She kept refocusing when she had to. She would see him Wednesday. It wasn't too long to wait.

Why then did it feel like a lifetime?

~~~~~

Tuesday afternoon Mark Leadbetter sat alone in his office. He felt like crap. That was the most precise way to describe how he'd felt since he'd kicked his oldest son out. He knew Phillip was staying with Greg. There was no reason to worry about him, fearful he was homeless or anything. He was housed, and he was safe. Hell, he was thirty years old! That knowledge didn't remove the regret Mark felt in treating his son like he had. Phillip had only spoken the truth to him. Every day of his life, he had done what his mother and father had told him to do. He'd never been a kid to argue or put up any kind of fight. He was now a grown man, and until he'd said that 'no', he'd not once said it before to his father. He was a good man. Mark knew that. He wondered inside if he wasn't so much angry at Phillip, as he might have been envious. Phillip had found the courage to say 'no'. Mark had never found that courage when he'd served his own father.

Rhett had seen Mark that morning and provided more details of the job. By the day, it was looking more and more likely that it was something small enough that they could handle, but big enough that it could be a worthwhile haul if they pulled it off. The thought of doing a job still excited Mark. That feeling was in contrast to the one that came from knowing that Stacey was disappointed he wanted to do it. In his love for her, he was conflicted about the job in question. She'd hardly spoken to him since Phillip had walked out. Mark felt that most of all. For three decades, she'd always supported him. She'd been there to lean on, to talk about plans, and discuss things when they went wrong. The thought that he might be losing her was enough to bring tears to his eyes.

As he sat in his desk chair and turned to watch the branches that moved in the wind outside the window of his office, he felt the tears come on again. They'd been coming on quite a bit recently. He was supposed to be a man who felt no emotion. He wasn't that man. He'd honed being able to hide his feelings over the years, but the thought of losing his wife's love, faith, and strength beside him, was enough to cause him to sob uncontrollably. He was the head of everyone now. He could just stop the job. He could declare that he would take part in no more jobs ever again. It would only be a few words that he'd need to say, and everyone would hear him. Making the change could be just that easy … except it wouldn't be that easy. He was a vital link in a chain that spread far and wide. People depended on his leadership and instruction.

The conflict was strong. He loved his wife. He didn't want to lose her. He also felt the pressure of his family's legacy. If he let anyone down, he was letting huge numbers of people down. How could he do that?

He'd faced some situations in his time that had scared the crap out of him. This one was going to be the hardest he'd ever had to consider, let alone decide upon.

~~~~~

Stacey paused outside the door to Mark's office. She could hear him sobbing. She knew he was in an impossible place, trying to keep so many people happy. Hearing him like that brought tears to her own eyes. She'd not felt like talking to him at all since she'd heard he wanted to do another job, but she loved him. Knowing he was in pain was more than she could bear.

She knew that apart from him, she was the only one in the house. All of their kids were out doing whatever it was that they did day to day. She was glad. She didn't want them to hear their father at that moment. The question was, what was *she* to do?

Another sound of another sob was all it took to melt her heart again. She couldn't bear his pain anymore. She opened the door slowly, closed it behind her, and walked up to him. As he looked up at her, his confusion was evident on his tear-lined face. Stacey held out her arms and guided him to stand. As she pulled him hard against her, she felt him let go completely as he wrapped his arms around her and let the sobbing out.

She'd never seen him cry in such a way before. There had been times when she'd seen his eyes water during their long marriage. There were times when he'd cried in joy - every time one of their children had been born, he'd held them in his arms that first time and openly cried with a huge smile on his face. Thinking about those moments, Stacey knew that she could never hate Mark, and she would never turn away from him. She loved him. He had conflict within him, but he was an incredible man and an incredible husband.

Mark found comfort in his wife's arms. She didn't say anything to him. She didn't try and coax him to stop crying. She didn't tell him everything would be alright. Just feeling her arms around him was enough. He let the tears out. Stress had been building in him for a long while. It had to all be set free. He knew that. If it wasn't, it was going to explode and not in a good way.

When finally he felt the tears slow and then stop, he remained still. He held his wife tightly, afraid to let her go.

Stacey felt the point where the crying stopped, and his body's tension lessened. She pulled her head away from his shoulder and looked into his eyes. Gently she tried to wipe away the tears down his cheeks, all the while seeing his eyes studying her face. It was impossible to be so close to him and not want to kiss him. She leaned up and engaged his lips with hers. She engaged his tongue with hers. They didn't move for a long time. Sometimes lovemaking was needed. Sometimes hard out fucking was needed. But at that moment, a long uninterrupted period of deep, passionate kissing was needed, tongue and all. It was a different kind of intimacy, and sometimes it was exactly what was needed above anything else.

Mark indulged in the blissful feelings coming from kissing his wife. He never tired of it. He loved all of their intimate interactions, but he knew that if ever he had to make a choice about sex with no kissing, or kissing with no sex, he'd take the kissing. There just wasn't anything like it. It had been a long while since they'd just kissed like they were, without it leading to more. Now and then, he had to be reminded that there was value in the simple things, just as much as there was value in the bigger things.

Stacey pulled away from him but led him to their bedroom. There she moved onto the bed, fully clothed, and welcomed him to lie with her. Neither moved toward anything sexual. Both remained silent as they continued their kissing marathon.

A long while later, the kissing eased off when they heard the front door open and close, and then a bedroom door open and close. Stacey lay on her side and faced her husband. As he lay facing her, she could see pain still in his face.

"I'm sorry I've hurt you," Mark said quietly as he gently reached up and caressed her cheek. "I would never intentionally…"

"I know you wouldn't," she responded, cutting him off. "And you haven't. I just can't bear the thought of losing you. There have been too many close calls lately. This long-running streak of no-one getting caught and no-one getting hurt is going to come to an end, Mark. It has to. Who will we lose when that happens? You? Me? One of our kids?"

Mark moved closer and pulled her to him.

"Tell me what you want me to do," he said.

"I can't tell you that. I don't *want* to tell you that, but, please, we have everything we need," Stacey said. "We don't need anything more. You and I have enough to live well enough for the rest of our days, and the kids are all going to be grown and out on their own. I want … I want to relax with you. I want to wake up each day and not have to worry about you. I want to lie around like this whenever we want to, without having to consider all the other people who depend on you. I want to fuck you senseless every morning, every afternoon and every single night…"

Mark smiled. She was making a serious speech, but that comment couldn't go past without some amusement or reaction on his part.

"I know you're scared," he said quietly, pushing

the comment aside for the moment. "I can retire anytime. I have no doubt that someone will happily step up and take over as head of everything."

"You say that, but when will you actually *do* it?"

He kissed her. He hated hurting her. He hated letting her down. And that thought of making love to her three times a day wasn't something that would leave his head in a hurry. He sighed, knowing she was right.

"This job is happening in a few weeks," he said quietly. "I can be part of it, or I can step aside and let someone else take the reins with a crew that I'm not on. Do I want to do it? Yes. Will I do it if it means losing you in any way? Fuck, no. You mean more to me than any jewelry. You must know that, Stace."

"Must I?"

"Yes!" he said forcefully as he wound his fingers into her hair and pulled her close for a passionate kiss. "You are my *life*."

"Mark, I've never told you to not do a job. I'm not telling you now to not do *this* job, but I've got a real bad feeling about this one. Maybe it means nothing. Maybe it means *something*," she said and paused, seeing the conflict on his face. "Please reconsider before you do this."

He watched her face as she spoke. The tears beginning to quietly form in her eyes weren't missed. He felt his heart break at the sight of them. He couldn't be angry or upset that she didn't want him to do another job. He'd wanted the same thing in recent times.

"Alright," he said softly as he nodded. "I'll call Rhett and Greg here and talk to them. If neither of them wants to step up, I know that my cousin Pete has questioned my leadership for years. I have no doubt he'll happily take everything over, including this job."

Stacey said nothing. She felt like she was forcing him to give up something he wanted to do. That didn't feel good, but if it meant that her husband and kids might be safe from something bad that was going to happen, she wasn't going to let her guilt alter the way things were now going.

Mark found resolve in his decision. Truth be told, he'd been over his position for a long time. The excitement of doing a large job had temporarily excited him. As he looked closely at his wife, he conceded that he really didn't need anything else. After all, the best things in life could be free. Certainly making love to Stacey was one of the biggest joys he had, and it cost absolutely nothing except his heart.

He pulled her to him again and kissed her deeply. Instantly he felt her wrap her arm around him and hold him tightly. A bedroom door once again opening and closing in the distance, followed by the front door opening and closing, was all the sign he needed that they were alone again, and they were *meant* to be alone again.

Stacey wasted no time. As soon as she heard the front door close, she pushed him onto his back and lay on top of him, kissing him with all the love she had inside of her. When she sat up and quickly pulled off her top and bra, she watched his eyes. No matter how much he saw her body, or how it changed over time, every time he looked at her like that, she loved it. She leaned forward, coaxing him to take her nipple into his mouth. The sensations made her let out a small moan in appreciation. She wasted no more time. Stripping off the rest of her clothes and telling him to do the same, she soon eased down on him and once again found the fulfilling joy that came from riding him like it was the last time she'd ever do so.

CHAPTER 22

After work on Tuesday, Phillip made his way back to Greg's place and took his time washing away the grime of the day in a long hot shower. Daisy was on his mind. So much so that he couldn't hold back from reaching down and indulging his body in self-pleasure with the assistance of plenty of soap. One more night, and then he would see her. They hadn't had any contact since she'd dropped him home Sunday. He wanted to see her, and he wanted to hold her. So far, she had no idea he'd moved out of the Leadbetter family home. He briefly wondered how she would feel about that. Not that he was completely free of them - he'd simply traded parents and siblings in for a distant cousin.

After climbing out, drying off, and getting dressed, he walked out of the bathroom and straight into Greg.

"We need to talk," Greg said, not particularly wanting to have the conversation he was about to have.

Phillip said nothing. He followed Greg into the living room, and both sat, facing one another. It was evident to Phillip that Greg was uncomfortable.

"Does this have something to do with my father?" Phillip asked.

"He isn't happy you said no to him," Greg replied.

Phillip let a long deep breath flow out of him.

"I know, but I'm thirty years old, Greg. I want my own family - my own wife, my own kids. I want my own *life*."

Greg nodded. He understood exactly where Phillip was coming from. There were desires inside of Greg that he'd had for years, but he'd put on hold in order to be a part of the great Leadbetter clan.

"I get that, but…"

"No. No buts. My father wants me to give all of my life to our family, but he never did. *He* has a wife. *He* has kids. Where's the justice in him thinking that *I* can't have those things?"

Both were quiet for a long while, feeling like they were in a hopeless situation.

"Look, your father is going to step aside, Phillip," Greg said, his face revealing the surprise at the news Mark had so recently given him. "He's made a promise to your mother, and I do believe he's going to abide by it. He has asked me to step up, but I've told him I won't. I don't want it either. So all power is falling to our cousin Pete."

Phillip continued to sit in silence as he processed what was being said.

"This isn't necessarily a good thing," Greg said quietly. "Pete ain't no angel, and he likes things rough. He thrives on it. He always has. He's killed, and he won't hesitate to kill anyone who gets in his way of what he wants." He paused as he saw Phillip's face reveal that what Greg was saying was really sinking in. "He's a loose cannon, and we all need to be careful now that he's got word that he's going to lead."

"He won't come here, to see you or me…" Phillip said with a tail of a question mark in the tone of the words.

"I … don't … know," Greg replied. "He knows about this event that's coming up where these jewels are going to be. He wants them, and he'll likely want a crew to step up and play their part in getting them."

Phillip felt his heart drop. He couldn't do something like that. He wanted to do absolutely nothing that could go wrong and put him in front of the cops.

Greg watched as he saw Phillip drop his head into his hands and then rub his eyes.

"I'll never be free, will I?" Phillip asked, his voice

reflecting the level of hopelessness he felt. "I'll never be able to have a normal life."

When he looked up, Greg could see tears in Phillip's eyes. It was enough for Greg to feel them come on as well. He knew where Phillip was. He'd been in the same spot two decades earlier. The difference was that he still had no-one he could associate with home. Perhaps Phillip was still young enough to have a chance at love, at the very least.

"Get away, Phillip," he said passionately. "You got a girl, right?" he asked and saw Phillip nod. "Go to her and lie low."

"I can't … I can't do that if there's a chance that someone's going to come after me. I'd be putting her in danger…"

"I've got as many supporters as Pete's got," Greg said. "I'll keep my ear to the ground, and I'll keep him distracted. This job that's coming up will keep him focused…"

"And what if he wants me to be a part of it? I can't do it. I don't want to be in prison…"

"I'll handle that. Rhett and I can handle things, so you aren't needed. Just get away and find some happiness where you can. Don't let yourself turn your back on what you want and then end up like me, old and alone."

Phillip blinked at what Greg was saying.

"You're hardly old!"

Greg laughed softly.

"I'm almost fifty. I've had a good life but I'm getting past my prime. I can feel it in my bones."

"You never wanted to settle down?"

Greg pondered that. His heart was full. He just couldn't say who it was full for - not with the way the gang felt and talked about certain aspects of society.

"This life has been my life. I made the choice when I was a teenager to commit to being by your

father's side then and as he took the family over.
Probably, I could have walked away. In hindsight, there
is a small part of me that *wishes* I'd walked away. But I
didn't. So here I am - but you don't have to be. You're
young enough to be able to start your own family if you
want to. Go and do it, Phillip, before it's too late."

Phillip watched as Greg stood and walked into his
bedroom, saying no more. As distant cousins, they'd
always gotten on well despite their age difference, but
they'd never opened up like that before. It left Phillip
slightly startled and more than a little bit confused and
wary.

He glanced at the clock. Nine o'clock. That was a
great time to go to bed. The sooner he got to sleep, the
sooner he'd wake up. Then it would be only a few hours
before he saw his beautiful Daisy again.

~~~~~

Daisy woke early Wednesday morning. Today
she was going to see Phillip! It was a crazy thing, to feel
so alive and excited. There was no reason why they
couldn't have seen each other or even just spoken on the
phone over the previous two days. Somehow, though, it
was nice having had a small amount of time where the
anticipation could build. And it *had* built very well
indeed. She'd purposely kept her hands off herself. The
next time she wanted to orgasm, she wanted it to be at
his hands … or tongue … or whatever part of his body
would bring it on.

She showered and dressed quickly as if doing so
would make lunchtime come around faster. She also let
herself smile and enjoy the simple feeling of just being
happy. She'd been pondering a question in her mind for
two solid days as she'd steadily worked through two
large piles of case notes. Always she had loved being a
lawyer. Always she had loved doing her job. But
something was changing in her, and she was fairly
certain that she didn't want to do it anymore. She wanted

a break from the law. Having a break away and then coming back to the office had led her to believe that she wanted to take more time to enjoy life, not just work every hour of every day. Maybe she'd go back to it. Maybe she wouldn't. But she was sure of one thing - she was going to tell her boss that she wanted to resign because there was something she wanted far more than working, and it was time she gave that idea far more serious thought than she had been.

~~~~~

After a morning of working on a ute at Enrique's, Phillip bounded out of the garage to go and meet Daisy at their usual spot by the fountain. When he arrived, she was already there, sitting quietly but somehow appearing extremely fidgety at the same time.

"Hi," he said to her, seemingly breaking her out of her gaze toward the flowing water.

Daisy turned to him and absorbed the sight of him. He was grubby but very, *very* sexy. She was tempted to run to him and not give a damn about her work clothing. From that, she held back. She had only just given her boss the news. It would be another two months before she would finish.

"Hi yourself," she said as she grinned at him.

Phillip moved forward and sat as close to her as he dared without making it possible for her to get greasy from his mechanic's clothes. After he sat, he looked at her in entirety from head to toe and back again. She was something to see. He didn't mind her being in that corporate wear again either - especially that skirt.

Daisy leaned in carefully and kissed him again and again. For a moment, she didn't care about words. She just wanted to feel his lips on hers. She didn't stop until she felt his lips turn into a broad smile.

"I missed you too," he said quietly against her lips before kissing her back.

Daisy pulled away and opted to not mention her

resigning from her job. It wasn't the right time or the right place. They would only have a short time before she would stand and walk one way, and he would stand and walk the other.

"How is your work?" she asked, deciding to pick a neutral place for their conversation to begin.

"Awesome," Phillip replied, still feeling incredible about his luck. "I am now working full time. Nine till five, Monday to Friday."

"Oh, that's amazing!" Daisy exclaimed, almost jumping into his arms and only restraining herself just in time. "You're really excited, I can tell."

"I am," he said, his broad grin perfectly expressing his happiness. "All these years, I was only able to work casually. Being asked to work full time is incredible."

"We have to celebrate," Daisy said with an almost shy smile on her face.

"And how would we do that?" Phillip said quietly as he moved his face close to hers.

"Without clothes," she dared to say, making him laugh out loud.

"I like your idea for a celebration."

"Phillip," Daisy said, her voice toning down and becoming more serious. "Will you stay with me tonight? Please."

"We both have work tomorrow. I don't want to get in your way…"

"You won't. I mean, we've done it before, gotten up and gone to work, right?" she said and saw him nod. "Am I asking too much? I just want to sleep beside you again."

Phillip kissed her softly.

"I want that too. Tell me what time to come to your place, and I'll be there."

~~~~~

As soon as the clock hit five, Phillip tidied his

workspace and made for the door.

"Someone's got a date," Enrique yelled out at him with a distinctive teasing tone in his voice.

Phillip turned and smiled widely at his boss before waving and walking out. He had a date alright, but first, he had to get home and have a shower.

When he walked into Greg's place, he was met with Greg and Rhett sitting at the kitchen table. Both were talking quietly, and the level of seriousness in their speech was obvious. They looked up when he entered. Immediately Rhett rose and walked to him.

"Hey, we've got your back," he said quietly as he held out his hand to shake Phillip's. "I agree with Greg. Find a safe place and stay there until this job's over, Phillip."

"When is it?"

"Seven weeks. It won't be that long before Pete starts rounding up troops, though. Be nowhere when that happens if you really don't want to do the job."

"Thanks," Phillip said, nodding. "I know I'm putting you two in a difficult position."

"No," Greg added into the conversation. "Your father is trying to leave too. Don't panic. You aren't alone in wanting to be out of all this."

Phillip said nothing more except to excuse himself. The words of Rhett and Greg played on his mind, but he was determined to forget everything about being a Leadbetter. All he wanted was some time to just be Phillip - Daisy's Phillip.

~~~~~

When she heard the apartment buzzer sound, Daisy felt her heart start to pound. It had only been a few hours since she'd last seen him, but even that felt like forever. She opened her apartment door. As she heard his footsteps making haste up the staircase, she couldn't help but smile. When he came into view, she had the largest grin on her face.

Phillip saw her and already felt his jeans tighten. She looked amazing. As he neared her, he could smell she'd just showered too. Emanating from her was an incredible scent of cleanliness and freshness.

No words were said as he reached her and took her in his arms. Happily, Daisy let him engulf her as his lips claimed hers. Nothing needed to be said. After a week of having so much sex, the previous couple of days had been too much. Into her bedroom, they both went. No words were spoken until much, much later.

"How are you?" Daisy asked eventually as she lay down on the bed beside him.

She'd just ridden his gorgeous body until both of them had reached their beautiful climax. Finally, an itch she'd been feeling was superbly scratched.

Phillip heard the question and laughed.

"I'm feeling really good," he said. "How are you?"

Daisy laughed in turn. "Beautifully fucked."

Phillip looked at her. He couldn't stop smiling. The contrast between spending time with her and even considering anything to do with his family was too great. He believed in family honor and loyalty but in his case, family was stressful. Daisy wasn't.

He guided her under the covers and turned onto his side to face her. It was a joy just to look at her.

"I moved out of my family home," he said quietly.

Daisy pulled away and refocused, not sure she'd heard right.

"Why?" she asked.

Phillip took a deep breath. It was a stall tactic to give him time to assemble words in his head.

"It was time," he said. "I can't talk to you about anything specific, Daisy, but it's time for me to make a break."

"Well, where are you living then?"

"With my cousin. Well, he's my dad's cousin, so I'm not sure what that makes him to me, but anyway, he said I can live with him."

Daisy processed the information. She was quiet for a long time, but Phillip could see her mind churning over. Finally, she spoke.

"Phillip, I want to ask you something. I … it's important to me that you answer honestly. Please don't answer this question with something that you think you *should* say…"

"What is it?" Phillip asked, intensely curious.

"Do you have any kids? Anywhere?"

The surprise was evident on his face.

"Not that I know of. *Why?*"

"Do you want kids?" she asked.

Daisy saw him smile softly at her as he nodded.

"I do."

"Would you like to … with me?"

Phillip was stunned. He took a long while to think about her question before he answered.

"Daisy, we hardly know each other," he said. "I love being with you but bringing a child into the world isn't something that should be done easily."

"Are you saying no?"

"No, I'm not saying no. I could easily spend every day of the rest of my life with you, and I could easily make and raise babies with you, but let's not rush there. I've just started working full time. I'd want to save a lot of cash before we do that."

Daisy felt disheartened. It wasn't the exciting response she'd wanted deep down inside.

"Okay," she said in almost a whisper.

Phillip felt for her. A part of him wanted to say yes and get on with the baby-making fun straight away. In the back of his mind, though, was where things might get complicated inside his family in the coming months. He didn't want her caught up in that. He needed to stall and get them both safely through that time, and he had to do it quietly.

"Hey," he said, caressing her chin while raising her to look into his eyes. "I'm not saying no. I'm just saying, let's wait, even just a few months. I need to settle myself in my work and in my life…"

"Live here," Daisy said unexpectedly. "Live here with me."

"I love the thought of being with you every night," he said, smiling. "Let's take it one day at a time, though, my beautiful Daisy. Please."

"Alright," Daisy responded. She was kind of glad he wasn't wanting to rush. It could only be a good thing if they kept things slow for a longer time before spending every single night together. "Could you eat me now, though?" she asked boldly with a twinkle in her eye.

Phillip laughed out loud, glad for her ease of changing conversation. He pushed her onto her back, kissed her passionately, and then happily moved down to bring her to her happy place once again.

CHAPTER 23

"Seven weeks," Greg said to Rhett and Mark as all three sat in Mark's home office. "Pete's got his own crew planning the job. The jewels will be at a high scale charity gala event. I've told him I'll be a driver, but I won't be inside. He's accepting of that, but he does want Sasha there."

"What?" Mark asked. In no scenario he'd considered might happen, had the presence of his short-tempered daughter been involved. "What the fuck does he want her there *for?*"

"A decoy," Rhett added in. "A distraction. He wants her there, dressed to the nines as a way to distract all the males in the room while Pete and his crew get to work."

Mark leaned forward on the desk and rested his head in his hands.

"I can't believe this," he said. "She's just gotten over being stabbed, for Christ's sake. She can't do a job like that…"

"Mark, she's going to have to. You know what Pete's like. If you try and prevent it, he'll lash out, and she'll be the one to pay. Let her go. I'll stay close to her," Rhett said, trying to ease his gang brother's mind. "I'll be inside as analyzer. I'm not going near the gems. I'll be on lookout duty, and I'll make sure she's always in my sight."

Mark remained quiet, but his head was full of conflict.

"Did I do the right thing, stepping down?" he asked quietly, more so to himself than the other men in the room.

"You did," Greg said quietly. "You've wanted to

make a break for a long time, Mark. Now you've done it."

"But now I've put my own daughter in harm's way…"

"No, you haven't. She's the perfect person for this role. Talk to her. I'm pretty sure she'll be eager to do this job."

"If it happens, you do look out for her," Mark said, looking straight at Rhett. "And *you* make sure she gets away safely," he continued, looking at Greg.

Both men nodded in response and hoped like hell they could see their promises through to reality.

~~~~~

Across town in the Stonewarden home, planning was well underway. The jewels they sought were coming to town in seven weeks. They would be present at a large black-tie gala event. For the Stonewarden boys, that meant tuxedos were coming out of hiding.

Each of the Stonewarden men would have their own part to play. Night after night for the seven weeks to come, they would assemble in their family home and go over scenario after scenario. They would all question everything. They would go to all lengths to consider every single 'what-if' they could think of. It was the Stonewarden way. Every possibility had to be considered. No matter how unlikely, every possible scenario had to have a planned outcome.

The only Stonewarden who was oblivious to everything was Charlie. Well into her pregnancy, no-one would dare mention the upcoming job to her. They never would have anyway, but definitely, with the state she was in, no-one would let even a sliver of suggestion of the job reach her. Mitchell had already spoken to Tom at the ranch. They were going to try and coax Charlie and Ash to have a romantic weekend away around the very night the gala was to be held. Mitchell wanted her far from the ranch too. If anything went wrong on the job, the ranch was their getaway location. If anything more went wrong and the cops tracked them, Mitchell wanted his daughter safely as far away as possible.

It was going to be a good job. Fitz was sure of that, so everyone was sure of it. His intel was always good. And if on the night it wasn't, they had each other to rely on someone feeling it was wise to abort. They'd worked well together for years. They'd work well together again.

CHAPTER 24

After spending the rest of the week in Daisy's apartment in and around his work, Phillip ventured home. Upon seeing his father, both of them did as they'd never done before. They moved forward and held each other tightly. When they broke apart from their manly hug, Phillip could see the regret on his father's face.

"I'm sorry, Phillip. I should never have treated you like that…"

"Dad, it doesn't matter. I've been here for too long anyway," Phillip said as he took a seat on one side of his father's desk, and Mark moved to the other side. "I'm starting over. I love you and Ma, I'm not ashamed to be a Leadbetter, but I need to live a different life."

Mark nodded.

"I know, and really I'm glad," he said. "Your mother and I both want to see you happy."

"And you two? Does Ma get to be happy too?"

"I am," he heard his mother's voice say from behind him. Instantly he stood and went to hug her. "Your father has stepped down, Phillip. Now we can live in peace. We'll stay here till Anya's out of school, and then we'll move on to somewhere where no-one knows us. I want the same peace you do. I don't want to worry about everyone all the time anymore."

Phillip heard the sadness in his mother's voice. When he turned to look at his father, he saw the look he was giving his wife. Phillip felt the strength of their bond. It had been hidden behind closed doors for most of his life, but now he could see it clearly. He hoped his father would stick to his promise. He hoped his mother would get the life of peace that was being promised to her.

"What about this woman of yours?" Mark asked, trying to lessen the seriousness in the room. "Will we get to meet her?"

Phillip openly cringed.

"No," he said. "Not for a long time yet anyway."

"Why, Phillip? Why won't you introduce her to us? Are you ashamed..."

"No, Ma. I told you before. It's complicated. There are things about her that will upset you..."

"She couldn't be any worse than we are!" his mother exclaimed, completely confused by his arguments. "What could she possibly have done that would upset *us?*"

"I'm sorry," he replied, sighing. "I'm not going to say. Maybe a time will come in the future when it might be alright for you to meet her, but not yet. Please trust me on this. I have good reason to keep you away from her."

Stacey nodded but said nothing more about it.

"Alright. For now, I'll just be glad that you've found someone, and you're safe."

"Please don't worry about me," Phillip said. "Keep *yourself* safe, Ma. From what Greg and Rhett have said, this upcoming job has everyone on edge. You two will get away out of town around then, right? Dad? You'll take Ma away and keep her safe..."

Mark hadn't even considered the option but instantly looked at Stacey. The thought that any crossfire from Pete getting irate about anything, in some way hurting Stacey, was enough reason for Mark to give serious thought to the idea. He nodded.

"I think you're right," he said as he looked at Phillip. He then moved his eyes to his wife. "We should. Let's take off for the week before..."

"Mark, we have kids..."

"Stace, we'll make Anya come with us. Rex, David, and Sasha can have a choice to come or not.

They're old enough now to make their own decisions."

Stacey nodded. She didn't care about her own safety but she had been worried about any outfall from Mark stepping down out of power.

"Alright," she said.

"I gotta go," Phillip said as he stood. He turned to his mother and hugged her tight against him. "Ma, please do go around that time. Lean on me if you have to. Check into a hotel here in town if you have to. Please don't just stay here in this house. *Please.*"

"We'll be gone, Phillip," Mark responded. "Take care of yourself and that woman of yours."

"Yes," Stacey said, feeling happier at her son's situation. "Bring me some grandkids."

Phillip laughed out loud. His mother had no idea just how close *that* wish might be coming true.

"If she's worth it, make an honest woman out of her," Mark added for good measure.

Phillip said nothing as he smiled and walked quietly out of the room.

Once Mark and his wife were alone again, Stacey turned to him.

"I can't shake the feeling. Something bad's coming, Mark. It's coming for us."

~~~~~

That night Phillip lay with Daisy in her bed, holding her tightly from behind.

"I love sleeping next to you," Daisy said quietly in her after-love glow.

"Me too."

"I'd like to do it every night."

Phillip grinned broadly against her shoulder.

"Me too."

"Can we?" Daisy asked as she rolled onto her back and looked at him.

Phillip calculated dates in his head. He loved the idea of living with her. First, though, he wanted to make sure she was out of town on the weekend of the gala.

"How about I sweep you away for a weekend of romance in a few weeks' time? Let's go somewhere neither of us have ever been."

"Just for a weekend?" Daisy asked.

"We both have work on. We could leave Friday night and come back Sunday night."

"Really? Can I choose the location?"

Phillip laughed and nodded.

"Yep," he said.

He didn't care where they went. He just wanted her safe.

Daisy turned onto her side again and moved so that her back was securely against his chest. Nothing more needed to be said. She let herself relax as a smile graced her face. She'd found an awesome man who she adored and who she truly believed adored her. Yes, he was rough. Yes, his family was on the wrong side of the law. Finally, she was in a place where she could look past that and focus just on him. That thought would keep her smiling for a long while yet.

Phillip held her even tighter. Now he'd found her, he wasn't going to do anything to risk losing her. He had no regrets about turning his back on the Leadbetter family. He'd wanted a better life for a real long time, and in his arms was a woman who inspired him to get on and live that life.

All he had to do was keep her safe.

It sounded easy. It sounded simple.

But with Pete Leadbetter now the master of the entire Leadbetter clan, there no way of knowing how anything was going to go. Perhaps nothing would happen, and everyone could live in harmony.

Perhaps that was exactly the opposite of what was about to happen.

EPILOGUE

The countdown to the next job was on. Six weeks. In six weeks, a hoard of gems was coming to the city, and not one but two groups had their crews assembling and planning. There were gems for the taking, and both sides intended to take them. Neither group knew of the other. Each assumed they'd be the only ones making a play to earn a great score.

It wasn't the most complex job the Stonewardens had done.

It was a far more complex job than the Leadbetters had done.

Generally, the Stonewardens aimed high.

Generally, the Leadbetters aimed low.

For the first time ever in their families' long histories, in six weeks, both were going to finally be in the same place … at the same time … with the same intention.

Anything could happen.

The End

~~~~~

FURTHER BOOKS
IN THE
FORBIDDEN CONFLICTS
SERIES

DIAMOND OF WAR
(FORBIDDEN CONFLICTS SERIES - BOOK #3)

James Stonewarden is a playboy. He has been since the moment he first started to notice girls. He loves them all, and they all love him. Why would he want to get himself into a relationship?

Sasha Leadbetter's a hot-headed young woman, known to the law for her quick temper and harsh ways. She isn't one to mess with - especially with the way she keeps a blade in her pocket. To her it's her security. It's something that makes her feel safe and comfortable. She's had it for so long that it's nothing for her to pull it out and hold it to someone's throat without any conscious thought.

Unaware of who each other are, or how their families are distantly interconnected through crime, the chance of James Stonewarden meeting Sasha Leadbetter is slim. But it happens.

A playboy and a young woman who has the mentality to kill. What kind of recipe could that result in? And what will happen when James identifies a car at Sasha's family home, that matches the description his sister Charlie gave after the supermarket shooting months earlier?

SAPPHIRE OF PREJUDICE
(FORBIDDEN CONFLICTS SERIES - BOOK #4)

Greg and Rhett. They've grown up together since they were teenagers. They've fought together. They've stolen together. They've even loved women together. But something deeper has existed in one of them for years. He's hidden it well. Being part of the great Leadbetter gang and family, the prejudice of certain situations has always been loudly expressed by many of its members - too many, and certainly enough to make anyone fearful of what would happen if feelings were revealed and brought out into the open.

A night has passed when finally, in a moment of wondering if he'd survive till morning, Rhett's taken the chance and kissed the person of his desire. Given their circumstances, what can they do, and where can they go?

Meanwhile, as Phillip Leadbetter continues on his path of happiness with his Daisy, someone from her past has grown obsessed with her and wants her back. To what degree will he put into effect a plan to get her back, and get Phillip out of her life forever?

~~ NOTE: This book does contain adult sexual content and LOTS of swear words.

EMERALD OF WISDOM
(FORBIDDEN CONFLICTS SERIES - BOOK #5)

When Mitchell Stonewarden lost his wife to cancer more than a decade ago, he vowed to never give his heart to anyone else. With all of his children now adults, and a new generation of Stonewardens having already begun, he's finally started to wonder - does he really want to be alone for the rest of his life? The handover of the family business to his oldest son, Vic, has seemed to be free of difficulty or issues - but has it? Mitchell knows little of his oldest son's private life away from the family. He is surprised by what is brought to his attention that he had no idea about.

While Mitchell finally starts to move on into a new chapter of his life, another of his sons - Max - is on his own path of discovery in life and in love. Previously well-known as 'Romeo' to his family and peers, he begins to wonder if Christy - a surprising addition to his life - has grown to become more important to him than any other young woman he's ever met. When her work at a homeless shelter tests the boundaries of her safety, Max's commitment to her is also tested, making him wonder if he will, indeed, end up hurting her.

Meanwhile, on the other side of town, the Leadbetter family is shattered by an unexpected turn of events that leaves Stacey wondering if she is going to lose the man she's loved for more than three decades...

THANK YOU!

Thank you so much for reading my book, 'Ruby of Law' (Book #2 in the Forbidden Conflicts Series). I greatly enjoyed writing this story and I appreciate your enthusiasm for reading it.

~~~~~

If you would like to make contact with me, please:
Visit My Website
http://authorannmpratley.wixsite.com/writingisbliss

Visit my Goodreads Author Page
goodreads.com/author/show/14777236.Ann_M_Pratley

Thank you,
Ann M Pratley